Bantam Crime Line Books offers the finest in classic and modern British murder mysteries.
Ask your bookseller for the books you have missed.

Agatha Christie

Death on the Nile
A Holiday for Murder
The Mousetrap and Other Plays
The Mysterious Affair at Styles
Poirot Investigates
Postern of Fate
The Secret Adversary
The Seven Dials Mystery
Sleeping Murder

Dorothy Simpson

Last Seen Alive
The Night She Died
Puppet for a Corpse
Six Feet Under
Close Her Eyes
Element of Doubt
Dead on Arrival

Elizabeth George

A Great Deliverance
Payment in Blood

Colin Dexter

Last Bus to Woodstock
The Riddle of the Third Mile
The Silent World of
  Nicholas Quinn
Service of All the Dead
The Dead of Jericho
The Secret of Annexe 3
Last Seen Wearing

Michael Dibdin

Ratking

Liza Cody

Head Case

John Greenwood

The Mind of Mr. Mosley
The Missing Mr. Mosley
Mosley by Moonlight
Murder, Mr. Mosley
Mists Over Mosley
What, Me, Mr. Mosley?

Ruth Rendell

A Dark-Adapted Eye
  (writing as Barbara Vine)
A Fatal Inversion
  (writing as Barbara Vine)

Marian Babson

Reel Murder
Murder, Murder Little Star
Murder on a Mystery Tour
Murder Sails at Midnight

Dorothy Cannell

The Widows Club
Down the Garden Path
coming soon: Mum's the Word

Antonia Fraser

Jemima Shore's First Case
Your Royal Hostage
Oxford Blood
coming soon:
Cool Repentance
Quiet as a Nun
The Wild Island
A Splash of Red

HEAD CASE

·

LIZA CODY

BANTAM BOOKS

NEW YORK · TORONTO · LONDON · SYDNEY · AUCKLAND

HEAD CASE

A Bantam Book / published by arrangement with
Charles Scribner's Sons

PRINTING HISTORY
Charles Scribner's edition published 1986
Bantam edition / January 1990

Published simultaneously in the United States and Canada

Bantam Books are published by Bantam Books, a division of Bantam Doubleday Dell Publishing Group, Inc. Its trademark, consist-
ing of the words "Bantam Books" and the portrayal of a rooster, is
Registered in U.S. Patent and Trademark Office and in other
countries. Marca Registrada. Bantam Books, 666 Fifth Avenue,
New York, New York 10103.

PRINTED IN THE UNITED STATES OF AMERICA

OPM   0 9 8 7 6 5 4 3 2 1

For Brian

HEAD CASE

CHAPTER 1

The morning began with a small domestic theft. Anna would have called it a loan but Selwyn was quite adamant.

"Don't, don't, don't take my morning paper!" he had bellowed after a previous infraction. "And don't tell me you haven't. I always know. You steal the print off the page, the power from the words. And besides, you fold it up again all wrong."

"What a fuss," Bea said, all wifely contempt.

"You'll never understand." Selwyn met contempt with disdain. "It's my paper, and it's fresh and crisp I want it, with the smell of ink intact. Not after her upstairs has read the new off the news."

Upstairs, right above Selwyn's sleeping head, Anna pilfered the news from the *Guardian:* there would be no peace summit, the social workers were threatening industrial action, the miners were already committing it, an old war hero was convicted of shoplifting, and Somerset were all out for 173. She poured another cup of coffee. Outside, the plane tree was beginning to darken into its dignified summer green and the daisies on the patch of grass looked in need of beheading.

Anna refolded the paper with great care. It did not look second-hand. She hoped Selwyn would never know, although he had an uncommonly sensitive nose for the unlikeliest things.

The new yellow client folder caught her eye. It contained a single sheet of paper: a Brierly Security interview form. Subject—Thea Hahn. Client—Mr. Rodney Hahn, civil servant, married. An address in Wimbledon. A paragraph followed describing a telephone conversation between Rodney Hahn and Martin Brierly.

1

Anna did not read it. She had already been told. Instead she gave her shoes a quick rub with a piece of Kleenex and checked her stockings for holes. She looked as neat and reliable as a representative of Brierly Security should when calling on a civil servant in Wimbledon.

Collecting bags, keys and *Guardian*, she blew a soft raspberry at the mirror and left the flat. She ran swiftly downstairs and out through the front door. There was no sign of Bea or Selwyn but it would never do to loiter in the hall in possession of a borrowed *Guardian*. Safely outside, she pushed the paper through the letter-box and left it at the rakish angle favoured by the paperboy.

It was already warm inside the car. There was a faint smell of plastic and axle grease. She rolled down the window, noted the mileage and turned on the radio. The Everly Brothers sang "Crying in the Rain" as she drove through sunny, early morning streets to Hammersmith Bridge.

The river already had a steamy, glassy sheen to it. It was going to be another scorcher. The traffic had not yet coagulated into rush hour, and most of it was coming in the opposite direction. Anna made it to Wimbledon in good time.

Ansel Grove was leafy, with big houses set well back from the road and protected by high hedges. Mr. Hahn's was hidden behind years of laurel growth and his lilacs were beginning to turn rusty at the edges. It was a low white house with the curved windows that always reminded Anna of school swimming pools.

She parked by the front door to avoid blocking the garage. A man appeared on the front doorstep just as she was getting out of the car. He looked at his watch.

"Right on time," he said, as if congratulating her on a difficult feat. "I'm Rodney Hahn."

"Anna Lee. Good morning."

He extended a creamy manicured hand and looked her over with sharp pale blue eyes. Anna shook the hand, hoping he wasn't going to say he had expected an older man.

"I was expecting someone older," he said, holding her hand a fraction too long. "Mr. Brierly assured me all his agents were very experienced."

"It's just the way I look," Anna said.

"Well, come through anyway," he said briskly. "We're having breakfast on the terrace."

He led the way into a wide hall with a terracotta tiled floor, through a shining regimented dining-room to the French windows which opened on to the back garden.

The remains of breakfast for two, pieces of croissant and eggy plates, lay on a white metal table. There were three chairs, though, and a third clean cup.

"Coffee?" Mr. Hahn asked. "Do sit. My wife will be down shortly."

He picked up a deep-necked, bell-bottomed coffee pot and poured some weak, tepid coffee.

"Wonderful," Anna lied gamely, studying him over the rim of her cup: tall, good-looking, beginning to grey in all the right places, well-cut sober suit, no skin showing between silk sock and trouser bottom. He was watching her too, a closed confident look with the beginning of a smile round his mouth.

He's going to tell me how he's never had dealings with a detective before, Anna thought, putting her cup down and getting ready to make a good impression.

"I've never actually employed a private detective before," he said, the smile breaking through as though he should be applauded for the absence of necessity.

At that moment, Mrs. Hahn appeared from the house. Anna stood up and was introduced. Mrs. Hahn was wrapped in peach-coloured silk and Mitsouko. Her hair was gilded, her nails tinted and her long slim shins looked French-polished.

"Do forgive the godforsaken hour," she murmured. "Rodney so much wanted to see you himself, and before work is the most convenient time."

"Meetings and so forth," Mr. Hahn supplied vaguely. "One's colleagues can go on rather."

Anna was rather overwhelmed by the picture of tasteful wealth the pair presented. Either Mr. Hahn was a
very superior civil servant, or someone had inherited
something. She cleared her throat and said, "Well now,
about your daughter . . ."

"Yes," Mr. Hahn interrupted quickly. "Thea. You
see, I don't think the police really know what they're
talking about."

"Who they're talking to, actually," Mrs. Hahn put in.
"Do you know, they suggested we contact the Salvation
Army?"

"The Salvation Army are very good," Anna said.

"Yes, but with drunks and dropouts," Mrs. Hahn
said. "Of course, I won't hear a word against them, but
there's no reason in the world why Thea should go to
them."

"She's quite young, isn't she?" Anna said, knowing
full well how old she was, but wanting the parents to
start talking about her.

"Just sixteen," Mr. Hahn said. "Valerie, have you
sorted out the photographs? Mr. Brierly said she would
need photographs."

"In the study, dear." Mrs. Hahn waved an immaculate hand, presumably in that direction. "And while
you're up, would you ask Mrs. Elder for more coffee?
This must be undrinkable."

Mr. Hahn went into the house, and Anna wondered
which of this smooth couple called the tune. Mrs. Hahn
seemed quite content to wait until her husband returned, so Anna said, "Thea's been gone for eleven
days now. Would you tell me what steps you've already
taken?"

"Well, the police, naturally," Mrs. Hahn said, turning her face up towards the morning sun and closing
her eyes. No breeze stirred the garden: leaves and
blossom hung motionless. She took a pair of sunglasses
out of her silk wrap pocket and put them on.

"Thea was lodging with a cousin at the time," she

went on. "Danielle Soper. You'll probably want to talk to her yourself. I've included a short list of relevant names and addresses in the envelope of photographs. I thought it might save time."

"Thank you," Anna murmured. "Does Thea's cousin live near Thea's school, or what?"

"Ah, well. Thea doesn't actually go to school," Mrs. Hahn said, still giving most of her attention to the sun. "Didn't my husband explain that to Mr. Brierly? No? Well, Thea was attending some lectures at the University of London, and private tutorials."

"I suppose one should describe Thea as gifted," Rodney Hahn said, returning through the French windows. He placed a thick white envelope on the table. "Her subject, basically, is mathematics. She could have begun at Cambridge last September, but neither we nor the authorities there thought it advisable. So she has been rounding out her education, so to speak, as a sort of external student at London."

"Oh," said Anna, rather flummoxed. "I had no idea."

"It would have been a somewhat complicated phenomenon to describe over the telephone," Mr. Hahn said coolly, "besides being irrelevant to the circumstances. Our daughter is not some sort of freak, as we take great pains to point out to anyone who might be overly impressed with her academic achievements."

"Of course," Anna said, feeling as if she were consoling him for a hardship. Perhaps having an exceptionally clever child was a hardship, although most of the parents she knew complained about the opposite.

"Ah, coffee," Mrs. Hahn said with evident relief. "Thank you, Mrs. Elder."

Mrs. Elder, a more motherly-looking figure than Mrs. Hahn, put a pot of fresh coffee on the table, nodded good morning to Anna, and left without a word. Mr. Hahn poured for Anna and Mrs. Hahn. His own cup stayed empty. He looked at his watch.

Anna said quickly, "So what steps have you taken in the last eleven days?"

"It has, in fact, been far less than eleven days," Mr. Hahn said. "We only came to the conclusion that Thea was missing last Thursday."

"Mrs. Soper thought she was with us," Mrs. Hahn put in. "While we, of course, assumed she was still with Mrs. Soper. It was only when Danielle phoned to ask why she had not returned for her Thursday lecture that we realized there was a problem."

"We contacted the police immediately," Mr. Hahn said, again looking at his watch. "And to cut a long story short, between their inquiries and Mrs. Soper's, it is generally agreed that Thea has not been seen by anyone who knows her since Thursday, eleven days ago. Now, I'm afraid I must leave you." He stood up.

Anna stared at him in surprise. She said, "There are two broad categories for missing people. Those who want to be missing and those who don't."

"I hope you aren't suggesting that Thea would put us to this trouble voluntarily," Mrs. Hahn said coldly, while Mr. Hahn said, "Yes, I see what you mean, but as I can think of no reason why she might wish to absent herself, I have no suggestion to offer."

Anna could not ruffle him or detain him. He aimed a kiss at Mrs. Hahn's perfect cheek and left. Anna said, "I didn't mean to upset you. It's just that sometimes kids go off for reasons that the rest of us wouldn't understand at all."

"You haven't upset me in the least," Mrs. Hahn said calmly. "And, as I pointed out to the police, it would be a mistake to assume that Thea is one of those disaffected dropout teenagers."

"So you think something must've happened to her?"

"If that is the only alternative to the first of your 'broad categories,' yes." A well-bred hint of sarcasm was unmistakable. Anna felt the first trickle of sweat down her spine. She shifted uncomfortably. Mrs. Hahn almost smiled.

To change the subject, Anna said, "How long has

Mrs. Elder been with you?" hoping to find someone in this elevated household she could talk to on her own level.

"About ten years, I suppose. Why?"

"I'd like to talk to anyone who's involved."

"Mrs. Elder is not involved," Mrs. Hahn said flatly. "However, if you think it might help . . ."

"And I'd like to look at Thea's room."

"Very well." Mrs. Hahn stood up and led the way through the house. At the top of the stairs she paused and said, "Since interviewing one's employees seems to be on your list of necessities, I should mention that my charwoman is coming at nine. She is not involved at all and I would be most displeased if you spoke to her. She does not yet know of Thea's disappearance, and I will not have family matters turned into neighbourhood gossip."

"She works for your neighbours too?" Anna asked, almost smiling in her turn. It was nice to see Mrs. Hahn's complacency slip, if only by a fraction. "How about Mrs. Elder?"

"Mrs. Elder lives in," Mrs. Hahn said stiffly. "I'll send her up. This is Thea's room." She opened a door that led off the hall at the top of the stairs. Anna went in alone.

CHAPTER 2

Thea's room was painted a quiet grey-green—the sort of colour a decorator would call "pussy willow." Against one wall stood a narrow bed, with antique brass bedrails, covered by a white crocheted cover. There was a large desk under the window, and a reproduction of Rembrandt's son Titus over the bed. Apart from a built-in cupboard and wardrobe, the rest of the wall space was taken up by bookshelves.

Thea had at her disposal a complete set of *Encyclopædia Britannica*, Dickens, Scott, Hardy, Eliot, Austen and the Brontës; and that was only the light reading. There were volumes by Kierkegaard, Popper, Russell, Locke, Hobbes. The closest thing to a comic was *Scientific American*. There were books about physics, metaphysics, geophysics, astrophysics, astronomy, and mathematics.

Anna gulped and opened the cupboard where she was reassured to find an array of ordinary clothes. She was relieved to see that the only hat present would fit a normal-sized head. The cupboard, in fact, was remarkable for what it did not contain. There were no jeans, for instance, nothing made of denim—no T-shirts with writing on them, no sweatshirts, no trainers. Nothing that a sixteen-year-old, of the sort Anna knew, would choose. Everything looked conservative and tasteful and everything was made from natural fibres. They were all the sort of garments Mrs. Hahn might have chosen.

Anna felt it was time to look at the head that wore the normal-sized hat. She was having difficulty imagin-

8

ing a young girl who had read all those intimidating books and unresistingly wore nice white cotton blouses and plaid woollen skirts.

She sat at the desk and tipped the photos out of the envelope.

The one on top of the small pile was a black and white studio portrait. The head was carefully halated, light catching hair, eyelids, and eyes—dark hair cut in a short, glossy page-boy, clear eyes, broad cheekbones, straight nose—a still, classical pose to a quiet, classical head. Only the mouth had a childish, indecisive look. It was the sort of photograph Thea's father might have in a silver frame on his office desk.

Anna sorted through the rest, trying to find one that showed Thea relaxed, unposed, or off-guard. Nothing. She stood between her parents in front of a rhododendron bush. She sat on the terrace in the garden with a book. She knelt on the grass with a spaniel she did not touch and which was anyway looking in the other direction.

"Mrs. Hahn said you wanted a word," Mrs. Elder said from the doorway. Anna swung round. She asked impulsively, "Which of these pictures would you say looks most like Thea?"

Mrs. Elder came across the room, round and short-legged on neat little feet. She looked over Anna's shoulder. After a pause she said, "Her father always liked that one best," pointing to the studio portrait.

"And you?"

"Oh, it's very like her," Mrs. Elder said noncommittally.

"Yes, but what's she really like?"

Mrs. Elder smiled and said, "Oh, she's a lovely girl—so clever, very polite. She never gives anyone any trouble."

"There's trouble now," Anna said, quite sharp in her disappointment.

"Poor girl," Mrs. Elder said. "I wonder what can have happened. I've never known the Hahns so upset."

"But was she unhappy or something?" Anna asked bluntly. "Could she have run away?"

"Oh no," Mrs. Elder said disapprovingly. "She'd never give us any trouble like that."

When Mrs. Elder left her alone, Anna looked at the list of names and addresses Mrs. Hahn had provided. There were only four, with Mrs. Danielle Soper's at the top. Anna made a note to ask about old school friends. Thea must have gone to school at some point. Then she started opening desk drawers. By now she was not expecting to find any girlish secrets.

Downstairs, she heard the front door open and close, and after a while, the steady drone of a vacuum cleaner. She listened to the ordinary sounds almost with pleasure. She had found nothing she could understand in the desk: notebooks filled with figures and symbols, computer printouts, ring files filled with pages of incomprehensible charts. It might have been ordinary, or even child's play to a mathematician, but it was nonsense to Anna who was looking for letters, diaries, or phone numbers. Even a dog-eared Valentine would have done. It was like looking for a pin-up in a stamp collection.

She gave up and went downstairs.

Mrs. Hahn, now dressed in a cream silk suit, was perched on the edge of a leather chesterfield giving Mrs. Elder instructions about lunch.

"Well?" Mrs. Hahn said as the older woman left, closing the door quietly behind her. "Did you find anything helpful?"

Anna had the impression she knew to the last detail what Thea kept in her room, so she held out the list and said, "Could I have the name of Thea's last school and any friends she stayed in touch with."

"The school, by all means," Mrs. Hahn said, and added another name and address to the paper. "But as to friends—well, you must understand that Thea did not mix with girls her own age. She was always several years ahead scholastically."

"But didn't she have any hobbies?" Anna cast around for something that might do. "Riding, music, dancing?"

Mrs. Hahn smiled and said, "I was fond of horses and dancing at her age. But Thea is afraid of horses. And of course young people don't dance these days. Well, not the sort Thea could be taught. She plays the piano quite well, I'm told. Oh, and of course chess."

"Of course, chess," Anna said. "Who did she play with?"

"Her father's quite good, I believe. But even he wasn't much competition for her. No, we have a chess program for the computer. Would you like to see it? It's in the study."

"No, thank you." Anna sighed. Perhaps the chess program was an important clue. But if it was, she wouldn't understand it.

CHAPTER 3

Anna found a free meter in Allen Street: an event rare enough to make her smile as she locked the car and walked up to the office on Kensington High Street.

Upstairs, Tim was leaning on the corner of Beryl's desk persuading her to part with some petty cash. Beryl had one hand clamped, vice-like, on the cash box while the other held a fistful of pink Kleenex. The first flowering of the grass had brought her hayfever into full bloom too.

"Oh, there you are, Anna," she said irritably. "The Commander said to see him. I'll ring through."

"Got one?" Tim asked, while Beryl was attending to the internal system.

"Yeah, Wimbledon."

"Toffs or rotters?"

"Toffs," Anna said decidedly. "Live-in housekeeper, cornflakes on the sodding patio, and don't wipe your nose on the napkins."

"Napkins eh?" Tim said, deftly pocketing three of Beryl's pencils while she was looking the other way. "How super jolly classy."

Beryl said, "Don't hang about all day, he's waiting."

Anna tapped on Mr. Brierly's door and went in.

Martin Brierly looked up and said, "Ah, Miss Lee. How did you get on?" He was thumbing through an IBM catalogue. The picture on the cover was of small computer hardware. The thought that he might buy one and make Beryl redundant made Anna quite cheerful. She sat down.

"They came well recommended, the Hahns," Mr. Brierly remarked. It was a statement with the hint of a question in it.

"Oh, good as gold," Anna said, implying that the Hahns would not have to sell the telly when Beryl sent the bill in.

Mr. Brierly looked satisfied. "First impressions then," he said, putting the catalogue down and lining it up neatly with his blotter.

"They're a bit overpowering as a family," Anna began cautiously. "Very top drawer. The daughter's some sort of genius. And they've no idea why she could've skipped. I mean, if she was unhappy or something, they aren't saying. I think good impressions is what they're good at."

"Well, we're used to that," Mr. Brierly said impatiently. "But all in all you'd say it was a good home?"

"I suppose so," she said even more cautiously. She and Mr. Brierly went by very different standards where home life was concerned. "But sort of cool. They aren't the sort of people to start screaming about getting their baby back, but even so they were just a bit cool."

"Not everyone is an emotional extrovert," Mr. Brierly

said with approval. "However, it sounds to me as if I'd better handle that side of it. They might appreciate the personal touch."

"Okay."

"Now, I've spoken to the department dealing with this. They've made all the usual moves—hospitals, hostels, etcetera. There'll be no conflict there."

Anna nodded. There was nothing worse than getting up police nostrils. The police could make a private operator's life unbearable if they thought they were being usurped.

"So what will be your first step?"

"Mrs. Hahn gave me a list," Anna said, producing it. "I'd better start on that."

"Fine. Leave a copy with Miss Doyle." He picked up the IBM catalogue again: a sure sign he thought the interview over. He was fanning himself with it as Anna went out.

She went down the corridor to the rec-room for a cup of tea while Beryl photocopied the list. Tim already had the kettle on when she got there. He had the paper open in front of him and was moodily giving the prime minister a moustache and spectacles. The nude on page three had already received some imaginative tattoos.

"I'm waiting for the travel agency to phone," he said. "West London Insurance's got some joker they want talking to. Only he's skipped to Jersey. So it's me for the land of the rising tomato."

"Nice one," Anna said. Jersey would be lovely in such a fine spring.

"Except Madame bloody Beryl's frigging idea of a suitable per diem over there's put the dampers on. I mean, St. Helier's not bleeding Clacton, is it? What's she expect me to do? Pitch a tent on the beach and take me own corned beef sarnies?"

"Just because you're mixing with millionaires doesn't mean you can live like them," Anna said, holding her nose and talking like Beryl.

"Chance'd be a fine thing," Tim complained. "Kettle's boiling. It's just you and me. Everyone else's out grafting."

It was very stuffy in the rec-room because the window on the south side had been nailed shut in winter as a vain attempt to keep the draught out. A couple of flies had a lazy dogfight round the light-bulb. Anna drank her tea quickly and left Tim to his grumbles and graffiti. Once started, he could moan for hours, and she didn't want to be around to hear.

Danielle Soper lived in a quiet Victorian terrace in Islington. Anna was admitted by a Portuguese au pair and two small boys who competed for the honour of showing her into the sitting-room. Mrs. Soper was fair and tall, like Mrs. Hahn, but far less poised. She had been writing a letter and seemed quite flustered by the explosion of two boys, the au pair and Anna into her privacy. There followed an embarrassing ten-minute fight while the boys were banished upstairs where they could wreck neither furniture nor conversation.

"My God," Mrs. Soper sighed when she and Anna were finally alone and the door had been shut on far off shrieks and pounding feet. "I used to be an organized person. I used to have a life of my own. Oh dear. They don't get it from me, I can assure you. It must be their father." She subsided on to a sofa, fanning her flushed face with her hand. "Aunt Valerie rang and told me to expect you," she went on. "Oh Lord, it's so awful. I'm sure she blames me. But I can't see how it can be my fault. Thea said she was going straight off to Wimbledon after her last tutorial. How was I to know she never arrived? I didn't even know she wasn't expected home. And that damned man didn't ring to say she hadn't turned up. It was a week before anyone said anything, and all the time I thought she'd decided to stay at home."

"Just a minute," Anna interrupted. "Thea said she

was going home? Did she take a bag when she left here?"

"Well, I didn't actually see her." Mrs. Soper blushed. "But the police asked me that too, and I checked so I do know she took her overnight bag."

"Was that normal? Did she spend most weekends at home? And I've seen her room at home. She wouldn't have needed to take much."

"Well, she always took her bag, I think. But she didn't always go home for weekends. Sometimes Aunt Valerie would ring and say she wanted her if she hadn't been back for a while."

"And she didn't this time?"

"No. She says not."

"Did Thea say she did?"

"Oh dear," Mrs. Soper said gloomily. "The police asked that too, and actually, I can't remember. I can't see what difference it makes."

"I suppose we're trying to make out whether she's run away or not," Anna said. "If she said her mother asked her to come home, but Mrs. Hahn didn't, it would imply she was lying to give herself some space to go off somewhere."

"How frightful," Mrs. Soper said. "I'm sure she didn't lie. Thea never gave anyone a moment's trouble."

"Everyone says that," Anna said thoughtfully.

"But it's true," Mrs. Soper protested. "She's so quiet and neat. She does exactly what she's told. And so clever too. I was hoping it ran in the family, but my two are the opposite." As if to illustrate the point, a door slammed upstairs and yells and bumps descended. The door burst open. One of the boys, scarlet-faced and furious, shot in screaming, "William took my train. William took my train. Tell him to give it back." William followed yelling, "He won't let me play with his train," at the top of his voice. The au pair added to the chaos, shouting in Portuguese, and obviously enjoying herself. Blows were exchanged on the Persian rug, under the coffee table and over an armchair. Mrs. Soper looked on helplessly and Anna had to restrain herself from picking the two delinquents up and chucking them out. Peace was only restored when the fight carried itself to another room.

"I can't wait till they go to school," Mrs. Soper said despairingly. "I can't think where all that aggression comes from. It must be their father. I know it's early but I could do with a drink." She poured herself a generous gin and tonic from the drinks cabinet. Anna accepted a lager.

"I never used to drink until just before dinner," Mrs. Soper said, sitting down again. "It's the noise I can't stand. I came from such an ordered home. Mummy and Aunt Valerie are sisters you know. And you'll have seen how nice the house in Wimbledon is. I'm always so ashamed when Aunt Valerie and Uncle Rodney come. I practically have to give the boys a sedative to make sure they don't let me down. And Thea was always such a model child. I don't know where I've gone wrong."

"It must be their father," Anna murmured, grinning. Mrs. Soper laughed. The level in her glass had dropped dramatically and she looked more relaxed. "I always say that, don't I?" she said. "I'm such a wreck at the moment. You see, the Hahns set such high standards. I used to be quite terrified of them as a child. And I know they blame me for Thea."

"They didn't give me that impression," Anna said to console her.

"Oh, they wouldn't say anything. It's just that they get more and more cold and withdrawn."

"Was Thea afraid of them, do you think?"

"Why should she be?" Mrs. Soper said, puzzled. "Thea never did anything wrong. I mean, if she had been a difficult girl or anything like that, I couldn't have let her stay here, could I? I've got enough to do as it is."

"Well, did she have a boyfriend?" Anna asked, searching for any of the normal reasons a girl might stay away from home. "Who did she hang around with? Did she go out in the evening much?"

Mrs. Soper shook her head. She took another sip of gin and tonic and said, "You see, you mustn't compare Thea with ordinary girls her age. She's gifted, and I think that's made her very shy of other young people. I think she was afraid they'd treat her as some sort of freak. She seemed more comfortable with older people."

"Well, what about other students at the University? They'd all be older."

"It's not as if she met many," Mrs. Soper said thoughtfully. "She wasn't a proper student. She just went to some of the lectures and had private tutorials with some of the professors. And besides, she's much too young for the ordinary students."

"Wasn't she very lonely?"

"I don't think so. I mean, she's never been gregarious. She had her books and she spent most of her time here upstairs reading. She's wonderful that way."

"What's wonderful about sitting alone in your room reading?" Anna asked.

"It's wonderful in *this* house," Mrs. Soper said emphatically. She got up and poured herself another drink. Anna produced Mrs. Hahn's list. She said, "Can you add anything to this? Anyone who knew Thea that Mrs. Hahn's forgotten or didn't know about?"

Mrs. Soper looked at the list. It was a short one; only five names and addresses including Mrs. Soper's own at the top. She said, "I'm afraid not. These three are her tutors. He's Geology," pointing, "he's Economics, and he's Literature. This must be her old school. Literature's the one who should have rung when she didn't turn up for her tutorial that Thursday afternoon."

"Who saw her last?"

"She had Economics in the morning, I think. But I don't know whether that was a lecture or a tutorial. I didn't see her when she left. Thursday's my morning for aerobics."

"What about the au pair or the boys?"

"They go to the park most mornings. No one saw her leave."

Anna asked if she could use the phone. Economics had been the last to see Thea, so she thought she'd start with him. He was expected home for lunch, his wife said. Anna could come at two. She was about to tell Mrs. Soper this when the sitting-room was invaded again.

"I'm hungry," howled William.

"Baked beans," yelled his brother.

"Fish fingers!"

"Fish fingers *and* baked beans," they both screamed and suddenly fell silent, awed at their agreement. Anna was awed too. She said goodbye and left hurriedly.

CHAPTER 4

Sun and dust cast a haze over Chalk Farm. London, Anna thought, needed its constant wash of rain. She stopped at Marine Ices for lunch. It hadn't rained for over a week and the people she saw through the window didn't know how to dress for heat so early in the year. Most of them only half-acknowledged the sun: below the waist, clad in winter suits or woollen skirts, above, in shirt sleeves or summer blouses.

G. C. G. Stickle, B.Sc. (Econ.), Ph.D. (London), lived in a ground floor and basement flat just off Englands Lane. The basement kitchen trapped the remains of winter and was chilly and dark. Mrs. Stickle, wiping furiously round an omelette pan when Anna was shown in, was persuaded to make two mugs of weak Nescafé. The kitchen table was strewn with Save the Whale pamphlets and books about cooking with a wok. There was no wok to be seen.

"A remarkable girl, Thea Hahn," George Stickle said, adjusting his gold-framed spectacles. He was a thin, shabby man of about fifty who looked as if he was influenced by his students in the matter of dress. His wife glanced at him sharply and started to mend a raffia lampshade. "Extraordinarily analytical mind, for a girl," he went on. "Truly phenomenal memory. She'll go far."

"I'm afraid she already has," his wife said, with a touch of satisfaction. Anna couldn't tell whether it was envy or pleasure at her own wit. She said, "Thea came here the morning of the day she disappeared, didn't she?"

"That's right," George Stickle said. "It was purely a private arrangement between her parents and myself. One can't afford to turn down private arrangements these days."

Mrs. Stickle let out her breath in an angry sigh and tugged at a strand of raffia. Anna said, "How was she? Was there anything different you noticed?"

"Not at all," he said, frowning. "She was very quiet. But of course she's always very quiet. And as usual, she'd done the work and completed all the reading. Unlike the other two, I might add. I wish I had more students like her. It might make teaching a positive pleasure."

"What other two?" Anna asked.

"Ah, well." He glanced at his wife. "I have two second-year students who are covering the same ground and we occasionally make up a tutor set."

"They were present on the Thursday morning?" Anna asked. "Who are they?"

"David Rietz and Mary Foley," he answered. "Mr. Hahn surely can't object to Thea occasionally sharing a tutorial, can he?"

"I don't see why he should," Anna said.

"I have their addresses somewhere in the study," he said, standing up. "I'd ask you in, but I'm correcting proofs at the moment." He left Anna and his wife sitting in silence. After a few minutes, Mrs. Stickle cleared her throat and said, "Repressed. Classic example of anal retention."

"What?"

"Thea Hahn. Over-achievers generally. Consume knowledge; give nothing back."

Anna scratched her ear and could think of nothing to say. Mrs. Stickle curled her lip and went back to her raffia work.

George Stickle returned with a piece of paper. "I hope it'll be of some use," he said, giving it to Anna. "Not that they fraternized much. But you never know." Anna thanked him. "No," he went on, "I'm afraid I can't remember anything unusual about the last time I saw Thea. She was as she always was. She didn't say where she was going or anything."

"If you think of anything else," Anna said, getting up to go, "or hear anything, would you let me know?" She gave Mr. Stickle her card. Mrs. Stickle sighed bad-temperedly and showed her out.

Sitting in the Renault, the plastic seat sticking to her legs, she consulted her list again. J. S. Tulloch, B.Litt. (Oxon.) lived in Maida Vale, which was near Notting Hill Gate where David Rietz lived, which was on the way home. Anna was hot and needed a cup of tea, so she started for Maida Vale. She was tired too. It wasn't the heat or the early start, but the feeling of being outclassed by everyone she had met that day. She had left school at sixteen with enough O-levels to satisfy the Metropolitan Police and that was all. People without much education, she thought, either despised it or over-respected it.

She knew that people with stunning academic qualifications could also be quite stupid in other ways, but that didn't stop her feeling very small in their company.

J. S. Tulloch's house was in a row which had no front gardens. A newsagent, a greengrocer, a launderette, and an Indian restaurant formed an unbroken line with the houses. Paper bags and dust billowed in the gutter with every passing car, and cats had come out on to the doorsteps to sleep.

The door was opened by a skinny boy of about sixteen. He was wearing a neat blue suit unequal to the length of his arms and legs. He said, "Mum's in the bedroom with my sister. I'll get her." His eyes were red-rimmed.

"It was Mr. Tulloch I wanted," Anna said.

"Oh." The boy was silent for a couple of seconds, his eyes fixed on her face. "You don't know, do you? My dad's dead. I thought you'd come to see Mum. People have been coming for days."

"Oh no! I'm very sorry," Anna said. It did not seem an adequate response. "Are you all right? Is there anything I can do?" That seemed silly too: she didn't know the boy at all. He said, "I wish there was something I could do myself. I just hang around answering the phone and opening the door. I can't even look after Mum. The house is full of people doing that."

"But later," Anna said. "You know, after the funeral, when everybody's drifted away." She was getting drawn in.

"No funeral," he told her, his eyes clutching at her like hands. "There won't be a proper finish to it. I was thinking, last night. Perhaps that's what funerals are for. Isn't that the point of rituals: to leave no doubt something's changed?" They were still standing on the doorstep. It seemed a curiously appropriate place for a conversation of that nature. Anna said, "I suppose so," and then, unwillingly, and because she couldn't leave, "Why won't there be a funeral? What happened?"

"He had an accident, swimming," he said, suddenly sounding very weary, almost bored. "They can't find the . . . him."

"That's horrible for you all."

"Yes. Half the time Mum won't believe it's happened. I wish she would. Hope is so pathetic." His eyes looked watery and he blew his nose on a not too fresh handkerchief. "What did you want my father for? Perhaps I can help."

"It was about one of his students," Anna said. He was so eager to be distracted. "Thea Hahn. She's gone missing."

"The Brain?" he asked. "Weird. She's only a few months older than I am. But she could've come from another planet. I only met her a couple of times. She scared the life out of me."

"Why?"

"Oh, you know, everyone was so impressed with her." He didn't seem able to concentrate. "And I don't know if I can even pass my O-levels. Dad'll never know now, will he?"

"Don't think about it like that. You'll only make yourself feel worse," Anna said sympathetically. She didn't know how to leave him. Eventually, she gave him her card and said, "Look, maybe in a few days you'll feel like a change of scene. Give me a ring or come round. What's your name, by the way?"

"Sam," he told her. "Do you mean it? I'd like to get away from the house sometime. Everyone here's so sort of suffocating."

"I mean it," Anna said, hoping she did. It was partly guilt about turning up at Sam's major tragedy on what now seemed to be quite a minor errand, but it was also Sam himself in his outgrown blue suit, at an age when he reacted like a child but was forcing himself to behave like an adult.

When she left, he opened the car door for her and thanked her for calling with an awkward formality that made her very sad for him.

CHAPTER 5

David Rietz was a person no one could feel sorry for. He was handsome, young, bright, and arrogant. He was also stoned. He sat in a battered rocking-chair with an expression of withdrawn pleasure approaching imbecility as he swayed to and fro. His girlfriend was on the unmade bed. She was in such disarray it was hard to tell where the bedding ended and her clothing began. A veil of smoke hung like mist close to the ceiling.

"Go on," he mumbled. "It's good stuff. Have some."

"Not now," Anna said, ignoring the outstretched hand offering a lumpy joint. She could tell it was good stuff just by looking at him. And if a window were opened the neighbours would know it too. With a favourable wind, so would half of north London.

"Go on," he repeated. "I can't talk to you if you're straight. Or are you afraid of being high?"

"Piss off," Anna said crossly. "You bleeding dopers are all the same."

"Yeah, leave her alone," the girlfriend chimed in. "You're such a fascist when you turn on." David's face melted into a dreamy sneer as he rocked back and forth. "Monstrous army of women," he said. "This one wants to know about the Brain, and tells me to piss off. That one wants me to marry her and insults me. You girls've lost your talent for manipulation."

"Want to be stroked or flattered or cajoled, do you?" the girlfriend said, assembling herself into something like order, "Well, how about this? You're a conceited, spiritually flabby, little turd. You're supposed to be among the academic élite and you'll probably end up with power and influence. Well, God help us all. I've had enough." She got up; the grubby skirt separating itself from the grubby sheets. He laughed and handed her the joint. She sucked in as much as her lungs would hold and held her breath. Exhaling with a long sigh, she flopped back down on the bed. He laughed again. "She does this once a week," he said. "She doesn't mean it. She's supposed to be among the academic élite herself, and she can't do without me."

"I do mean it. That's the tragedy," she said, lying down and closing her eyes. "Who's Thea Hahn, anyway?"

"A profound question," David said, staring up at the ceiling as if a wonderful film were projected on it. "Maybe the girl with amber eyes will enlighten us."

"Me?" said Anna, who had had just about enough of the two of them. "All I know is she's missing. I've never met her. You have. In fact, you must be one of the last to see her if you left George Stickle's together."

"Worthy old George," David mused, "a prince among plodders. And you must be a princess of the same ilk if you don't know that the Brain was unknowable."

"I don't want a bleeding character analysis," Anna said acidly. "Just where she went after the tutorial: who was she friends with. Boring facts like that."

"Ah, the facts," he said with an exaggerated sigh. "The things known certainly to have occurred, the data of truth. Dear stranger, there are none."

"Cobblers," Anna said, getting up. "I'll talk to you sometime when you've dried out."

"You're welcome to try," he said, gazing at her. "Next time come when I'm alone. We could explore the facts of life if it's facts you're pursuing."

The girlfriend said nothing. She looked as if she had passed out. Anna said, "Fact off!" and left. She thought she could hear mocking laughter all the way down the stairs. Life was too short to waste chunks of it on the likes of David Rietz. She got in the car and drove home.

Her flat was hot and stuffy. The plants were drooping. Anna opened all the windows and filled the watering can. There were sweet basil seedlings growing on the kitchen windowsill which she had forgotten to water that morning. She hadn't made the bed either. Early starts made for neglect.

She watered the plants and straightened the bed. Then she made a pot of tea. Even tardy virtue demanded some reward. Tea, she thought, could be the answer to all ills: if you're cold it warms; if you're hot it cools; if you're low it picks you up and if, as now, you're frustrated it gives you something to do.

Drinking, she wandered round her living-room looking with pleasure at the minutiæ of her life: all perfectly ordinary and understandable—the Japanese bird print on the wall, Hockney's Splash over the fireplace, the stereo, records, the shelves she'd made, the rather worn Turkish rug bought at auction.

Selwyn tapped on the door and came in without invitation.

"I'm a completely ordinary person, aren't I?" Anna said, without looking round. She knew it was Selwyn because he always tripped over the doormat.

"Not at all," Selwyn said, surprised. "You've raised mere competence to an art. Got any beer?"

"In the fridge."

Selwyn disappeared into the kitchen and Anna could hear him rummaging. Something fell on the floor; she hoped it was only the butter. Selwyn was accident prone—or, as he preferred to explain, inanimate objects had it in for him. He emerged, looking flustered, with a beer can. "Er, um, scrambled eggs tonight," he said, by way of apology. He sat in an armchair while Anna cleaned up the eggs.

"What's the attraction of ordinary?" he asked when Anna had washed her hands and stopped swearing at him.

"Oh, I don't know," she said, finishing her tea. "I've just been talking to a doped-up wally who calls his economics professor a prince of plodders."

"Makes a change," he said, burping and splashing beer on his shirt where it joined the marmalade and dried tomato pips. Selwyn's food tended to bite back. "I mean, it's a bit better than shoplifters and the usual low-life you mix with. What're you doing this time?"

"Looking for a young genius."

"Look no further," Selwyn said, spreading his arms expansively and pouring a generous tot of beer on to the Turkish rug.

"Young?" Anna said through clenched teeth as she mopped the rug. "Genius? You can't even get beer into your mouth without causing a flood and your poems

don't even rhyme. Bea has to fill in your tax forms and I
have to mend your sodding typewriter. Don't talk to
me about genius."

"Speaking of which . . ." Selwyn said sheepishly.
"Bea made me promise to mow the lawn, only the
round thing's come off the front of the mower and it
won't go back on. And if I don't do something about the
grass she says I can whistle for my supper."

"Well, tough," Anna said. "You've just broken mine.
Why should I help you earn yours?"

"Oh, come on, Anna," he wheedled. "It's going to be
chicken salad and chocolate mousse. You know I love
chocolate mousse. There'll be enough for you too. Isn't
that better than eggs?"

"It might be," she said grudgingly. Bea did indeed
make a delicious chocolate mousse. "Only, if I mend the
mower, you'll find some way of making me use it."

"I won't," he promised without much conviction.
"But if I did, it'd only be fair. We do let you sit in the
garden, after all, and you don't pay rent or rates for
it—just out of sheer neighbourliness."

"Neighbourliness, my eye," Anna snorted. "I'm always mowing your grass."

"Also," Selwyn said with a combative gleam in his
eye, "you've been at my newspaper again. I could
charge you for that too."

CHAPTER 6

In the morning Anna phoned Elgin Underwood. He
was not a full-time lecturer at the University, he told
her, more a specialized crammer. He had only seen
Thea half a dozen times. Yes, she was exceptional. No,
he didn't know anything about her except that she had
been doing a course on Art History and Appreciation

but had given it up, because she thought Geology was more in her line.

Anna was interested. It was the first time she had heard of Thea exerting a will of her own. She asked who had taught the course. Elgin Underwood did not know. Anna was welcome to come and see him that afternoon if she thought it would help. Anna didn't. She called Danielle Soper.

"That's right," Mrs. Soper said. "A woman. Ex-Courtauld. Lynne something. I've probably got the address somewhere."

"Can I come round?" Anna asked. "I ought to look at Thea's room too."

"If you hurry," Mrs. Soper said. "The boys are out for a while and when they get back I'm going shopping." She sounded as if she planned her day to avoid her own children. Anna wanted to avoid them too so she left her coffee undrunk and drove straight to Islington.

The house was unnaturally quiet. Mrs. Soper let her in and showed her to Thea's room. The door was locked.

"It's to keep the boys out," she said, producing a key. "They got in once when Thea first came to us. She was most upset. They don't mean any harm. It's just that everything they touch breaks or tears. I keep my own room locked too."

Like Thea's bedroom in Wimbledon, this room was immaculate.

"Did she clean it herself?" Anna asked, looking round at the straight lines of books and papers. Not even a handkerchief was out of place.

"As I said yesterday, she was absolutely no trouble at all." Mrs. Soper sighed. "I could have had three more like her in the house and never known the difference. Even the policeman who came was impressed. I'll go and find that address for you."

Anna sighed too. The neatness looked impenetrable.

She looked under the pillow, ran a hand under the mattress, opened all the drawers, searched the wardrobe, shook out the books, and found not so much as a toffee paper.

"This just isn't natural," she said when Mrs. Soper came back. "I can't find anything to tell me she exists apart from what she stuffs in her head. And that's all Greek to me."

"What are you looking for?" Mrs. Soper asked.

"I don't know—anything," Anna said. "You go through most people's pockets and you'd find a bus ticket, receipts, an envelope—something'd tell you where they'd been, what they spent their money on. Then one thing leads to another."

"Thea's always been a tidy girl." Mrs. Soper looked puzzled. She wasn't used to someone being criticized for tidiness.

As a last resort, Anna opened the single drawer of Thea's work table, and found two empty notebooks and a ream of clean paper. Underneath the paper however was a framed photograph of Mr. and Mrs. Hahn. The glass was broken.

"Oh dear," Mrs. Soper said when Anna showed her. "The boys must have smashed it. Thea wouldn't want broken glass on her desk."

"Mmm," Anna murmured going to the door. "Can I use your phone again? I want to see that art historian."

The art historian was in fact a painter and picture-restorer. She had a studio at the north end of West End Lane, really a ground-floor flat with hardly any furniture. The railway could be heard but not seen and the north-facing windows looked on to a tangled green garden.

Lynne McCain was in her forties and might have been beautiful if she had taken the trouble. She was dark but growing grey, slim but clothed in a shapeless man's shirt with no collar. She had long, well-shaped hands but her fingernails were dirty.

She produced mugs of strong tea five minutes after Anna arrived and sat cross-legged in a crumpled old sofa completely relaxed, listening to Anna's questions. Anna liked her immediately.

"It was her parents' idea," she said, after a while. "A little art to balance the maths and science. They said they were worried she was specializing too young. Fair enough, the girl was a visual illiterate. And they paid well."

"But?" Anna asked, wandering round touching all the strange objects that were part of Lynne McCain's trade: a tailor's dummy draped in red velvet, some plaster casts of a man's hands, a light-box, etched zinc plates, sea shells, strangely coloured stones, pots of paint, tubes of paint, brushes.

"Oh well, painting," Lynne said with a shrug. "You either do it or you don't. If you're not drawn to it one way or another, no amount of theory's going to help. I mean, I could give her a book about Giotto, for example, and the next time I saw her she knew all about Giotto but it didn't mean any more to her than $e = MC^2$ does to me. I should've taken lessons from her. At least I'm interested in the implications of $e = MC^2$."

"Were you supposed to teach her to paint—as well as the history stuff?"

"That was the general idea." Lynne frowned, remembering. "It was quite ridiculous. The poor girl simply froze the minute I put a pencil in her hand. She didn't do a thing, so finally I showed her slides instead. A waste of time, as in the end we both agreed."

"Why did she freeze?"

"She didn't say. But after watching her a while I thought it was because she didn't know how to get it right."

"But, surely," Anna said curiously, "that's what you were there to show her."

"Ah, well . . ." Lynne smiled. "Perhaps that's where she knows more about it than you or I do. You see, I can show her something: how to look, or how to use a line, or how to catch reflected light, but I can't show her how to get it right. There's no such thing really. You can break every rule in the book and still, if you're lucky, make something beautiful. The only thing you can't do is get it right. Well, you can, but it's such a subjective right that it hardly exists."

"Which might be exciting or scary, depending on your point of view," Anna suggested.

"It's a funny business, this," Lynne said, nodding. "You can get really old people, in their eighties say, who the rest of the world would call great and you can see they're still learning: still trying and failing at things they couldn't master when they were eighteen. You have to be very persistent or very passionate or maybe a bit dim. I don't know."

"Thea isn't dim."

"No." Lynne agreed. "But I thought she was frightened."

"What of?"

"She didn't say. Maybe nothing specific. I was just rather sorry for her."

"That's funny," Anna said thoughtfully. "Everyone else seems to envy her."

"I did a drawing of her if you're interested." Lynne got up and rummaged in a portfolio. "Here."

Anna looked. It was a pencil drawing. The shape of the head and the features were familiar, but Lynne had seen and conveyed in a few lines something none of the photographs showed. Anna couldn't quite put her finger on it, but it was something unexpectedly pathetic and vulnerable. Lynne put the drawing away again. She said, "Well, I wish I could help. It's not what she's like that's important now: it's where she is."

"Quite," Anna said, pulling herself together. "I've got a couple more people to see, but so far nothing leads anywhere." She was suddenly worried. It wasn't unusual to feel anxious about someone she'd never met. If she was looking hard enough for a person she always got a bit involved. But talking to Lynne and especially seeing the drawing gave her a sense of urgency.

CHAPTER 7

Kids missing from homes all over England often come to the West End. It is impossible to know from a quick glance which ones are being searched for and which are not because a lot of them look lost.

Anna, driving through to Southwark where Mary Foley had a room, watched them wandering the streets or sprawled under Eros with a specially sensitive eye: kids looking pale and tired, kids stoned at eleven in the morning, kids looking as if it had been weeks since they'd had a proper meal or a bath. It was a fine day again and she saw them everywhere; all somebody's sons or daughters.

Mrs. Hahn was certain Thea was not a dropout. But Anna knew that children left home for any number of reasons, and without money or family support they could look dirty, exhausted, and starved in a matter of days.

She crossed the river at Waterloo Bridge and picked her way around behind the station.

Anyone looking at the house where Mary Foley lodged might be forgiven for thinking that she too was down and out. It was a squat with boarded-up windows, flaking paint, and cracked plaster. The stairs were sagging and looked as if a stamped foot would turn them to match wood. But Mary was a university student, eking out her grant.

She was lying on a mattress, finishing an essay, surrounded by books.

"Oh yes, Young Genius," she said, cheerfully making room beside her for Anna. "Gone walkies, has she? Weird. I didn't think she had it in her. Made me sick, she did. Took me blood, sweat and tears to get where I got and she doesn't have to lift a finger."

"When you left the Stickles', the last time you saw her, did you talk?" Anna moved a book that was digging into the base of her spine. "Did she say where she was going?"

"She hardly ever said a word," Mary said. "Don't really remember. She might've said something about an English tutorial. Or that might've been another time. Ask David Rietz, they went off in the same direction. But watch him. He may be very clever but he's a bit of a bastard."

"Was something going on there?"

"There's always something going on with Dave. But don't ask me. I hardly talk to him either. He really screwed up a friend of mine last term. Fancies himself a bit of a stallion. Trouble is, so do a few of my mates."

"And Thea?"

"Who knows? I wouldn't've given her credit for anything more than brilliant thoughts on lofty subjects. But still waters, as they say . . ."

"Yeah." Anna got to her feet.

"Ask David," Mary said picking up a pen. "Sorry I can't help. Some of us have to slog to get through exams."

Anna left her reassembling her essay and trod back down the tottering staircase to the warm sunshine.

By now there were more people than ever on the streets. The bright day had sucked people out of their homes or offices like water out of a sponge and the journey to Notting Hill Gate was slow and sticky. When she got there David Rietz was out. There was nothing to do but wait for him. After an hour she was so bored she rang the office.

Beryl said, "Where are you, for heaven's sake? Don't you ever check in?"

"The Gate," Anna said. "Why?"

"Come in immediately."

"Why? I'm busy," said Anna, who only seconds before had been wondering how on earth to survive the tedium. Beryl's managerial skill often had that effect.

"That girl you're looking for. She's turned up, no thanks to you," Beryl said, not attempting to conceal the smugness. "There's someone here wants to talk to you. So come in right now."

Anna said, "Oh all right," and rang off feeling deflated.

It should have taken two minutes to get from Notting Hill to Kensington High Street but by the time Anna raced up Brierly Security's stairs she had already spent twenty fruitless minutes trying to find a legal parking space. As Beryl did not count parking fines as legitimate expenses and Anna usually had rotten luck with traffic wardens she was on the verge of losing her temper. Only the sight of Bernie Schiller's comfortable bulk at the top of the stairs saved an outburst.

"Count to ten, love," he advised, grinning at her flushed face. "Don't go running in like that. Puts you at a disadvantage."

"One . . . two," Anna panted. "How're you doing, Bernie? Three . . . four."

"Medium rare," Bernie said. "I've got the afternoon off. Two days in court—what a waste of time."

"When you've quite finished," Beryl snapped, coming out of her office and standing hands on hips in the corridor. "You are the limit, Anna, always off somewhere, never phoning in. You'll have to pull your socks up. The Commander's getting in some bleepers to try next week."

"Bleepers!" Anna cried outraged. "You'll be having us on leads next."

"Unreliable things, bleepers," Bernie said calmly, winking at Anna.

"Oh, very," Anna said, with a snort of laughter. Beryl

looked puzzled. She said, "Well, go in for goodness sake. They've been waiting for you half the morning."

Anna knocked on Mr. Brierly's door and went in.

Martin Brierly was sitting with his back to the window. His visitor, on the opposite side of the desk, was drinking coffee and grimacing as if it was not his first cup. With evident relief Mr. Brierly said, "Miss Lee, this is Mr. Embury, the Hahns' solicitor."

"How d'you do," Anna said, shaking hands.

Without any preamble at all Mr. Embury said, "I have here a letter authorizing you, as a bona fide employee of Mr. Rodney Hahn, to take charge of his daughter, Thea." Anna stared at him. She had never seen a neater man. He looked as if he had used a plumb line to achieve the exact arrangement of his tie. Even the rims of his spectacles gleamed waxily. He obviously didn't think his words needed any explanation, so Anna said, "To who?"

"Whom," Mr. Brierly said absently. Then collecting himself he went on, "Thea is in hospital in Dorset. The letter will empower you to move her. It appears Miss Hahn suffered a fit . . ."

"Small fit," Mr. Embury corrected. "Nothing to concern yourself with. The details of where she is and where she should be relocated appear on the appended document." He proffered an envelope with a sheet of thick white paper clipped to it. Anna took it. She said, "What was she in Dorset for?"

"Mrs. Hahn received information as to her whereabouts by telephone this morning," Mr. Embury said stiffly. "There has, so far, been no explanation. And I am to convey to you Mr. Hahn's request, that you should at no time gossip with the hospital staff and/or anyone else who might show an interest in Mr. Hahn's private affairs."

"Does he have many?" Anna said before she could stop herself.

"That's quite unnecessary," Mr. Brierly said hastily.

"Mr. Embury, we have a reputation for confidentiality and discretion. Miss Lee is utterly reliable." Mr. Embury looked at her without any confidence. Anna looked at the sheet of paper. She said, "It'll take me five or six hours there and back."

"I'll inform both the hospital and the nursing home," Mr. Embury said. "You will be expected in both places. When you have carried out your instructions, telephone Mr. Brierly immediately."

"I suggest you be on your way," Mr. Brierly said quickly. "Enough time's been wasted already." He looked discomfited. If anyone threw their weight about in his office, he wanted it to be himself.

Anna left. "Sod 'em all," she said out loud on her way down to the street. Johnny Crocker overtook her on the stairs. He said, "Have you heard about the bleepers? Bloody liberty, I call it."

"Unreliable things, bleepers," Anna said, cheering up.

"Eh? Oh yeah, good thinking."

"Bernie's idea," Anna told him.

"Crafty old fox," Johnny said approvingly.

CHAPTER 8

Anna took the M3 out of London, the A30 past Salisbury's featherlight spire and then jogged south-west down to Britmouth. She was partly occupied with the route and partly occupied by what she'd say to the girl they called the Brain when she met her. How do you start a conversation with a sixteen-year-old, gifted in pure maths and astrophysics? Seen any good films lately? Which end of the bath do you sit? Her own thoughts demonstrated nicely how isolated a girl like Thea could become if ordinary people were too intimidated by her reputation to chat to her about ordinary things.

Sun slanted in through the windscreen as the afternoon wore on. She stopped for petrol and a sandwich
about thirty miles after Salisbury. The sandwich was
tightly swaddled in plastic and took longer to unwrap
than to eat. But the view was terrific. She had parked
by the roadside and a patchwork of ochre and green
fields spread out around her like a blanket on a lumpy
bed: acres of unpopulated country set aside to produce
grain. Nothing stirred except the occasional hawk hanging and floating. She could imagine mice and rabbits
cowering between the stalks.

The nearer she got to the coast, however, the greener
it became: smaller fields, thicker hedges, more trees,
and pasture dotted with munching cows. Small torna-
does of starlings wheeled over the cows.

Britmouth was long and thin, and divided into two
halves by the river. Anna stopped on the edge of town
to ask directions. She found the hospital on the west
side: a brick building looking as if it was held together
by black pipes and built tactfully next to the cemetery.
It was now well into the afternoon.

The lobby was cold and dim. A few people, carrying
bunches of flowers and paper bags full of fruit, wandered uncertainly through. Anna presented herself and
the letter at reception.

"I don't know anything about that," the receptionist
said through a mouth like a crack in a wall. "Take a seat
over there. I'll try to find someone who does." She did
not try very hard. It was a quarter of an hour before a
middle-aged nurse tiptoed to Anna's side.

"This way," she whispered in the undertone used by
professionals in echoing public buildings. "You have the
ambulance outside? Where's the attendant?"

"Just me," Anna said, mystified. "What're you talking
about?"

"I'd've thought you'd've laid on proper transport,"
the nurse said primly, leading the way through hollow
corridors to a flight of concrete steps. They walked up

two flights and along another corridor to a small
waiting-room.

"In here," said the nurse. "I'll ring for Doctor."

Anna opened the door and went in. Thea Hahn was
sitting slumped in a plastic chair staring at the green
vinyl floor. She did not look up.

"Thea?" Anna said tentatively. "I'm Anna Lee. I've
come to take you home." There was no response. Anna
stood, at a loss, in the middle of the room. The nurse
came back. She said, "Doctor's just looking up the
medication chart. You'll have to sign, you know."

"Okay." Anna was looking at Thea who still hadn't
moved. She said, "Come on, love. We're going home."

"She won't answer," said the nurse loftily. "She's
been a very naughty girl."

"What're you talking about?" Anna said. "And how
did she get those bruises?"

"If you're going to raise your voice, you'd better
come outside," the nurse said, opening the door. "We
don't want to upset the patient."

Out in the corridor, Anna said, "Look, what's wrong
with her? I was told she'd had some minor fit."

"I wouldn't know about that," the nurse said. "You'll
have to ask Doctor." She looked up and down the
corridor. No doctor appeared. After a while she went
on, "That child should never have been let out on her
own. She isn't responsible."

"What do you mean?" Anna asked.

"Well, she's retarded, isn't she?"

Anna bit her lip and opened the waiting-room door
again. Thea was sitting in the same position. Anna went
over to her and studied her face closely. She was identical to Thea Hahn. But the nurse was right, she looked
apathetic and half-witted. White stuff had collected in
the corners of her eyes and something that looked like
crusted drool caked her lips. The glossy cap of page-boy
hair hung lifeless as a flag on a still day.

Anna went back to the nurse, shutting the door softly

behind her. She said, "Does she have any identification on her?"

"Everything will be handed over to you when you sign the release."

After a few minutes a doctor appeared, white coat open and flapping, glasses at half-mast, hands in pockets. "Come to take our patient home?" he said in the patronizing voice doctors use when talking to laymen.

"Yes," Anna said. "What's wrong with her?"

"I'll just take a look, shall I?" he said, and disappeared into the waiting-room. The nurse followed, shutting the door neatly in Anna's face. He came out after a while and set off briskly down the corridor saying, "You'd better come to my office. There are some forms. Someone from Admin should've come but I suppose it's up to us as usual."

His office was about half a mile away, a cubbyhole between the sluices and Sister's room. He produced the forms after a vague search in what looked like a sea of paper. Anna said, "Before I sign, please tell me exactly when she was brought in, by whom and in what condition."

"I don't have the admission forms," he said, surprised and impatient. "Sister keeps them."

"Then please get them, or Sister," Anna said drawing herself up to her full height. Obviously she had to put on some show to get any answers. "I have to drive with Thea for the next three hours, and I'd like to know what to expect."

"I'll see," he said reluctantly and left her alone for another ten minutes. When he came back he had another sheaf of papers and his glasses had slipped even lower. He said, reading from the top sheet, "Well, it says here, she was admitted at about eleven yesterday morning. She was brought in by the police. They had been called to the shopping precinct where she had had what was described as an epileptiform attack. As to the results of our examinations, I suggest her doctor at . . ."

he consulted the letter Anna had brought, "at Adam House gets in touch with me in the usual manner."

Anna took a deep breath and said, "Well, thanks most awfully, Doc. So if anything happens on the way back to London, like her throwing herself out of the car and having an 'epileptiform attack' in the fast lane, I can tell the police to get in touch with you. Right?"

"That's extremely unlikely," the doctor said coldly. "She's been sedated."

"Terrific. And that leads me to another observation. There are bruises on her face and arms. Her parents are going to want to know why. So would you like a full-scale inquiry or would you like to tell me simply what's wrong with her?"

"I find your manner most objectionable," he said, colouring like a ripe plum.

"I won't tell you how I find yours," Anna said. "You're annoyed enough already. Why don't you just simmer down and give me the information I need. It won't hurt. It will hurt if Mr. Hahn decides to sue. He's got a lot of clout you know."

The doctor buried himself in his papers again. His colour faded from plum to mottled grey. "This is confidential information," he said, at last. "We are not responsible for the bruising, I assure you. However—the results of an EEG showed generalized, irregular, slow activity accentuated by overbreathing, some of which may be epileptogenic. She was catatonic when admitted but soon showed signs of delusional behaviour."

"Such as?"

"Apparently she made animal noises and hid under the bed. There was also evidence of hyperventilation and profuse sweating, and during this period her speech was bizarre to say the least. The nursing staff suggested that the episode might be an hysterical, attention-seeking ploy. She was sedated and has been withdrawn and apathetic ever since."

"Is that all?"

"We are not a psychiatric hospital," the doctor said stiffly. "We are not equipped to assess this kind of patient in forty-eight hours. Now if you don't mind, I have other patients to attend to. You can find your way back, I take it?"

"Thanks," Anna said briefly and took herself back to the waiting-room. The nurse was on guard outside tapping the toe of her highly polished black shoe on the ground. "Everything signed?" she asked, opening the door.

"Yes," said Anna, realizing that in the heat of the moment nothing had been.

"You'd best be on your way then."

"Yes. Where are Thea's shoes?"

"She was brought in barefoot," the nurse said and added primly, "The National Health does not supply shoes."

"Would the National Health lend us a blanket?" Thea was wearing a blue cotton singlet and a thin skirt. Her legs were bare. She did not look at all like Mrs. Hahn's carefully dressed daughter.

"I'm afraid I can't authorize that," the nurse said.

"I'll send it right back."

The nurse shrugged. "Sorry," she said. "The paperwork alone would take hours."

"Okay, we'll manage." She did not want to take on the might of the National Health over a blanket. She took Thea's hand and said, "Come on, ducks, let's get out of here."

Thea sat still. Her eyelids were waxy and heavy. "Where are my glasses?" she said slowly and thickly.

"You didn't have any glasses," the nurse said. "Don't be difficult now."

"But I can't see." Her voice sounded as if it was coming up from a deep well. "I can't see what I want to see."

Anna had a pair of sunglasses in her bag. She dug them out and gave them to Thea. The nurse sniffed.

"You shouldn't humour them," she said. "It's a rod for your own back."

"Well, it's my back," Anna said crossly. Thea put the glasses on. Her coordination seemed poor and the glasses hung crazily from one ear. Anna straightened them. "Let's shift," she said, again holding Thea's hand. "This place is driving me up the wall."

This time Thea came. She walked unsteadily, like an old woman, but eventually Anna got her outside into the sunlight. She opened the car door and tilted the driver's seat forward. "You'd better get in the back," she suggested. "I don't know what they've given you, but it looks as if you need somewhere to sleep. Are you hungry at all?"

Thea didn't answer, but she crawled obediently into the backseat and lay curled up. The car was stuffy with trapped heat. Anna rolled down the window on her own side and made sure the passenger door was locked. The nurse handed her a polythene bag. "Her things," she said, standing back from the car. "Drive carefully. You'll be all right: she's sedated."

Anna drove fast out of Britmouth and stopped at the first convenient lay-by. Thea was still curled up and looked as if she was asleep. Anna opened the polythene bag. It contained a cream canvas shoulder-bag. She unzipped it and found a purse, empty except for a few pence, and a brand new passport. That was all. She started the car and headed for London. Behind her, in the west, clouds were piling up like meringue. The good weather was breaking up.

CHAPTER 9

The sun had set in a stormy sky when Anna drove through the gates of Adam House. In spite of the dark she had the impression that it had once been a senior churchman's folly. Narrow gothic windows looked over a gravel car park and the curved doorway was faced with stone.

She woke Thea and led her into a huge mosaicked hall. A heavy oak table stood in the middle. A woman in spotless white overalls came round it to meet them. She smiled and said, "Thea! How nice to see you again."

A door opened behind her and Rodney Hahn, with Mr. Embury at his shoulder, came through. Thea suddenly gripped Anna's hand and howled like an animal in pain—a high, piercing sound, totally unexpected. Rodney Hahn stopped, his face yellow with shock. Mr. Embury turned round and walked back through the door. The woman in white laid a hand on Thea's arm and said, "Hush now, dear. You're alarming your father."

"Ow-wow-wow-wow!" Thea howled, backing away holding Anna's hand in a grip like a navvy's. Anna had to back away with her.

The woman in white made an urgent gesture to Rodney Hahn, and he followed Mr. Embury out of sight. Two men appeared through another door. One of them said, "Do you need any help, Mrs. Grayle?"

"Not yet," Mrs. Grayle said calmly. "But perhaps you could tell Dr. Frank that Miss Hahn's arrived."

Anna stopped Thea's retreat by putting her arms round her. Thea howled into her ear. "Give it a rest, ducks," Anna said into a mouthful of hair. "I can't hear myself think." Sweat trickled down her ribs. The howls gradually died away. Mrs. Grayle said, "Why don't you come upstairs, dear? We've got a lovely room ready."

Thea wrapped both arms round Anna, clinging as if to a log in a flood. "At least have a look at it," Anna said. "If you don't like it we can always find another one."

They made undignified progress across the hall—Mrs Grayle leading, Anna and Thea locked together. In the same manner, they went upstairs.

From what Anna could see of it, Adam House was more like a country hotel than a nursing home. Thea's room was cosy with brightly coloured curtains and a matching bedspread. There was a comfortable armchair by the window and a round table in the corner. The only thing that spoiled the impression was a spy-hole in the door.

"What do you think?" Anna asked, talking randomly. "Think you can stick it for a few days?" She felt she was cheating. But there was nothing else to be done. Thea relaxed her hold and scrambled under the bed.

"Don't worry," Mrs. Grayle said. "She'll be all right now."

Anna knelt and lifted the bedspread. Thea was curled up as she had been on the backseat of the car. Her thumb was in her mouth. She was still wearing Anna's dark glasses.

"Don't worry," Mrs. Grayle said again. "Dr. Frank'll be along in a minute."

"The doctor in Britmouth gave her something only three hours ago."

"Oh, he may not give her anything else," Mrs. Grayle said comfortingly. "He'll probably let her stay under the bed if she feels better that way. This always looks worse than it is, if you aren't used to it."

"Well, I'm not used to it, and it looks preposterous," Anna said, getting up. Her legs were shaking.

"You've coped very well." Mrs. Grayle had pink and white skin and pale-blue eyes that sparkled with intelligence. "You might as well go downstairs now. She won't come to any harm. I promise."

Anna decided to believe her: having no experience, she could not trust her own judgement. She went slowly downstairs to the hall where she found Mr. Embury leaning nonchalantly on the table. He was thumbing through a copy of *Country Life*. Rodney Hahn had disappeared. Mr. Embury looked up as she approached. He said, "Mr. Hahn has gone home. Most distressing for the poor chap. I'm to convey his thanks to you for transporting his daughter."

"That's okay," Anna said. "I'll probably talk to him tomorrow."

"I think not," Mr. Embury said coldly. "Now that Miss Hahn is safe, he won't be requiring the services of Brierly Security any more."

"Even so, I'd like to know why he didn't mention that Thea had had mental trouble before. That's the sort of thing he should've told us."

"Miss Hahn is suffering from mental exhaustion." Mr. Embury straightened his already vertical tie. "She has not had mental trouble, as you so crudely put it."

"Well, this isn't a country club," Anna said, annoyed. "And she's been here before."

"How do you know that?" he asked, frowning.

"I'm a bleeding detective, in case you hadn't noticed." They stared at each other in mutual hostility for a few seconds. Mr. Embury cleared his throat and said, "Mr. Hahn did not think the matter relevant. You were not required to psychoanalyse his daughter: merely to find her. Which, I might add, you failed to do. The incident is now closed and best forgotten. Or do you want an apology?"

"Or do you want a kick in the slats?" Anna said, losing her temper completely. "Of all the rude, pompous pronks I've met, you take the gold." He looked at her, open-mouthed. She said quickly, "Look, I've had better days. Why don't I just go home before I say something I'll regret?" She swung away from him and marched out to the car.

Her hands were sweating and she fumbled with the keys. It was not Mr. Embury alone that had made her so angry. He was simply the last straw. But the knowledge did not make her feel less frustrated. She had made a bad day worse, and she was in no doubt that every word would get back to Mr. Brierly. Bad reports always did. It was another of Murphy's famous laws.

When she got home, she found Bea Price sweeping the hall. "You're back late," Bea said. "Had a good day?"

"Unforgettable," Anna replied grimly. "How was yours?" Bea did the accounts for an electrical supply firm in Shepherds Bush. They were due for an audit and what with the extra work that entailed and Selwyn's artistic temperament Bea was looking a trifle threadbare.

"Bloody terrible, it was," she said. "One of the partners kept me back an hour after work with the books."

"Why don't you let Selwyn sweep the hall? You look knackered."

"Let him?" Bea's eyebrows disappeared into her hair. "The time it'd take me forcing him I could sweep seven halls. Come in and have a cup of something. You don't look too fresh yourself. Look at him," she added as they went into the sitting-room, "Lord Muck himself, at his ease."

Selwyn was stretched out on the sofa watching the boxing on television. "At my ease, woman?" he cried indignantly. "I'll have you know I'm suffering. It's ulcers, I'm sure of it."

"Ulcers are for workers and worriers," Bea said tartly. "That's wind, you've got. You ate your bubble and squeak too quickly." She vanished into the kitchen. Selwyn got up and turned the television off. "Boxers," he grumbled. "More like belly dancers, these are." He had a fat, sedentary man's contempt for anything other than total excellence in athletes. "Well, young Leo," he went on, "found any geniuses today?"

Anna sat down in one of Bea's tidily upholstered chairs and leaned her head back. "Not really," she said. "I didn't find her: she just turned up. And when I went to fetch her the hospital she was at had her tagged as retarded. Which is how she acted. And then when I got her to the sodding nursing home she freaked and hid under a bed. And then her father's solicitor came over all poncy and I insulted him and he's bound to blow the gaffe to Mr. B. So all in all it was something of a catastrophe."

"But apart from that, what's she like?" Selwyn persisted. He didn't listen to one word in ten.

"How should I know?" she said dully. "She's gone round the twist, poor thing."

"A mad genius, is she?" He was interested, at last. Probably identifying, Anna thought unkindly. Bea returned with two mugs of hot milk and honey. Anna didn't much like it: it was too greasy and sweet. But she was tired and hungry so she accepted it gratefully. The doorbell rang.

"It's yours," Bea said, going to the window. "Bit late, isn't it?" Years of small town life in Dyfed had made her adept at twitching curtains without being seen. She demonstrated her skill. "It's just a lad," she reported to her waiting audience. "All hands and feet."

"Cradle-snatching again, Leo?" Selwyn hooted.

"Eff off," Anna said. "I'm out."

"Looks ever so miserable," Bea said with the comfortable compassion of one who is not about to be tested. Anna got up reluctantly and, throwing the Prices a long-suffering glance, went to the front door.

Sam Tulloch stood on the doorstep, shoulders hunched in the human shape of apology. It had begun to rain in the last few minutes and large drops fell on his bare head.

"I know it's late," he stammered. "I walked, and it took longer than I thought. It's not important, honestly. I just wanted to see you." The rain fell harder. Anna sighed. "Come in," she said, as warmly as she could manage. She had no doubt that Bea, invisible behind her curtains, was missing nothing.

CHAPTER 10

The night air had the clean peppery smell it gets with the first rain after a long dry spell. Anna sniffed it appreciatively and left the window open a crack while she made a pot of tea and two thick ham sandwiches. She took them in to where Sam sat, sunk in dejection, in an armchair.

"The man from the insurance company came today," he told her. "He kept calling me 'sonny' and in the same breath telling me I had to be the man of the house. They all do that. I wish they'd make up their minds."

Anna poured the tea and gave Sam a sandwich. "Is the family going to be all right for money?" she asked.

"Oh yes," Sam said bitterly. "It seems Dad was worth more dead than alive. I was thinking about leaving school and getting a job. Only now I won't have to."

Anna sensed his disappointment. He wanted to make a heroic contribution to the family but the chance had been denied him. She said, "Maybe it is best to take your time on decisions like that. There aren't too many jobs going for people without qualifications."

"I'd've found something," he said stoutly, his mouth full.

"Of course you would," Anna agreed quickly. Sam looked gratified. He ate and drank in silence for a while. Then he said, "They're going to have a memorial

service at the College chapel. It's not a funeral but it's
better than nothing. Then maybe they'll all realize he's
not coming back. The thing I can't stand is my mother
saying, 'But he's only gone for the weekend.' And then
she cries and that starts my sisters off too. The police
sent his things back this morning, including all the notes
he'd taken to work on. And my mother went round
saying, 'But he'll need his notes.' It's driving me mad.
He was doing the foreword to a new book about the
Metaphysicals. And he went away to get a few days'
peace and quiet. It's the students, you see. Mother
blames them."

"How?" Anna asked wearily. It was late and she was
hoping he'd soon talk himself out.

"He could never say no," Sam said. "He let anyone
who wanted help or advice come to him. So if he
needed time for his own work he had to get out of the
house to do it." He sounded half proud of his father,
half ashamed. But because his father was dead he couldn't
admit to the shame.

"Wasn't Thea Hahn supposed to have a tutorial with
him just before she went missing?"

"Yes. I looked at his appointment diary after you left
yesterday. She was down for Thursday the 12th. But
she didn't turn up. That's what I was going to tell you."
He blushed. He had forgotten his own excuse for coming.

"Thank you," Anna said, carefully ignoring the blush.
"Does your mother blame her too?"

"Oh no. Thea was a private student and her father
paid. It was all the others, she says, who took advantage
of his good nature. She says he had time for everyone
except us. But that's not true really. I think she just
resents him not taking us when he went to Stony Point.
But if he'd taken us he wouldn't have got any work
done. He mightn't have died either," he added misera-
bly. "I'm a better swimmer than him. I might've been
able to save him."

"What happened?" She could see Sam wanted to tell
her.

"It was the day he got there. He went swimming after lunch. There's a guest house he stayed at, near the cliff, and when he didn't come back the landlady sent her son to look for him and he met a boy who said he'd just seen a man in difficulty in the water. He was running for help, you see. But when they got down there, there was no sign of my father. Just his clothes where he'd put them on a rock. They called the police, and all sorts of people turned out to help, but they never found him."

"Have you ever been there?" Anna asked.

"Once. We all went on holiday to north Devon and stayed there for a day or so. It's very wild and rocky. Mum didn't like it. She wouldn't let my sisters swim, but I went in with Dad. It wasn't dangerous if you were careful." He broke off and his words hung like accusations.

"Even very careful people have accidents," Anna said quickly. "Or maybe there was a freak wave."

"Or maybe it was Friday the 13th." Sam sank his head in his hands.

"Don't get morbid," Anna said. It was time to say something wise and comforting. Her mind went blank.

"How can I help being morbid?" Sam said, looking up.

"Grief is one thing." She started putting plates and mugs back on the tray. "But getting morbid makes a bad time worse. Life is precious. And now you know how short it can be you don't want to waste it being morbid."

She took the tray out to the kitchen. Rah-rah-rah, she thought. Why is it impossible for one person to lift another? Pep talks were so pitifully inadequate. She leaned against the jamb of the kitchen door looking at Sam. "Don't give in," she went on as confidently as she could. "I know you're having it rough at home. But sooner or later you've got to start paying attention to life rather than death. And you just have to grit your teeth and get on with all the stuff you have to get on with—school and day to day things. If you're strong enough to do the simple things well, maybe you'll give your family something to be going on with too. It's a lot harder than jacking in school and getting a job. But it should be worth more in the end."

"Do you think so?" he asked. "Like Pilgrim?"

"Like Pilgrim," she said firmly, wondering what on earth he was talking about. "Start now." It sounded like good advice, but she didn't understand why.

"Yes," he said, getting up. "I should be going. It'd be really cruel to make my mother worry about me now." Sam had found his own inspiration, Anna thought, puzzled but relieved. She showed him out and told him again to come back if he felt in danger of being submerged.

She went to bed and a long time later dreamed that Thea was drowning: sinking under the dark green waves, twisting and turning on her way to the bottom. Anna dived in after her, but Thea became entangled in a forest of seaweed. She escaped by growing a monstrous, scaly tail and swimming away. "Life is precious," she told Anna, who was swimming with her. "You have to adapt to survive." She flicked her horrible tail and corkscrewed down to the ocean bed where Anna couldn't follow her.

When Anna woke up it had stopped raining but the rooftops were wet and shiny. The leaves dripped lazily and looked clean again as she crossed Holland Park on her way to work.

In the rec-room Johnny, Phil, and Bernie drank coffee and gossiped.

"Anyone interested in a watch?" Johnny asked. "A mate of mine's come into a gross of quartz rotaries. With everyone into digital he's having a hard time shifting them."

"Come into?" Phil scoffed. "This isn't the same mate flogging tapedecks last year? Or those manky cutlery sets the year before?"

"Different bloke entirely," Johnny said, so blithely

Anna could tell he was lying. "Come on, lads. Only fifteen quid apiece. Would I see you wrong?"

"Would you see us right?" Phil turned to the back page of the *Sun*.

"Have they got Roman numerals or proper numbers?" Anna asked in spite of her cynicism. Her own watch had been taking an eccentric view of time recently.

"I'll bring one in to show you," Johnny said triumphantly. He obviously hadn't laid eyes on them himself. "Only twelve and a half nicker seeing as you're a friend. It'd be a pony down the market."

"There's one born every minute," Phil said.

"They aren't hot, are they?" Bernie put in quietly.

"Not even warm," Johnny assured cheerfully. "Stand by me."

Beryl came in with the morning post which she distributed like a beauty queen blowing kisses. The change in the weather had brought her relief from hay fever and she had powdered her nose extra thickly in celebration.

"You're starting that supermarket account this morning, aren't you?" she said to Bernie. "If you want any help, Anna's free today."

"That'd come in handy," Bernie said. "Fancy it, Anna? Someone's on the fiddle and the owners want to know who?"

"Okay," Anna said. She enjoyed working with Bernie.

"Don't forget your report on the Hahn job. Not that you did much." Beryl couldn't resist a dig, but this time Anna didn't mind. If that was all Beryl could think of to dig about, it meant Mr. Embury hadn't yet complained. If he had, Beryl would've been the first to tell her about it.

For two days she worked with Bernie around Valuemart in Dagenham. She wore several different hats, jackets and heights of heel, drifting around the aisles and through the checkout. Sometimes Bernie stood with husbands waiting by the window. Once or twice he came in himself and bought baked beans and bread with Anna.

By the end of the week, they were fairly certain that there was more than one fiddler. They spotted two cashiers who regularly rang up less than the proper amount on the till but asked for the right money and then pocketed the difference. This was done only when the old, the shortsighted, or women with loaded trolleys and toddlers came through. The shop did not employ packers, so anyone with large amounts of shopping and a couple of screaming children was in far too much of a muddle to compare her receipt with what she'd paid.

More serious was a fiddle being run by the manager. They quickly noticed that three of the girls systematically rang up items not present in the customers' shopping baskets. "They aren't taking the money," Bernie said, after watching carefully for several hours. "The only other thing they can be doing is making up for a stock shortage. I think it's tea and instant coffee they're ringing up. Go round again and see what price they are."

So Anna drifted round again and memorized the prices of tea and instant coffee. Sure enough, whenever someone already overburdened with goods and children went past one of the three girls, an extra item, fictitious tea or coffee, was added to the bill.

"They're probably nicking crates of the stuff and selling it privately," Bernie told her. "It's probably such a large quantity, the manager can't put it all down to shoplifting or damage, so they have to get it through the till somehow. The manager has to be involved."

"It's not fair, is it?" Anna said. "The people who're paying for it are the ones who can least afford it—big families with whopping food bills."

"I think we've got enough to be going on with," Bernie said with a sigh. "If we go back to the office we can draft up a prelim and stick in a couple of recommendations and see if the owners want us to go into any more detail."

"Agreed!" said Anna whose dislike for supermarkets had lately grown to positive aversion. "That's a sodding awful shop. I'll recommend they employ packers at the very least. They won't though, will they? They'll probably just fire a few people and pat themselves on the back. Problem solved."

"Till next time," Bernie agreed.

Back at the office, Beryl greeted them at the top of the stairs with a sneeze and an ominous smile. As usual, her first blow was below the belt. "Dear oh dear, Anna," she said, eyes shining with anticipation and hay fever, "whose nose have you been getting up this time? The Commander's in an awful paddy. You're to go in double quick. It'll be your cards this time, I shouldn't wonder."

"Having a loverly time. Wish you were here," Anna muttered, drawing a deep breath and making for Martin Brierly's door. Bernie patted her shoulder and said, "I'll be in the report-room with the first aid kit."

Mr. Brierly stood by the window gazing out over Kensington High Street. He did not turn round. "I asked to see you, Miss Lee," he began quietly, "because Mr. Embury had the goodness to inform me of your contretemps with him on Wednesday. Fact of life, Miss Lee: we acquire some of our most valued clients from solicitors. They are men to be respected. We do not alienate them by offering to 'kick them in the slats,' which, I believe, was your colourful expression. Correct me if I'm wrong."

"It had been rather an upsetting day," Anna murmured feebly. Mr. Brierly swung round on his heels. His round face, usually the picture of blandness, looked stormy.

"That's no excuse, Miss Lee," he said. "However trying a day has been, we should keep the interests of the firm in the forefront of our minds."

"It's a reason, not an excuse," Anna said, in the firm belief that if she was on her way out she should go out punching. "And as for respect: Mr. Embury has the rottenest manners this side of the Thames."

Mr. Brierly lowered himself stiffly into his swivel chair and laid his arms on his desk, fingers laced, thumbs revolving at speed. "Actually, the man is insufferable," he said surprisingly. Anna could only suppose that he had been more annoyed by Mr. Embury than he was with her. If that was so, it would be fortunate if Mr. Embury had recommended her dismissal, because Martin Brierly, in his own bland way, could be as bloody-minded as anyone she knew. He continued, "But I want to warn you in the strongest possible terms that you have been sailing very close to the wind indeed."

It was going to· be all right. Anna could afford to grovel a bit. She said, "I'm very sorry, sir." Sir was always a good move. "I shouldn't have lost my temper."

"I rang Mr. Hahn after speaking to Mr. Embury and fortunately he had been in touch with the nursing home. They are of the opinion that you managed rather well in the circumstances. That being the case, I suggest we say no more about it."

Anna did not speak to Beryl as she passed her office on the way to the report-room, but she sang "I did it my way" very loudly. She knew Beryl would be listening and, with any luck, gnashing her teeth.

"First aid," Bernie said, pouring her a mug of tea. "You look bloody but unbowed."

"I bowed a bit too," she admitted, settling down beside him at the cramped desk. "I even scraped."

"Good tactics," Bernie grinned. "A little tactical forelock-tugging never went amiss. Now let's get on with it, shall we? If you start on the advice, I'll finish off the findings and, God willing, we'll be home by supper-time."

CHAPTER 11

The house Anna lived in was on the cusp between Shepherds Bush and Notting Hill, two of London's most populous villages, but in the back garden, sheltered by walls and the city's secret greenery, it could have been deep in the country. Selwyn and Bea lounged under the plane tree. The grass for once was neatly trimmed, and Selwyn was relatively sober. It was a beautiful evening, warm without the weight of summer.

Bea lay back in her gaily striped deckchair, looking at the sky and lazily sipping white plonk. For a change she was not wondering aloud about blocked gutters or whether the brickwork needed repointing or nagging Selwyn to mow the lawn. "Perhaps we should build a barbecue pit," she said dreamily, which, in its way, was far worse. Anna shuddered. Bea would have wonderfully practical plans about any new ventures. Selwyn would have baroque fantasies; and Anna would probably have to mix the cement and steer a tactful course between the two.

"Something curved and hibachi-like," Selwyn mused. "Nature abhors a square." The process was beginning already.

"There aren't two days a year you could use it," Anna said with more hope than conviction.

The sound of a bell ringing came faintly through the open back door.

"More bereaved boys," Selwyn said. "Get me a refill on your way, Leo, or better still bring the bottle."

"No chance," Anna said, staying firmly rooted to the grass. "I'm not playing good Samaritan this weekend."

55

Selwyn held out his empty glass like a begging bowl and looked round for support. Bea closed her eyes and feigned sleep. The doorbell rang again. Selwyn struggled reluctantly to his feet. "What a dismal pair of handmaidens you two turned out to be," he complained as he ambled into the house. Bea and Anna exchanged a glance of complete understanding which turned to anxiety as they heard sounds of conversation from inside the house.

"The rat!" Anna protested. "He's gone and let someone in."

"It's revenge," Bea told her. "You should've brought him that bottle when he asked. A lazy man's like a wasp. He stings when disturbed."

The lazy man appeared, bottle in hand, at the back-door. "Someone for you, Leo," he said smugly. "A patrician, he is, in a thousand guinea suit. Handsome too. Better hop along, Leo. Rich and handsome's more than you deserve. I left him in the hall."

In the hall, Anna found Rodney Hahn looking bewildered. "He said I didn't look much like a bereaved boy, but to come in anyway," he said as she showed him upstairs. "He said you were a heartless apology for a handmaiden and had probably perforated his ulcer."

"Don't pay any attention," Anna said, opening the door for him. "He's a poet and he's got wind, not ulcers."

"I'm sorry to come unannounced." He looked around, his expensive clothes and mildly patronizing glance making Anna's flat look small and underfurnished. In spite of that, he seemed several degrees less confident than he had in Wimbledon.

"I should have phoned, I suppose," he went on. "But there's something I want to discuss personally. I did speak to Commander Brierly, though, and he gave me your address."

"Well, sit down," Anna said. "Can I get you something? There's lager, tea or coffee." He shook his head.

"Nothing, thank you," he said. "Something has happened." He sat for a minute, his face expressionless, giving Anna no clue as to what was going through his mind.

"I suppose," he began with an effort. "I suppose you didn't happen to come across any hint of trouble—in Britmouth, I mean."

There had been nothing *but* trouble in Britmouth, as Anna remembered it. "What sort of trouble?" she asked carefully.

"Well, er, trouble with the police." Rodney Hahn studied his manicure and did not meet her eyes. She repeated, "What sort of trouble?"

"This is probably quite absurd," he said. "However, when Dr. Frank at Adam House phoned Britmouth General—in the normal course of events, you understand—he was told that the local police had been asking some rather strange questions of the staff there." He stopped, and Anna waited. He was behaving, she thought, like a man who didn't want to discuss his piles with a doctor. She would have to wait and see whether pain or embarrassment would win.

"I can't believe anything serious had occurred," he went on. "But I thought you might have heard some talk while you were down there."

Anna said, "Look, I really can't help unless you tell me what the trouble is."

He sighed and nodded. "Perhaps, after all, I could have a glass of lager?" he suggested. But when she brought it, he didn't seem to know what to do with it. After one sip he put the glass down beside his chair and forgot about it.

"I'd like to assure you that, until now, there has been no hint of any scandal in my family," he said after a while. "All this is undoubtedly nothing but unpleasant rumour: but I am quite at a loss as to how to deal with it."

"Well, if you want *me* to deal with it," Anna said, patiently, "you'll have to tell me about it."

"Yes. Well. On the morning my daughter was taken to Britmouth General a man was found shot to death in a hotel bedroom in Southampton. Britmouth is only a few miles from Southampton. The police constable who conveyed my daughter to Britmouth General during her fit apparently thought he heard her say she had killed someone. As I said, it is quite absurd. My daughter was suffering epileptic convulsions. She might have said anything. You cannot take seriously the . . ."

"Just a minute," Anna interrupted. "Is there any connection between Thea and the man who was shot?"

"None that I know of."

"I mean, have the police made any connection? Who is he?"

"I don't know—to both your questions."

"Do you know what Thea's exact words were?"

"No. What Dr. Frank told me was hearsay—third-hand hearsay at that."

"Has Thea ever had a fit before or has she ever been violent?"

"Of course not!" Mr. Hahn said, pink with indignation. "Whatever do you take us for?" He stopped and then, seeing her expression, added, "Well, yes, she has been to Adam House before—as an outpatient. Dr. Frank was treating her for some small signs of nervous strain."

"Okay. Now, do the police have any reason, other than what you've told me, to connect her with Southampton?"

"I don't think so."

"What about you? Has she said anything to you or Dr. Frank?"

Rodney Hahn looked at his nails again. "I haven't exactly seen her since you brought her in on Wednesday night and neither has her mother. Of course we are acting on Dr. Frank's advice."

"Of course," Anna said politely. "Well, would Dr. Frank let me talk to her?"

"I think so," Mr. Hahn said, looking up at last. "In fact he's waiting in for your call now."

"I see."

"I thought it would be more efficient if you talked to him directly before going to Britmouth. I spoke to Mr. Brierly about that too. He wants you to telephone him as well."

"I see," Anna said again. Rodney Hahn had been rather busy, and Selwyn had opened the door to a ruined weekend when he'd let him in. She sucked in her breath and said, "Do I have your permission to talk to whoever I want about whatever's necessary, this time?"

"I suppose I should apologize for Mr. Embury," he said, inspecting his gold cufflinks. "He has the family's best interests at heart, but he must have seemed a trifle overprotective. In fact he has drafted a letter, to anyone it may concern, stating that you are my representative. It will be delivered here tomorrow morning by hand."

"Not his own hand, I hope," Anna murmured under her breath. Aloud, she said, "All right. I'll call Mr. Brierly and Dr. Frank. Then we'll see what's to be done. Is Thea any better now?"

"I'm told she's coming along nicely," he said in the abstract way of someone whose business is concluded and whose thoughts have moved on to more interesting things.

Dr. Frank, when she called him about half an hour later, took a different view. "She's a very sick girl," he told her with a refreshing absence of jargon. "I don't want to throw diagnoses around. It's not really possible anyway at this stage, and words like schizophrenia or hysteria are very imprecise terms for a whole range of conditions. Let's just say she's very, very disturbed."

"Well, would I upset her any more if I spoke to her?" Anna asked. "I wouldn't want to do that."

"In fact, it might upset you more than it upsets her," he said surprisingly. "You could say that her speech and behaviour have become a form of self-protection. Well, that's one way of looking at it. I don't know how much sense you'll make of her, though. What she says might sound like random ravings, but it's more as if she's using a code or a scrambler. It can take a lot of imagination understanding the disturbed." He laughed suddenly. "I'm only a poor old shrink; sometimes I think I'd have to be a poet or another patient to interpret some of the things they say."

"Can I bring a poet with me?" she asked quickly.

"Are you serious?" Dr. Frank said, sounding amused.

"Yes." For one thing she had qualms about seeing Thea alone again; for another, she thought perhaps Selwyn was better equipped to deal with the unreasonable than she was.

"Well, I don't suppose it'd do any harm," he said. "The attention might even help her. I'll expect you tomorrow morning then."

Anna thanked him and rang off. She went downstairs wondering how she could persuade Selwyn he was the best man for the job without insulting him.

CHAPTER 12

Far from being insulted Selwyn was exuberant. "I thought one day you'd have to call on my particular talent," he said triumphantly. "It's about time you showed a little respect for something other than the practical. Of course it's not your fault, young Leo. You've none of the Celtic blood required for an appreciation of the Mysteries."

"You'll have Celtic blood all over your nose if you don't stop waving your arms about," Anna said crossly. They were driving past the Old Deer Park on their way to Hampton Hill. It looked green and inviting.

Selwyn had suited his dress to the weather and wore
a fawn-coloured linen jacket that stretched tighter across
his waist than his chest. He had also insisted upon his
straw hat although Bea said it made him look more like
a candidate for Adam House than a visitor.

" 'Great wits are sure to madness near allied,' " he
sang out, ignoring Anna's pleas for better vision. " 'And
thin partitions do their bounds divide.' "

"What great nitwit said that?" Anna asked, thinking
of Thea sucking her thumb, huddled under th bed. "It's
just like bloody poets to glorify a miserable condition."

She turned off the main road into an area of suburban
quiet and leafy gardens. Now that she could see it by
daylight, Adam House was a bigger place than she
thought. Set in two or three acres of its own ground, it
seemed even more exclusive because two sides of the
property faced a golf course. The other houses on the
same road were smaller but equally well protected by
large gardens and high walls or hedges.

Adam House itself had a touch of B-movie gothic
about it. There were narrow, stone-surrounded windows, all of which were leaded and some, Anna noted
uneasily, which were barred. She glanced at Selwyn as
they went through the church-like doors into the vaulted
hall.

"It looks the part," he whispered. His eyes gleamed
with satisfaction.

"So do you," she whispered back. A sign on one of
the doors said "Reception." Anna knocked and went
through. She found Mrs. Grayle seated at a mahogany
desk writing in an appointment book. Mrs. Grayle got
up immediately and came round the desk to shake
hands. Anna introduced Selwyn.

"It's good to see you again," Mrs. Grayle said to
Anna. "I'll have one of the boys take you up to Dr.
Frank's room."

Dr. Frank's room was on the third floor. They were
led there by a quiet young man who walked with a

limp. Anna could see Selwyn trying to figure out whether or not he was a patient. This was difficult as nobody they met was in any sort of uniform. "It's funny," Selwyn whispered piercingly, "when you know you're in a nut-hut, everyone looks like a loony."

"Shshsh," Anna said. The young man turned round and grinned which did nothing to reassure her.

They were shown into a panelled waiting-room. A few of the comfortable leather chairs were already taken, and the young man motioned to Selwyn to sit down. He led Anna through another doorway into a passage. Several more doors led off this, each with a doctor's name painted on it. The young man knocked at Dr. Frank's, and then went away.

A man of about fifty opened the door. He had toffee-brown eyes, eyebrows like furry caterpillars, and curly greying hair. He was eating a tomato sandwich. Half the sandwich was in one hand and his mouth was full of the rest. He did not look much like a psychiatrist to Anna who had been expecting something altogether more formal.

"Hello, I'm Anthony Frank," he said through a shower of crumbs. "Come in. Sit down. Anna Lee, isn't it? There were a couple of things I wanted to get clear before you see Thea. All right?"

"Fine," Anna said, looking round. It was a small room, casual to the point of untidyness. The walls were decorated with cork tiles on which were pinned a riotous patchwork of drawings and photographs.

"You see," Dr. Frank went on, "Thea's father and I may be at cross-purposes, which is natural enough since he is part of Thea's problem. While I hope I can be part of the solution. I know he wants you to go back to Dorset to clear the family name. And I suspect that he wants to be told that nothing of any importance occurred there. I, on the other hand, have come to believe that something did. If I'm going to be of any use at all to Thea I should know what it is. Mr. Hahn, if he runs true to form, won't want me to.

"I've agreed to let you see Thea because I think maybe you can help her. Mr. Hahn is employing you because he thinks you can help him." He spread his hands and smiled disarmingly.

"If push comes to shove, I'm supposed to go with the client," Anna told him, smiling in return. "But since I don't know what I'll find in Dorset I can't make any promises one way or the other. What I want to know is—if Thea really has been in some bother, and the police really are after her, where do you stand?"

"If push comes to shove, I go with the client too," he said. "I'm not absolutely sure what the legal position is, but I'd do my damnedest to keep the police off my patient's back."

They stared at each other in silence for a moment. Then Anna said, "Well, we seem to be on the same side at the moment."

Dr. Frank laughed. "Thea calls you Cat Anna," he said unexpectedly. "It didn't seem so apt two days ago. Shall we go down now?"

They found Selwyn where Anna had left him in the waiting-room. A small man in a tidy business suit and bedroom slippers was seated next to him and whispered earnestly in his ear. Selwyn was now looking a little nervous. He leaped to his feet when he saw them and followed them out to the stairs.

"Who was that chap?" he asked, as they went down to the first floor. "He says there are unicellular tax men in the drinking water and they get into your cardiovascular system and give you heart attacks."

Dr. Frank laughed and said nothing. Anna said, "He's probably a doctor." Dr. Frank laughed again. He knocked at Thea's door and went in without waiting for an answer. Anna and Selwyn followed.

The room was bright with sunshine. A posy of wild flowers and feathers stood in a vase on top of the dresser. It was as cosy as Anna remembered it. Thea, she thought, was looking better: the bruises at least had faded and her hair was clean and glossy. She was sitting by the window, staring out at the garden. Only her left hand, which was bent stiffly inwards at the wrist, and her eyes, glassy as a doll's, looked at all abnormal.

Dr. Frank said, "I've brought Anna and her friend Selwyn to see you. Do you feel like talking to them?"

Thea got up slowly, and gravely shook hands with both of them. "Will you sit down here, Anna?" she said, pulling another chair over to the window. "I'm glad you've come to see me. You're the white knight who guards the white queen in the white night."

Ignored, Selwyn and Dr. Frank sat side by side on the bed. Anna said, "It's nice to see you too."

"I was very young when we first met," Thea said, looking very seriously at Anna who could almost feel herself being sucked into her eyes. "I've grown up a bit since then. Do you still like me, now that I'm bigger?" she continued after a short pause. "I took your sunglasses, didn't I? Did you mind?"

"Of course not," Anna said. "You seemed to need them more than I did. You can keep them if you like."

"The white knight's shield." Thea looked out of the window again. Anna felt relieved. She glanced over at Dr. Frank who smiled encouragingly. She asked, "Do you remember being in Britmouth, Thea?"

At first it seemed as if she hadn't heard. She stared fixedly out of the window. Anna was about to repeat the question when Thea said in a low expressionless voice, "Remember? Remember. Between us we remember everything. We're programmed to remember. We have a nine hundred and ninety-nine K memory. The question is, do you have access to our memory. Do you have the password?"

"No," Anna said, jolted. "Can you help?"

"It's difficult," Thea said sadly. "But it's not my secret alone. There are four safety devices. Devious devices."

"Four?"

"The dog, the bird and the stag. All white. And also the black weird who garbles the output. You can't get into the file without placating all four."

"Well, what about you?" Anna asked, out of her depth. "How do you get access?"

"There is only a labyrinth," Thea said patiently. "The labyrinth is only the housing, but as I say it's well guarded—by the four and sometimes more. In fact, sometimes there are ninety-nine characters per second. So you have to be quick. It's a question of aligning the ports and setting the parameters. After that, there is a password, and after that you have to be able to read the printout which may be quite unintelligible. That's the work of the weird. It all depends on how dependable you are."

"What about Southampton?" Anna asked. "Is that one of the passwords?"

"Southampton was the gateway," Thea said, and began to cry, rocking back and forth, tears pouring out of her eyes. Anna was appalled. She hurriedly gave Thea her handkerchief and squatted on the floor in front of her stroking her hand.

"How many deaths does the Saviour die," Thea cried. "After Christ rose again at Easter, it was wonderful, but what's the point if they crucify him again next year? Once a month the sun kills the moon. How long can it go on?"

"Not long," Anna said. "Please don't cry." She looked furiously at Dr. Frank. Thea stopped crying as suddenly as she'd begun. She wiped her eyes with Anna's handkerchief. "The white knight's favour," she said in a tired little voice. "Can I keep it?"

"Yes." Anna stood up and patted Thea's shoulder with a hand that felt as if it belonged to someone else.

"Tired?" Dr. Frank said from the bed.

"Yes." Thea nodded. Anna nearly said yes too but realized just in time the question was not for her.

"Well, why not relax a little before lunch." Dr. Frank

got up quietly and went over to the window. "Just let your head roll around on your shoulders. That's it. Breathe deeply. Feel your feet and hands go heavy. You don't have to hold your hand like that, Thea. Let it go. That's right."

Anna crept away and stood by the door, while Dr. Frank put Thea through a relaxation exercise, and when she was quite still he picked up her wrist as if he were feeling her pulse for a few seconds. He waggled her floppy hand and then let it drop into her lap.

"No more speeding till after lunch," he admonished. She smiled weakly and said in a tiny voice, "Can Anna come back sometime? I won't hurt her, will I?"

"She can come if she wants to."

"Will you come, Anna? I'll try not to harm you. Will you bring me something to read?"

"What would you like?" Anna asked, wishing fervently she was on the other side of the door.

"You choose," said the little-girl voice eerily.

"All right. Goodbye now. I'll see you soon." Anna opened the door and went out. With indecent haste Selwyn shot out after her and they waited silently in the passage till Dr. Frank followed a few minutes later.

"Well done," he said as they went down the hall. "She seems to trust you."

"What's the little-girl stuff?" Anna said, ignoring the compliment. "And why did Britmouth General say she was retarded? They did an EEG, you know."

"I know." Dr. Frank stood still for a moment as if deciding what to say. "It must be obvious to both of you that Thea is hiding. At Britmouth she was hiding behind a retarded person."

"Do you mean she's faking it?" Selwyn asked hopefully. He was very pale, Anna noticed. Dr. Frank said, "Not at all. As Anna said, the EEG results were of a very dull person. If you had tested cortical or galvanic skin responses, they would have been very dull too. But if you did the same tests today, your findings would be completely different. The difference would be as marked as between separate individuals. I can't give you any satisfactory explanation, I'm afraid, because I don't claim to understand it myself. All I can say with any certainty is that she is totally disintegrated."

"Which seemed to be what she was saying about herself," Selwyn said, looking longingly towards the door and the car parked outside, "if you take all that computer nonsense as metaphor, that is. Ninety-nine characters per second! I thought perhaps she was playing word games."

"Well, she is and she isn't," Dr. Frank said.

"Is all this quite new?" Anna asked curiously. "I mean, what were you treating her for before?"

"Not this, anyway," he said, choosing his words carefully. "I was most shocked by the development. It's what leads me to think there must've been some trauma."

"Can you cure her?" Anna found that she was almost pleading. She cleared her throat and moved towards the open door. Selwyn and Dr. Frank followed.

"I can probably help her," Dr. Frank said, again very carefully. He eyed her shrewdly. "Will you come again?" he asked.

"I'm bringing her a book, aren't I?" she said quite tersely. She did not want to be tied down on the subject. Nor, from the look of him, did Selwyn. Dr. Frank seemed to understand. He said no more but accompanied them to the car and saw them off.

"Nice bloke, don't you think?" Anna asked as they turned on to the Chertsey Road. But Selwyn, for once, didn't want to talk. He sat morose and silent until Hammersmith.

"Do you know what she meant about the dog, the stag, and the bird?" Anna said, hoping to jog him out of his depression before they got home. They were idling in a traffic jam. A poster on the hoarding beside them offered to fly them to Australia in less time than it would take to drive the couple of miles home.

"Depends if she's been reading *The White Goddess* or not," Selwyn said flatly. "According to Graves, the dog guards the underworld: the lapwing is a taboo bird that lures deceitfully and camouflages her eggs. I can't remember about the white roebuck but it's got to do with hiding something. If you ask me, she was telling you in an allegorical sort of way to mind your own business."

It was Anna's turn to keep silent.

When they got home, Selwyn got out of the car and without a word stumped up the steps to the front door. He had forgotten his keys so he had to wait for Anna to let him in.

"What is Cat Anna?" she ventured as she turned the key.

"Why don't you read a book once in your life?" he snapped, pushing past. "Cat Anna was a seventeenth-century witch."

CHAPTER 13

The road climbed the gentle, arable side of the scarp before plummeting down the steep, wooded side to the sea. Anna stopped the car at the top from which she could see the two halves of Britmouth laid out on either side of the river below. She had to fill in Thea's two missing weeks, and was wondering how to go about it. She had failed when starting from the point of Thea's disappearance. Now she could start from the point of her appearance on Wednesday. But the two-week gap was very wide, and there was nothing to fill it except the growing certainty she shared with Anthony Frank that something remarkable must have happened to change the brilliant girl she had been looking for into the isolated, mad one she had found.

The only lead she had was the police officer who had delivered Thea to Britmouth General, PC Mason. But since it was probably his follow-up inquiry that had made Rodney Hahn panic, she would have to tread carefully if she wanted to avoid making matters worse.

Thoughts of Selwyn intruded: his unusual silence, his bad temper. The reason had emerged when Anna was getting ready for the journey to Britmouth. Bea came up for one of her little chats. She had been washing her hair when Selwyn returned home, and it was still in heated rollers. She sat uncomfortably on the edge of Anna's bed and gave her a halting, embarrassed lecture on the subject of her husband's poetic sensitivity. Anna admitted that taking him to meet Thea had been a mistake and they had agreed that he shouldn't go again.

"He didn't really want me to come up and say this," Bea said awkwardly. "He thought you'd say he was soft. But when I insisted, he practically pushed me up the stairs so's I wouldn't miss you. Most upset he is. He wanted to help, but I really don't think lunatics agree with him."

Anna was sorry for upsetting Selwyn. Although she had known him for years now, it was still impossible to predict what he would be upset by and what he would enjoy. Privately though, she was even more sorry she now had no one who might help her with Thea. However upset he had been by her, Selwyn had at least had some insight into what she'd meant. Also Anna herself could hardly claim to be unaffected by Thea. She had simply needed the company as much as a possible interpreter.

Selwyn, Bea told her, had promised to look for a replacement. But Anna was not enthusiastic. By and large Selwyn's friends were even less reliable than Selwyn himself.

Now, three and a half hours later, it was time to get acquainted with PC Mason. She started the car and zigzagged down between the trees to the town.

She found the police station near the centre of town, close to the river. It was a low, square building, blackened by exhaust fumes. Inside were the usual worn lino, the usual strip-lighting augmenting the usual meagre windows, and the usual bored desk sergeant. She hoisted her most innocent smile and began to make inquiries.

Tom Mason, she learned, was off duty. He would be up at the cricket ground opening for Britmouth XI against Charbarrow. Britmouth were going to paste Charbarrow something terrible even though one of Charbarrow's spin bowlers had tried out for Hampshire fifteen years ago. After some gentle nagging she also learned that the cricket ground was at the north end of town and in fact she had already passed it on her way into the centre.

Retracing her steps, Anna found it on the last flat ground at the very outskirts of town. Not absolutely flat, a groundsman assured her. The pitch was on a slight slope which a clever captain could use by putting his fast bowlers on at the uphill end. Tom Mason, he told her further, had already succumbed to a devilish tricky in-swinger for only eleven runs.

He was sitting disconsolate on the grass beside the pavilion. "I must've taken me eye off," he was saying to a small boy standing contemptuously nearby. "Never take your eye off the ball." The small boy looked at him with the expression of one who would never dream of being so silly if only he were big enough to hold a bat, and wandered off without a word.

"That's my boy," Tom Mason explained morosely when Anna sat down beside him and introduced herself. "I always seem to get out quickly when the missus brings him along. I don't know why. Must be trying too hard or something. But I do wish she'd leave the lad at home."

Anna sympathized. She was glad he was out but she wished he had scored more than eleven. Twenty-five or thirty, she thought, might have made him more amenable. She told him that Thea's father had sent her to find Thea's luggage. It seemed to be the approach that would excite least curiosity. The last thing she wanted was for him to be too curious.

"Her luggage?" he said, thoughtfully. "She didn't have none that I recall. Nor no shoes neither, poor kid. Just one of them little shoulder things they do carry."

"Where did you find her exactly?"

"In the precinct, just outside Woolworth's," he told her. "Someone rang in and said there was a kid sick and acting strange, see. Said she'd been rolling around on the floor and knocking herself about. But when I got there she was on her feet and talking a mile a minute."

"She's very sick, poor thing," Anna said without much emphasis.

"She seemed lucid enough to me." He stopped. A ripple of applause had spread from around the pavilion. The batsmen were taking three runs. "Nice shot," Tom Mason exclaimed clapping too. "We'll have the beating of 'em yet. No, she was lucid all right," he went on, his eyes still fixed on the white figures out on the pitch. "Too lucid you might say. Said she'd been through a gate somewhere and a bull'd attacked her. Then she said, no, it hadn't been a bull, it was a man and she'd killed him.

"I was trying to calm her down, see, to get her into the car. So I says, 'Don't talk so daft.' But she wouldn't have it. No, she says, she killed this man. Well, later on in the afternoon I heard they'd got a murder in Southampton so I got to thinking, but by the time I went back to the hospital she'd been transferred to London."

"Who did she say she'd killed?" Anna asked.

"Said it was her father. I don't know, though. When I asked what she'd done with him, she said she'd eaten him. I know it sounds funny now, but she really sounded like she believed what she were saying. But it's the oldest trick in the book pretending you're barmy."

"She isn't pretending," Anna said decisively. "And her father's alive and well in Wimbledon."

"Ah well, there you go," he said almost regretfully. "Still, there was that murder."

"What've you heard about that?" she asked, affecting idle curiosity.

"I do believe them chaps in Southampton're still trying to find out who he is. But he was shot in the neck. Chambermaid found him in his room that morning. Been dead since the night before. It's a big hotel, the Continental Gateway, and there'd been some convention or other. But nobody actually heard the shot. You wouldn't credit it, would you? All them folk about but no one hearing."

A burst of clapping from the visiting team interrupted him, and hid Anna's involuntary reaction to the name of the hotel. The applause was joined bravely by the home supporters only a few seconds later. The batsman who had so recently taken three runs was coming in, a self-conscious, annoyed grin on his round, red face. He had been caught at mid-on.

"Bad luck, old man," Tom Mason called as he passed, and then turning to Anna added, "Should've kept 'un down. He will try to whack a short ball to kingdom come, silly bugger. Always hooks 'em up. Where'd you say that kid'd been taken to?"

"Well, I don't know, exactly," she replied blandly. "Tell you what though, the one who knows all about it is the family brief, Mr. Embury." It was obviously time to go, so with a great show of helpfulness she wrote down Mr. Embury's telephone number for him. It was giving away nothing at all, she reflected with a smirk of amusement. If Mr. Embury wanted to be a conceited, upper-class stonewall, he might as well practise his art where it would do some good.

The Britmouth XI were at 39 for three when she left. In other circumstances, it would have been a pleasant way to spend a sunny afternoon: sitting in the grass by the little white pavilion, great chestnut trees shading that side of the boundary and the woods rising up the hillside behind. Instead, she turned the car back towards the middle of Britmouth.

The precinct was an area that looked as if it had been developed in the 'sixties by someone who hated the soft lines and embellishments of the older part of town. Nearly all the shops were now shut and Anna walked through it almost entirely on her own. She found Woolworth's, a blank wall of glass and locked doors. There was nothing to see and no one to talk to so she went on out of the precinct, and into the empty car park that backed on to it. On the other side of the car park was a bus station.

This was more or less deserted too. She wandered around looking at notices and route maps. Buses, she saw, went to and from Yeovil, Lyme, Exmouth, Weymouth, Bournemouth, Poole and Dorchester. The 369 was a direct route between Britmouth and Southampton.

The only building open for business was the ticket office. Anna opened the door and went in. A fat greyhaired woman sat behind the counter chewing peardrops and reading *True Love* magazine. Anna said, "Excuse me. A friend of mine came through here on Wednesday and left a bag on the bus. Could I have a look at the lost property, please?"

"Lost property's Monday to Fridays only," the woman said without looking up.

"I know it's a bother, but I've come rather a long way," Anna said cajolingly.

"Mondays to Fridays," the woman said, chewing happily. "I only sell tickets." She turned a page. Anna clenched her jaw. "You see, my friend left her false teeth in the bag," she said with a rising sensation of impotence. "She hasn't had a square meal since breakfast Wednesday morning. It's really urgent I find them."

"I'm tickets. It's more than my job's worth to open

lost property," the woman explained, turning another page. "Come back Monday."

"Well, can I see the supervisor?" Anna asked. The woman looked up at last. She smiled. "Supervisor's off till Monday," she said and popped another peardrop into her mouth. Anna knew when she was beaten.

She stamped back through the precinct to her car in a thoroughly bad temper. She was not going to stay in Britmouth till Monday and she didn't want to come back either. Life seemed to be nine-tenths full of doing things she didn't want to do because of someone else's recalcitrance. She was about to get into the car when she noticed a second-hand bookshop still open. She went in. An old man with a plump tabby cat on his knee sat in a rocking-chair at the back. He was fast asleep and the sound of gentle snores reverberated round the rows of dusty books.

Anna walked quietly. She didn't want to wake him unless she found something to buy. Choosing a book for Thea was going to be a problem—her bookshelves were already filled to bursting with classics and textbooks. Eventually, thinking of Thea's little-girl voice, she went to the children's section, and after a long search found a tattered copy of *Big Tiger and Christian*, a book that had enthralled her when she was about ten. Even if Thea didn't like it, she thought she could read it again herself. She woke the old man to pay for the book and went out into the afternoon sun clutching her prize. She felt better now: better able to face the long drive home knowing she would have to turn round and come back on Monday.

CHAPTER 14

It was quite dark when Anna arrived home. The Prices'
windows were lit and the sound of 'fifties bebop, muted
by glass and curtain escaped into the street. She knew
before she opened the front door that Selwyn was having one of his ad hoc parties. These were foisted on the
neighbourhood only once or twice a year, but they
were usually memorable. Such occasions customarily
began with just one or two people invited to supper.
Selwyn would go to the pub, ostensibly to boost his
wine cellar, and, after one or two drinks to give him
confidence, he would issue invitations to anyone unfortunate enough to be present. The resulting social mix
was always eccentric and often quite unmanageable.

The front door was unlocked. Anna went in and
found that the party had spilled out of the Prices' flat
and risen like water in a tube halfway up the stairs to
her own door. A few people, like the greengrocer, an
elderly neighbour, and the local district nurse, greeted
her noisily. She didn't recognize anyone else. A good
smattering of neighbours was always present, as the one
sure way to get an invitation was to ring up and complain about the noise.

Selwyn blundered into the hall, his hair on end and
his face flushed with sociability and Algerian red. "Leo!"
he roared. "Don't dither. Come in. There's someone I
want you to meet." He grabbed her sleeve and edged
his way into the sitting-room.

The furniture had been pushed back against the walls,
but even so the space provided was barely enough for

the crush of people. They had Dizzy Gillespie on the hi-fi playing "Swing Low Sweet Cadillac," and some ill-assorted couples were shuffling in the middle of the room with total disregard for the beat. The rest were doing what is always done at parties: drinking, smoking, and shouting. Anna recognized the Mediterranean beauty from the Italian restaurant round the corner cheek to cheek with the young telephone engineer who was a Queens Park Ranger's supporter and who had had his eye on her for months. Now, undeterred by her numerous and protective family, they were making a night of it. A man she knew to be one of the High Street bank managers who drank at Selwyn's favourite pub was talking to a group of assorted women, one of whom was a hairdresser and another who was married to the greengrocer. His own wife was nowhere to be seen.

Following Selwyn, she nearly tripped over Sam Tulloch who was sitting on a cushion at the feet of the middle-aged actress who had been an old flame of Selwyn's before she had seen the light and married her agent.

"Hello, Pilgrim," Anna shouted. "What're you doing here?"

"He's soothing my battered ego," the actress cried. "Do you know the darling actually knew me from one of my old films on telly. And so young!"

"I came to see you, actually," Sam yelled from the floor. He was looking tipsy and slightly baffled. "Mr. Price asked me in to wait."

"I'll be back in a moment," Anna said, drawn on into the crush by Selwyn's grip on her sleeve. They stopped momentarily by Bea, just long enough for Selwyn to thrust a glass into her hand and Bea to fill it with something that made her eyes water. Bea was wearing her best blue silk and a lop-sided smile. She would complain tomorrow; tonight she was out to enjoy herself.

"Can't you find someone younger for Sam?" Anna shouted.

"Sam's too young for someone younger," Selwyn bellowed back. "An older woman's the best he can expect at his age."

"Forty people, at least," Bea said happily. An unknown young man with a floppy cravat flung his arm round her and kissed her cheek, pleading for wine and a dance. Bea pushed him away but only so that she could fill his glass. Selwyn snorted and moved on until he reached the window and could go no further. He nudged a broad back, and as the stranger turned round, said, "Quex, this is Leo. Leo, this is Quex."

"Hello, Quex," Anna said cheerfully, hoping Selwyn wasn't on one of his matchmaking missions again. Every so often he took an impertinent interest in her love life. If there were gaps, he bought forward candidates to fill them but Anna hadn't met a good one yet.

"Quex is a colleague," Selwyn confided at the top of his voice. Whether this meant he was a poet, someone who worked on the magazine that occasionally published Selwyn's work, someone he'd been a student with, or simply drunk, Anna couldn't tell. He certainly didn't seem any drunker than anyone else at the moment and he was definitely on the sober side when compared to Selwyn. His eyes were so dark that Anna couldn't see the pupils, and he seemed to be smiling, but she couldn't be sure about that either as the lower half of his face was hidden by a curly brown beard.

"It's all right. I've told him about the ulcers," Selwyn thundered, drifting away, a plump redhead attached to his arm.

Quex said, "He told me he was helping you with a case but had to give up on account of his ulcers." She could see he was smiling now because she caught the gleam of white teeth. He looked like a pirate.

"Wind," Bea shouted as she struggled past in the arms of the floppy cravat.

"Do you dance?" Quex asked, taking her arm and drawng her towards the middle of the room.

"No," she said.

"Nor do I," he told her and began to sway in time to the music. Anna, hemmed in from all sides, swayed with him. Everyone was now dancing to "American Pie."

"You're not exactly beautiful," he said over the top of her head, "but I must say you're rather dashing."

"I'll be rather dashing out of here if you don't loosen up a bit," she complained into a mouthful of black cord jacket. He obligingly relaxed his arm.

"Selwyn invited me round to dinner to explain your problem." He had to bend to talk into her ear. "I wasn't expecting anything like this."

"No one ever does," Anna shouted. "Not even Selwyn."

"We need more booze!" Selwyn's voice boomed above the din. "There's not enough left to drown a mouse in."

"Come on," Quex said, leading off towards the door. "That sounds like the job for us." Anna followed willingly. She was dying for want of space and air.

The night was warm and fresh. As they sauntered companionably to the off-licence Anna told Quex a little about Thea Hahn, and he told her a little about himself. "I used to work at a day centre for mentally handicapped and other misfits," he said, sniffing the breeze with obvious delight. "Peculiar behaviour doesn't freak me. And I'm in roughly the same trade as Selwyn when I'm ashore. So if he could help, then probably so could I—without it giving me ulcers, that is."

Anna laughed. He seemed to have a shrewd grasp of the situation in spite of Selwyn's explanation. "Merchant seaman?" she asked.

"Rigger," he answered shortly. "North Sea." He didn't seem inclined to follow this up so they walked on in silence. At the off-licence they bought several flagons of red and white wine. The object was quantity. Nobody would appreciate quality except perhaps the bank manager who, when they had left, had been doing an impression of an elephant eating a bun, and was by now

too far gone to care. The flagons were heavy and Anna
had a hard job carrying two. Quex however managed
two in each hand. He was a very big man.

They were greeted at the front door with cries of joy
and were forced to begin pouring there and then, so
that by the time they regained the epicentre of the
party their burdens were noticeably lighter. Duty done,
Anna went off in search of Sam. She found him where
she had left him, only now he was fast asleep, mouth
agape against the lovely legs of the Italian beauty. The
Italian beauty was too engrossed in snogging with the
telephone engineer to notice. The actress was dancing
with an Indian and Bea was dancing with the bank
manager. Selwyn, who was dancing by himself, had a
carafe of white clasped to his chest and Floppy Cravat
was boogying with the greengrocer's brother. Anna soon
found herself doing something that only vaguely resem-
bled dancing with Quex.

The party might have gone on till daylight if it hadn't
been for the Italian brothers. They arrived mob-handed
to carry the beauty away to safety. One of them punched
the telephone engineer on the shoulder by way of a
friendly warning. He responded. Selwyn hid under the
nearest table and Sam woke up and punched the Italian
beauty by mistake.

When things calmed down a little, all the Italians
were gone, Bea was nursing skinned knuckles, Sam had
a bloody nose, the back pocket had been ripped from
Anna's jeans, and Selwyn was fast asleep under the
table.

Sam said, "What a fantastic party!" and went out to
the kitchen to help Quex dispose of the broken glass.

Not many guests were left and those that were had
either joined in the fight or slept through it. Surprisingly, everyone seemed to agree with Sam. Anna began
to help Bea clear up. More people left. Happy to witness a fight, they did not have stomachs strong enough
for the aftermath. Someone offered to take Sam home

and he left thanking Bea over and over again for a wonderful time.

When things were more or less straightened out, Bea made coffee for the survivors and Anna made a small pile of foreign objects they had found on the floor, between cushions, kicked into corners: a bunch of keys, a shoe, a wallet, three ties, a shawl, five odd earrings, an envelope of snaps, a comb, and a toupee. Quex bet Anna that no one would have the nerve to claim the toupee.

After coffee, and while Bea and Quex were carrying Selwyn off to bed, Anna slipped away. She was very tired. Her own flat looked like a model of peace and good order as she got ready for bed. She was just about to turn the light off when someone tapped on the door. She got up to answer it, and found Quex, hairy and massive, leaning against the banister rail. He looked wide-awake and ready for three more parties. He came in, saying, "You didn't say, in the end, if you wanted me to help you with Thea."

"I hadn't made up my mind." Anna ran her fingers through her hair and wondered if the night would never end. "I think maybe you could, if you're interested, but I ought to square it with Adam House first."

"Oh, I'm interested all right." He sat down on one of her armchairs and regarded her with his inscrutable black gaze. "You could ring them first thing in the morning and we could pop over there after breakfast."

"Could we?" She was somewhat fuddled, but not fuddled enough to fail to wonder where he intended having breakfast.

"Yes," he said. "I thought I could stay overnight. If a thing's worth doing it's worth doing now."

"It might be more convenient that way," Anna admitted. "The sofa's quite comfortable."

"I wasn't thinking exclusively of convenience." The white teeth flashed briefly. He was so big, Anna thought, he'd be very hard to shift if he didn't want to go. She said, "Well, I'm sorry, but convenience is all I'm offering."

"We got on pretty well downstairs," he said reflectively.

"As far as we went," Anna said abruptly. "I'd have to know you a lot better to get on any further."

"Ah well, the sofa looks fine." He reached over and pummelled the springs with his fist. "If a thing's worth doing it's worth doing later on too."

"Big if," Anna said and went to get blankets and a spare pillow.

CHAPTER 15

Quex was outrageously affable in the morning. Anna, who had only slept for five hours and was nursing a headache, had to empty the fridge to feed him. As well as having an enormous appetite, she thought, a big man could metabolize alcohol faster, and thus not suffer from the hangover which might have made his presence bearable.

"Are you always this quiet in the morning?" he asked while consuming the vast quantities of toast which followed the cereal, eggs, bacon, and tomatoes. "I like people who're quiet in the morning."

"So do I." Anna swilled down an aspirin with her coffee and watched with morbid fascination as slice after slice disappeared into the curly brown beard.

"Wonderful coffee too." He was now three-quarters of the way down the second pot. "I've certainly known less comfortable quarters, even if the sofa is a bit short."

The sofa was six foot eight inches long. Anna knew because she had had to measure it to see if it would fit round the bend in the stairs when she had first moved in.

"Have you phoned Adam House?" he asked when no

apology for the length of the sofa seemed to be forth-coming. Anna nodded. In fact as soon as she had caught on to his appalling good humour she had begun to make plans for its disposal.

"Whenever you're ready," she suggested politely. But he insisted on washing up, whistling "Modern Major General" while he did so. Anna went away to brush her teeth and remained hidden in the bathroom till the whistling stopped.

At least he had his own car, an old Jaguar with rounded ends and graceful curved lines. Anna, in her Renault, followed it to Fulham where he stopped to pick up a cassette recorder. They had agreed that, if it looked as if Thea was going to take to him, Anna would leave them together. Quex was confident that she would, and Anna, while not imagining that anyone could posi-tively dislike him except perhaps in the early morning, was hoping for the best.

After Fulham, she led the way through Richmond and Twickenham to Adam House.

They found Thea in the garden sitting on the grass by a bed of azalea bushes. Several people were spending Sunday morning strolling round the grounds or sitting in the sun. Some of them were probably nurses, though as usual, Anna could not tell which.

"It's Cat Anna," Thea said in sepulchral tones as if to an unseen companion. "She's brought another familiar."

"Hello, I'm Quex," he said dropping into the grass like a brown bear. Thea didn't look up. She was hunched over, holding her elbows like an old woman in distress. She had more moods than trees had leaves, Anna thought, sitting down too. The book she had bought seemed inappropriate now. Thea took it anyway, and hugged it to her chest. "I'm writing my own book now," she informed them. "But thank you anyway."

"Can I look?" Anna asked, and Thea moved her legs to reveal a notebook hidden under them. On the first page she had written what looked like a list. It read,

"I-dentity, Id-entity, Eye-dentity, Aye-dentity, I-don'-tity." Quex, reading over Anna's shoulder, gave a shout of laughter. Thea giggled reluctantly. On the next page, in a completely different hand was written,

A hilarious Mathematical progression of hours.
In one,
A positive element of electric Mischief
Illumines momentarily a figure,
Gargantuan,
Whose Shadow is for a split second
Burnt into the wall behind.

He has been there for one hour.

Now is not the time.
That was yesterday and will be tomorrow.
In one hand he weighs his past
And in the other his future.
"Someone has cheated me," he cries in disgust.
And another two seconds pass by unnoticed.
God did not create him.
He is a self-made man with no roots
And only three green shoots.
But the white spear of detached electricity,
Not caring who made him,
Unmakes him.
Strikes him.
And neatly and equally, with scrupulous justice,
Severs past from future.

"Who wrote that?" Anna asked. She recognized the list as being Thea's writing. The poem, if that was what it was supposed to be, was in a much freer more florid hand.

Thea giggled again. "The hype-writer," she said. "The one who is not Hahn-made or even Hahn's maid."

Quex plucked a long stem of grass, and lay back

sucking it and gazing at the sky. He said, "Anna's got to go now."

Anna got up. Thea jumped up too and stood clinging to Anna's hand.

"I'll be back. Don't worry," Anna said. "And I'm leaving you Ursa Major here for company. He eats a lot but he's very nice really."

"The white knight's familiar?" Thea said uncertainly.

"That's right," Anna said. "He is a bit familiar, but he grows on you."

Quex gave another loud bark of laughter. "They're both at it," he said. "Sit down and talk to me, hype-writer."

Thea sat down again and Anna left them together. She did not believe for a moment that Thea had written the passage she had just read. Apart from the obvious difference in writing it wasn't possible that a girl who wouldn't even attempt to draw a picture could make up a thing like that. But whoever had written it and whatever it meant, if it meant anything at all, it had an ominous ring to it. She hoped it was that kind of thing Quex could sort out for her. He had a tough row to hoe, she thought, and he was welcome to it.

In the meantime she wanted to talk to David Rietz again. Tomorrow she would be back in Dorset and there wouldn't be time.

She drove home, left the car outside her house, and without stopping to go in, walked to Notting Hill Gate. The streets were full of people doing the odd, aimless things they do on Sunday mornings: fetching the paper, waiting for the pub to open, going to the park with the dog and children. Anna passed several family groups carrying small boats to sail on the Round Pond or model aircraft to fly in Kensington Gardens. There was hardly any breeze so the kite brigade was missing, but everyone else was out to make the most of the day. Even the churches were doing good business, with women in their smart spring hats and men in tight collars standing apart from their secular neighbours on the church steps.

Deeper in Notting Hill people sat on their doorsteps or the bonnets of their cars chatting, or with their windows open listening to music drifting out on to the streets. The group around David Rietz's front door had Lynton Quasi Johnson on their tape-deck, and Anna edged past to the tune of "Di Black Petty Booshwah." She climbed the sleazy stairs and knocked on his stained and blistering door. After a while the door opened a crack and David's girlfriend peered suspiciously out.

"Remember me?" Anna said. "I was here on Tuesday, talking to David. Can I come in?" The door opened wider and Anna went in.

"Sorry," David's girlfriend said. "I thought you were one of the bloods from downstairs. They're always hanging around bothering me when Dave's away. I wish he'd get a place somewhere else." She was wearing a grubby green kimono and had obviously just got up. She got back into bed and pulled the greyish sheet up to her shoulders. "There's a kettle over there," she said. "Put it on, will you? I can't function till I've had some coffee."

In the corner, partly hidden by a screen, was a sink and a single gas-ring. Anna filled a horrible, blackened kettle and lit the gas. There were two dirty mugs on the draining-board concealed under some tinfoil containers which had once held a Chinese meal and now had the calcified remains of rice and sweet-and-sour pork clinging to their edges. She tipped a half-eaten spring roll out of one of the mugs, rinsed the mug, and looking for the coffee, said, "Dave's away then?" She found a jar of powdered coffee, crusted, and with the lid off.

"He went rushing out after you left. I thought he was running after you. Didn't you see him?"

Anna chipped out a spoonful of coffee. "After me?" she asked. "Hasn't he been back since?"

"I thought he rather fancied you," the girl said, yawning loudly. "I thought he followed you. He's always trying to wind me up like that. I hate him really."

The kettle was boiling and condensation ran down the wall and window. Anna poured the hot water into a mug. There was no milk, only a few sour-smelling milk bottles. She said, "You're out of milk. Do you want sugar?"

"Shit. Oh, all right, sugar."

What had once been sugar lumps had dissolved and then recrystallized into a shapeless, rock-hard mass at the bottom of the box. Anna broke off a shard and put it in the mug. She gave the mug to the girl.

"He didn't catch you then?" The girl sipped the coffee, wrinkling her nose in disgust. "Where's he gone, I wonder? He loves to be mysterious. He loves hurting me. I should go home really. I don't know why I bother with him—he's such a bastard. Pass my fags, would you. I can't function without a smoke."

Anna handed her the cigarettes and opened a window. The girl said, "He's so good-looking though. Don't you think he's good-looking? And very bright. He's one of the top three in our year. Don't you really go for brainy men? I mean, why does he have to be such a shit?"

"Search me," Anna said, bored. "Look, I'll give you my card. Perhaps you'd ring me when he gets back."

"I might," the girl said, "or I might not. I could tell from the way he looked at you he fancied you. Couldn't you tell?"

"No." Anna went over to the door. "But you should've been able to tell from the way I looked at him there's nothing to get in a twist about."

"Don't you like him?" The girl fingered Anna's card and looked surprised.

"Not a lot." Anna opened the door. "In fact blokes like him piss me right off. Give me a ring, eh?"

"You're not going, are you? Couldn't you stay and talk? I can't function without someone to talk to. You could tell me what to do about Dave."

Anna went out but poked her head back round the

door. "You've got enough brains to get a university place," she said. "So you must have enough to know what to do about nerks like him."

The girl sighed and said, "Of course you're right. I must enjoy it deep down. Do you think I'm a masochist?"

Anna shrugged and closed the door. She wanted to go home and lie down. Her headache had suddenly got much worse.

CHAPTER 16

The rest of Sunday was only remarkable for what did not happen. David Rietz did not call. Quex did not come back. The Prices did not emerge from the downstairs flat. And Anna's headache did not subside until, in despair, she went to bed before ten o'clock.

She was in Britmouth bus station again by eleven-thirty the next morning, feeling as wonderfully fleet of foot and optimistic as she usually did on the morning after the morning after. It was the euphoria of *not* waking up with a hangover that always worked like a charm.

Today the shopping precinct and bus station were alive with shoppers and travellers. Anna opened the door of the lost property office and went in. This time she was met by a cheerful man with nearly all his teeth missing and a paunch like a beach ball. Her inquiry was hampered by the fact that she could not describe Thea's luggage or even say how much there was. But when she said she thought her friend had lost her shoes too, the man's face lit up in a smile of recognition.

"Oh, right you are," he said, thumbing through a small book of dockets. "Off the 369 from Southampton. Tuesday. Gotcher. Must've had her head in the clouds that day, your friend." He lumbered into a recess at the back of the office and came back with a tartan bag and a pair of canvas running shoes. "Still," he went on, pushing them across the counter, "you'd be surprised what people do leave on buses. Chap last year left a dead dog. He was taking it to the taxidermist, would you believe. 'Course, we thought it'd been dumped, and the council took it away to the tip. Ever so upset he was. Said he'd sue but he never did do. Sign here."

There was a name tag attached to the handle of the bag but it had no information on it. Anna said, "I'd better look inside first. I wouldn't want to nick someone else's luggage." She unzipped the bag. Inside, clothes were tangled like a nest of eels.

"Bit untidy, your friend," the man said as Anna tried to sort through the mess.

"Not usually," Anna said. "But she hasn't been well lately." She found a book of Montaigne's essays. "To Thea, on her ninth birthday, with love from Mummy and Daddy," was inscribed on the flyleaf. 'Struth, Anna thought; Montaigne for her ninth birthday present: no wonder the poor girl was only flying on one engine. She said, "This is it all right," and signed the man's docket.

She carried the bag and the shoes out to the car, and placing it carefully on the front seat beside her, she began to take everything out item by item, shaking each garment thoroughly before folding it and putting it on the back seat. Mostly the clothes were sensible Wimbledon things. But there was also a black nylon dress with a low neckline and a gilt chain for a belt which would have made Valerie Hahn's hair stand on end. When the bag was empty, Anna searched the toilet case, and found, lying among the usual jumble of nail scissors, brush, toothpaste, deodorant and soapbox, a packet of contraceptive pills only half full.

She put everything back in the bag, and fighting off a depressing sense of inevitability started the motor and turned the car towards the coast road and Southampton.

*   *   *

The Continental Gateway was a sawn-off tower block of a hotel separated from the main route to the docks by a small public garden. It had not been located there for quiet or the beauty of the view, but for its proximity to the ferry, and it had the impersonal air of a place only used briefly by people on their way to somewhere much more attractive.

In keeping with this the lobby looked much like an airport lounge and had been designed for commerce rather than comfort with a boutique that looked like a duty-free shop on one side and a booth for passport photographs on the other. Attached to the booth, alongside the sample pictures of smiling faces and children with teddy-bears, was a police poster showing the head and shoulders of a man and a headline under it saying, DO YOU KNOW THIS MAN?

The picture struck Anna, as such pictures always did, as half-familiar. On the one hand it was as if she had never seen anyone like him in her life, and on the other it bore a resemblance to someone she didn't know very well and couldn't remember. The eyes looked sleepy and glassy and she realized, having seen many such pictures before, that the photograph was of a dead man, his head turned three-quarters to the right to hide a wound. Anna had often wondered how useful posters like that were. They had such an impersonal quality that she didn't know how anyone could recognize even a close relative from them.

She went over to the reception desk and booked a room. As she signed the register she asked, "Who's that on the poster?" The clerk, a thin freckly man, said, "He was found shot in his room a week ago Wednesday. The police put that up a couple of days ago. I wish they hadn't, there's been nothing but questions ever since."

"Bad for trade?"

"The opposite," the clerk said disgustedly. "People fight to stay here once it got round there was a murder. Sick, I call it." He handed Anna her key and rang for

the porter although she only had a small overnight case
and didn't need anyone to help her carry it.

The porter was an elderly youth with a dirty collar
and onions on his breath. In the lift on the way to the
fourth floor he said, "Interested in the murder, are you,
Miss?"

"Oh, well, murder," Anna said vaguely, gazing at the
lighted numerals that flashed one, two, three as they
went up.

"Show you the death room for a tenner," he suggested out of the corner of his mouth.

"I'm not *that* interested."

"Seven's me final offer," he said as they arrived at the
fourth floor. She followed him through the doors and
down the passage saying, "You must be making a for-
tune. Who in her right mind'd pay that much?"

"You'd be surprised," he said, sneering. He opened
the door to her room and tossed her bag on one of the
beds. "Call it a fiver and I'll take you straight up there
now."

"Oh, why not?" She delved in her purse with a show
of exasperation and passed him the note. It vanished
into his sweaty fist and he led the way back down the
passage.

They took the lift up to the next floor, and then the
firestairs to the sixth. "They cleared this floor when
they'd finished questioning people," he said, padding
down the long carpet. Everything he did looked stealthy.
"But it'll be back in use in a couple of days. Management nearly did their nuts: not that we was that full at
the time." They stopped at 627 and he produced a
bunch of keys and unlocked the door.

The room was an anticlimax—just a tweedy carpeted
box with two unmade beds and a bathroom leading
off it.

"This here's where he died," he said, showing her
one of the beds. "Shot in the throat, he was. You can

see the blood stain on the mattress. And there's more on the carpet where he slid down on the floor."

There were indeed rusty marks on the bed and the carpet below.

"He was found on the floor," the bellboy continued in an authoritative voice. "Lying on his side, see. I can show you."

"Don't bother," Anna said quickly. He was getting down on one knee to demonstrate, but she stopped him. "Who found him?"

"Chambermaid," he said, standing up, disgruntled. "You can have her story too if you want. Two to me, five for her. She can tell you about the long hair on the pillow in the other bed and the weird noise in the night."

"What about them?" She took a last look round and went to the door.

"Two to me, five for her," he repeated firmly. He came out after her and locked the door behind him. "Fuzz're looking everywhere for the mystery woman. Well, Jackie saw her with her own eyes. She told all to the fuzz and she won't tell no one else who ain't come across with the ready first."

"Quite a little business you've got between you," Anna said sourly as they went downstairs.

"She's into personalities: I'm into technicalities," he confirmed proudly. "Only you women ain't that keen on technicalities. If you was a man now, I'd've let you in on the death weapon, etcetera. Women only want to know how the body was etcetera."

"So what was the weapon?" Anna asked. "As if you'd know."

"9mm Luger," he replied promptly. "The manager picked up the bullet case and it said Luger on the bottom. Besides, one of the girls in the bar's seeing a copper from the local nick, and he told her. Word gets around in a place like this."

Try stopping it, Anna thought. She said, "Well, if

you know so much, how about telling where the wound was, and how come the police're treating it as murder. Could've been suicide, couldn't it?"

He fingered the right side of his neck and said scornfully, "Nah. So where was the gun, eh? A Bonnie don't shoot hisself in the neck and then trot off and dump the gun."

They had arrived back at the fourth floor. Anna said, "Lucky for you: there's no bunce to be made out of suicide."

"You're not wrong," he said seriously, preparing to take the lift back to the ground. "You want me to send Jackie up? It's . . ."

"I know, two for you, five for her. I'll let you have it when she comes." She went to her room and locked the door. After washing her face and hands she telephoned the office to tell Beryl where she was.

"How long?" Beryl asked without any pause for small talk.

"Maybe only today," Anna said. "Maybe till tomorrow. It depends."

"Well don't hang about. You're not on holiday. And keep a proper record. One I can actually read. And don't forget receipts."

"Yeah, yeah," Anna said. Beryl never once let an opportunity slip for giving obvious instructions. It gave her such pleasure to have someone she could treat as a subnormal delinquent that Anna often felt it was her role in life to be offered to Beryl as a scapegoat. The men were mollycoddled or flirted with but Anna actually thought the sharp end of Beryl's tongue was preferable. Beryl flirting was a sickening spectacle.

She ambled over to the window and looked out. The sunlight stained the concrete buildings beyond the dock wall yellow and the sea was a hazy blue-grey that merged with the sky without any clear horizon. The view would be just the same from two floors up.

Jackie was not the prettiest sight either. She had a

body that would provoke more sympathy than lechery and eyes like the oily glaze on puddles in a garage forecourt. Whatever charm she might have possessed was overwhelmed by her pink uniform and the expression on her face, which was like someone who is about to enjoy telling her best friend of her husband's affair with his secretary.

"Well?" she said in a nasal whine and with a chilly smile. Anna parted with more money and the smile warmed by half a degree.

"It was like this," Jackie said, sitting on a bed, thick ankles crossed, pink hands folded like a Sunday school teacher. "It was seven-thirty Tuesday morning, right? Chap in 627 had ordered tea and a continental, right? So I'm outside with the tray. So I knock, right? No answer. Well, of course I think he's still asleep, so I knock again, and get out my key. I'm his morning call too, you see. 627 had a call in for seven-thirty, right? I unlock the door and go in. It's only what I do a hundred times of a morning. I wasn't expecting anything different. So I go in with my tray, right? And there he is, see, all crumpled up between the beds in a pool of his own blood. It gave me such a turn I spilt the orange juice, didn't I?"

She paused for dramatic effect. Anna said, "So what did you do?"

"Well, I rushed out and along to the sixth-floor linen room. There's a phone there, see. I couldn't use the room phone, could I? I'd've had to step over him to get to it and I couldn't of done that. So I phoned down to the desk and said there'd been an accident in 627. Then I went back."

Again the breathless pause which Anna filled by asking, "What did you do that for? Weren't you scared?"

"Oh I was, I was. But supposing he was dying for want of help? It was my Christian duty, wasn't it?"

Anna murmured something that might have been "in a pig's ear" but which Jackie took for admiration. She continued smugly, "I knelt down by the deceased, well, I didn't know it was the deceased then, did I, and I touched his hand." Her hand went out and withdrew as if burned. "Cold as a witch's heart, it was. And stiffer'n a board. So I thought to myself, this poor soul's beyond mortal help now. And I said a little prayer for him, like. I was crying, too. Ever so soft-hearted, I am."

"I bet you are," Anna said, straight-faced.

"And then the manager comes up. In his pyjamas he was, and white as a ghost, and he says, " 'Hello, this other bed's been slept in." It had too. And on the pillow was this shiny blonde hair. And he says to me, he says, "Who was it in 627?' So I told him Mr. Jones, because that was the name on the breakfast order. Well by this time Des'd come up. You met Des. And he'd already had a look in the register. So he says, 'Jackie's right,' he says, 'That's Mr. Jones. He booked two rooms. This one, and the one next door for his niece.' And I could see him thinking, we heard *that* one before. Which we have. Anyway the manager goes next door, but it's empty. Gone. Cleared out. But Des'd seen her when he brought the bags up, and I seen her when I done the towels, and she weren't nobody's niece, not in a million years. Golden hair down to here, she had. And bosoms out to here." Jackie's hands were describing something hardly ever seen, even on the screen. "And a look in her green eyes that was cold and cruel," she went on, with a look in her own that was calculating to say the least. "Anyway, when the police started questioning everyone on that corridor, the couple in 626 opposite swore they heard sobbing and running footsteps at two o'clock. Heart-breaking, they said."

"Is that when the police reckon he died?" Anna asked, wide-eyed.

"Some time between one and two-thirty in the morning," Jackie confirmed. "I got to get back to work now or Mrs. Molethrop'll have my hide." She got up, straightening her rumpled skirt. Anna got up too and stood innocently between Jackie and the door. "Well, I really enjoyed that, Jackie," she said, with a sad smile. "Brilliant. Almost worth a fiver. But I didn't pay for a fairy story, did I? So unless you want to start again, I'll have my money back, please."

CHAPTER 17

"What's wrong?" Jackie asked with almost academic interest.

"Well, for a start, his hand wasn't stiff as a board, was it? Not after only six and a half hours at most." No one who hadn't been there could say that for sure, but Anna thought it a good beginning.

Jackie creased her brow. "No?" she said. "Oh well, most people like that part. You're not a copper, are you?"

"No, I'm not. More people than coppers can recognize a naff tale when they hear one. Also, if the people in 626 heard sobbing and footsteps, how come they didn't hear the shot? If you don't give me the right stuff, I'll spell your name wrong in my article. I mightn't even mention your name."

Jackie sat down again. "You're writing an article? Honest?" she said enthusiastically. "Why di'n't you say so? Well it's not my fault. Des said you was just another punter; and we tell them what they want to hear, don't we?"

"Des was wrong," Anna said flatly. "Go on about the footsteps."

"Oh, well, there was this storm that night." Jackie wrinkled her nose in disgust. "And no one heard nothing. It's Jacqueline, with a Q, P-O-W-I-S. Aren't you going to write it down? The bloke from the *Chronicle* had a tape-recorder."

Anna tapped her forehead. "Total recall," she said impressively. "And what about this long golden hair? Even if the curtains had been open you wouldn't've seen it on a white pillow without a microscope."

"That's what they call local colour," Jackie explained. "But that other bed *was* rumpled, I swear. And the police took the pillowcase and sheets away for testing."

"Which makes the blonde next door a bit suss, doesn't it?" Anna went on inexorably.

"Yeah, well, actually she was dark. And she could've been his niece—straight up—she was that young. But no one remembered seeing her much. She was a no-body. But one of the waitresses says he had dinner with a biggish woman in a red dress who wasn't the niece. A bit brassy, like. And that gave me and Des the idea for a sort of scarlet woman. But, honest, the niece'd cleared out in the morning. And the police've put out a description."

"Oh yeah?"

"It was in the local paper, if you don't believe me. Age about fifteen to twenty, they said. Dark brown hair. Pale. About five foot five tall. I didn't see her myself but Harry on the desk did, and Des brought the bags up. The trouble is, she wasn't the sort'd stand out in a crowd. Des hardly noticed her. And she didn't have her dinner downstairs. She had a sandwich brought up. But she was in the bathroom when it came so the girl who brought it didn't see her either."

"It's not much of a description," Anna said, thinking it was both too vague and at the same time too close for comfort. She badly wanted to know if Thea had been in the room next to 627 but she didn't want anyone else to know she wanted to know. And, anyway, was it simply her own involvement that made a description, which could have been of thousands of girls, fit the one she most hoped had not been present? She said, "How about the woman in red? Do the police want to talk to her too?"

"Already done it," Jackie said, looking at her watch. "Look, I got to go now, I really have. Mrs. Molethrop'll be having kittens."

"One more thing. The chap in 627, didn't he have any identification on him?"

"No wallet, no cheque-book, no passport. Nothing. If that girl shot him she must've cleaned his pockets out after. Must've been why she did it if it wasn't a crime of passion." Jackie looked wistful. "I'm not saying it wasn't mind," she added more cheerfully. "I mean, why else would he call himself Mr. Jones and fake his address? Her too. She was supposed to be Miss Susan Jones. I ask you!" She got up and went to the door.

Anna said, "Real Joneses do exist, you know." And then as Jackie was leaving she went on, "The waitress, the one who saw the woman in red, can you ask her to come up?"

"Carmen?" Jackie said, stopping in the doorway. "You're never going to put Carmen into your paper?"

"Just background," Anna said hastily. "No names. Not important enough."

"It won't be till about five," Jackie said, mollified. "I'll tell her." She shut the door behind her, and Anna waited till her footsteps faded down the corridor. Then she went out too.

With so many lies and exaggerations flying about like party balloons it was time to look for some outside verification. Normally, the last place you'd look would be the back numbers of the local papers. But Anna did not have a contact on the local force, and even if she had, now was not the time to use it. Police information always had to be paid for in kind, and the only currency she had was far too vulnerable. It would be so easy to do more harm than good.

She went instead to the library and pored over last week's newspapers. After the first "Horror Hotel" headlines, the mundane facts which emerged were very much the same as Jackie's second version and Des's

technical details. A man had been found shot in the
throat. The murder weapon was a Luger. The wound
was a near contact wound. The gun was missing. The
police were treating the incident as murder. The assailant was thought to be well-known to the victim. The
police were not too sure about the identity of the victim, but they had issued a description of a young woman
they wanted to question. They had interviewed a Mrs.
Patricia Westerman from near Woking in Surrey who
was said to have shared the victim's last meal. But as it
turned out they had merely shared a table when the
hotel restaurant was crowded due to a Rotary convention.

All this left Anna with more facts, certainly, but with
none of her personal questions answered, and none of
her doubts resolved.

She surrendered the papers to the librarian and with
a sigh of relief went out into the warm streets to find a
telephone. When she found one that worked, she called
Directory Inquiries who eventually gave her Mrs. Patricia Westerman's number and address. When stuck
for a lead, try the yellow pages, she thought, not for the
first time.

There was an hour left to kill before five. Anna was
feeling hot and sticky and more than a little stale. It had
been a long day already. She went back to the hotel to
wash and change her shirt. The lobby was crowded
with a coach party of tourists on their way to Le Havre
by next morning's ferry. She caught sight of Des and a
couple of other porters working overtime stacking cases
near the lifts and wondered how many tourists he would
entice to the death room. Perhaps he catered for coach
parties too. She took a bleak look at the packed lift and
started briskly for the stairs.

By the time she reached her room her shirt was
clinging in a damp wad to her armpits. Her overnight
bag was where she had left it, on the end of one of the
beds. She opened it, and then, hand outstretched to
take the clean shirt, she stopped. When she had packed

it, the shirt was lying neatly over the sponge-bag and clean set of underwear. Now the underwear slightly overlapped it. She looked further. Nothing was missing: there was nothing worth stealing anyway. But everything was just marginally disturbed. Her first thought was to make sure she hadn't left any of her Hahn notes in there. But they were all safely in her shoulder-bag.

There was nothing to be done about it. No harm done—just an unpleasant feeling, an ironic one too: she, who so often had occasion to finger through other people's possessions, hated it when the same treatment was dished out to her. She shrugged wryly and took the clean shirt to the bathroom. She filled the basin with cool water. While the tap was running she began to undress.

It was a small bathroom with no windows, made more claustrophobic by the hot-pink shower curtains that hung in front of the bath. A large mirror over the basin gave the illusion of more space, but Anna was not fooled and left the door into the bedroom open so that she could breathe.

It was not so much a sound that made her turn—it was hardly even a movement—just an odd feeling on her bare skin like a change in air pressure. And it was more a sense than a certainty that made her put her hand to the narrow gap where the shower curtains met and rip one of them aside.

He was standing in the bath, bent slightly forward, one eye closed in the act of squinting through the opening. He was wearing the uniform of a hotel porter, but his flies were undone.

Anna snatched a towel off the rail and held it to her chest. He opened the eye that had been closed. A look of sick embarrassment crossed his face. Anna could feel a similar expression on her own. They were only eighteen inches apart.

She stepped back, almost politely. For a second, he stood motionless fumbling with his zip, and then he straightened up and leaped for the open door.

When he ran, Anna's first instinct was to chase him. But the instinct died immediately. A women caught unexpectedly without clothes is not at her most self-assertive. She may feel humiliated, angry, frightened, even aggressive, but she does not think clearly except about covering herself up.

Anna slammed the bathroom door and struggled into shirt and slacks, fingers slipping on zip and buttons. Her face was flaming. She swore steadily and nastily under her breath.

When she emerged from the bathroom a few moments later she found the door into the corridor wide open. A woman in a black and white uniform stood in the doorway. She said, "You shouldn't leave your door open, you know. Anyone might come in."

"You're telling me!" Anna said, stuffing the rest of her shirt under her waistband. "A porter just left. Did you see him?"

"Miles?" the woman said, giving Anna an odd look. "He was just getting into the lift as I was coming out. Do you want him back?"

"Do I . . .? Er, no," Anna said. She buttoned the collar of her shirt even though it was a bit tight. "Miles who?"

"Miles Gancitano." The woman's questioning look gave way to a sly smile. "Didn't he say? Bit of a dish, isn't he?"

"What?" Anna stared at her. "Look, who the hell are you?"

The woman looked offended. "Carmen Ockney," she said. "Jackie said you wanted to see me."

"Carmen? Jackie? Oh shit." Anna turned abruptly away. "Well, come in and close the door." She stationed herself with her back to the window and Carmen came over and sat on the stool in front of the dressing table. Anna said, "So, you're the one who saw the man who was shot with the woman in red?"

"Jackie said your paper pays for services rendered."

Carmen kept the knowing smile intact. It was a well-fed, smooth, thoroughly corrupt smile. "Say a fiver?" she went on. "Not what your paper'd pay Miles, natch. I ain't that serviceable."

Anna drew in a deep breath. She went over to Carmen, grabbed her elbow, and yanked her to her feet. "What a nasty little mind you've got," she said, propelling her to the door. "As far as this hotel goes though, I'd say you were about average." She opened the door and pushed the startled waitress out into the corridor. "On your bike! I wouldn't pay a bent farthing for any smut you had to offer," she added as she shut the door on Carmen's outraged face.

"Idiot!" she muttered to herself as she gathered up her possessions and stuffed them back into her bag. "Idiot. Always taking it out on the wrong person. Idiot." Her face was still burning as she left the room, closing the door with a furious crash behind her.

CHAPTER 18

There were plenty of things she could have asked Carmen, and Anna thought angrily about them in the hour and a half it took to drive from Southampton to Woking. She also thought just as savagely about the theory that peeping Toms were inadequate men who were rarely dangerous. Peepers were not rapers, so the theory went. But almost any man, if he wants to, can do harm to almost any woman. And that had been Anna's most pressing sensation when caught undressed at close quarters with Miles Gancitano. Probability went out the window and left possibility far too dominant.

He had run, so the theory in this case held. She could most likely have done him more harm than he ever intended her. But she had been too busy feeling foolish, outraged and frightened. It was humiliating enough for any woman to be spied on, but for Anna, herself a professional watcher, it took on an aspect of catastrophic failure. She felt ridiculous.

And now she was threading her way through the leafy, golf course-lined outskirts of Woking. And that too might have been unnecessary if she had had her wits about her and not, in a fit of temper, thrown Carmen out of her room.

She stopped the car outside a tidy suburban house. It sat like an egg on a lettuce leaf in the middle of a nicely groomed lawn which was in its turn edged by rose beds. The roses were not in flower yet, but each plant was carefully mulched around the roots.

Anna looked at it with distaste. She had got to the point, in her mental confusion, where she could almost hear the ribald laughter if she ever told anyone in the office what had happened, so at the moment she would have looked at anything with distaste. But the evidence of a well-ordered suburban existence struck her as exceptionally affronting. She would have liked to see the clean cream stucco defaced with rude graffiti.

As she sat in the car trying to collect her thoughts to a degree where she could usefully face Mrs. Westerman, a mottled, idiotic-looking English Setter emerged from the next door garden, ambled over to the Westermans' gatepost and lifted its leg. It stared around with a satisfied expression and ambled back into its own garden. Anna laughed out loud. It was one of those things that meant absolutely nothing but made all the difference in the world.

She got out of the car and went up the path to the front door with almost a skip in her stride. The doorbell chimed the first four notes of a tune. Anna was trying to decide whether the tune was "The Bluebells of Scotland" or not when the door opened and a middle-aged man in carpet slippers and spectacles looked out. He was wearing a sleeveless Fair Isle waistcoat over a smart white shirt. Just back from the office, Anna thought. In her friendliest tone of voice, she said, "I wonder if I could speak to Mrs. Westerman, please."

"Not selling encyclopædias are you? Ha ha," he said jovially, stepping back and opening the door wider. "Because if you are, we've already got a full set. Not that I find any use for them, mind. No, my wife's the intellect around here. Open University and all that. Self-improvement, what."

Anna assured him that she was not selling encyclopædias or anything else and he opened a door off the hall and called. "Patsy! Someone for you, my love. Can I offer you a glass of sherry or something?"

"Er, no thanks, I'm driving," Anna said, wondering if he thought she was a friend of his wife's.

"Very sensible," he said in the same tone of empty jollity. "Drink not, wink not, prang not, clink not, I always say, ha ha."

"Are you in advertising?" Anna asked.

"Whatever made you think that?" he said surprised, and they looked at each other vacantly until Mrs. Westerman appeared. She was a dark bouncy woman wearing a butcher's apron over a frothy summer dress. She looked about ten years younger than her husband but probably wasn't. A woman who had worked hard on herself, Anna thought. Mrs. Westerman looked inquiringly at her husband and said, "Good evening, Miss er er . . .?"

"Miss er er?" Mr. Westerman said, looking inquiringly at Anna.

"Lee," Anna said. The Westermans looked at each other. Anna said, "I've just come from Southampton and . . ."

"Conservation, Hugh. We'll go into the den," Mrs. Westerman said. "Didn't you want to prick out the tomatoes?"

"Tomatoes? Oh, right," he said turning to leave. Anna followed Mrs. Westerman upstairs to a spare bedroom which had been converted to a study. Directly opposite the door was a poster, pinned to a chipboard panel, which featured an enlargement of a modest blue butterfly and the legend "South Coast Conservation Corps." A neighbouring poster said that the Woking and District Thespians were presenting *She Stoops to Conquer*, and a third advertised an exhibition of local watercolours. The table by the window was artfully strewn with piles of unused ruled pads, Open University publications and books. The only one whose title Anna could read from the doorway was about the pictorial significance of George Herbert. If Mrs. Westerman was into self-improvement, Anna thought, she was tackling the problem on several fronts. She said, "I'm not actually here about conservation, Mrs. Westerman."

"I know you're not, damn it," Mrs. Westerman said crossly, turning round, hands on hips. "Your chief assured me that if I made my statement to him my reasons for being at that bloody hotel would be treated with confidence and no one would come to my house without telephoning first and making an appointment."

"I wasn't told," Anna said apologetically.

"I've a good mind to ring up and complain," Mrs. Westerman said, her finely pencilled brows meeting in an angry dip over her nose like a bird drawn by a child. "That's the trouble with you people. The right hand doesn't know what the left hand's doing."

Anna nodded complete agreement: at present even the left hand didn't know what the left hand was doing.

"I mean, think of the embarrassment," Mrs. Westerman continued. "It was all a chapter of accidents. How was I to know the meeting had been cancelled? And how was I to know the chairman's wife was in hospital after a car accident? I was only keeping him company, after all. He's a very educated man, you know. Someone I thought I could look up to. But even educated men drink too much and get oafish, as I've found to my cost. Think of it, a man with all his qualifications passed out in that bloody hotel bedroom, and me forced to dine alone. It would never have happened if that damned secretary had rung in time to stop me leaving. She knows I've got a long drive. It was sheer inefficiency, but Hugh'd never understand. He simply doesn't have the imagination."

"And Mr. Jones?" suggested Anna, who was having difficulty with her imagination too.

"Well, you know what it's like; a woman alone in a crowded restaurant. There was that damn convention, and I'd no sooner sat down when those two louts came to share my table. Mr. Jones was on his own too and didn't look one over the eight like all the rest so I went over and asked if I could join him. For protection, you understand. I don't make a practice of soliciting strange men in restaurants. You still don't know who he is then?"

Anna shook her head. "What did you talk about?" she asked. Mrs. Westerman took a packet of Rothmans from the table and lit one. "Do we really have to go through all this again? I told Chief Superintendent Whatsit everything twice. Someone wrote it down and I signed it. Surely you can look it up."

"Not very easily," Anna admitted. "Suppose you start from the beginning."

Mrs. Westerman looked at her with sudden suspicion. She took a forceful puff on her cigarette and said, "You aren't from the Hampshire police at all, are you?"

"I never said I was," Anna said innocently.

"You never said you weren't either." Mrs. Westerman blew smoke out through her nostrils. "So who the hell are you? Oh my God, you're not a bloody reporter, are you? What paper? You can't print a word I've said. I'll deny it. I'll ring your editor. Who is he? I'll complain to the Press Council.' She started to cough on the smoke, eyes watering furiously. Anna said, "Calm down. I'm not a reporter. I'm a private detective making inquiries on behalf of a client."

Mrs. Westerman went on choking. After a while she managed to say, "What inquiries? Who's your client?"

"I'm afraid I can't tell you that. But she's someone who's very ill at the moment and needs me to look after her interests. Your story might really help her."

"Well, you've got a frightful nerve," Mrs. Westerman said, clearing her throat noisily and wiping her eyes. Mascara had smudged into little black horseshoes under her eyes. "Getting me to divulge confidences under false pretences. If you don't get out of my house right now I'll call the police."

"Okay," Anna said mildly. There wasn't much point arguing. That was the trouble letting people assume things that weren't true: once they tumbled they naturally felt as if they'd been had, and even more naturally became hostile. "But," she went on, "I don't see how telling me what you know about Mr. Jones could possibly harm you, and it might very well help my client. I wouldn't let any of it get out."

"I am not obliged to talk to you," Mrs. Westerman said. Her tidily lipsticked mouth set in a thin straight line. "What you want to know is not my concern. I've got my marriage and my reputation to think about. This is my house, and I'm asking you to leave. That's my right."

You had to be very careful not to cross the middle classes, Anna thought ruefully on the way downstairs and out through the front door. They not only knew their rights but they could be painfully articulate about expressing them. Worse, if they decided you were taking a liberty, they knew just who to telephone when they wanted to complain.

She concluded that today was not one of her better days and turned for home.

CHAPTER 19

It was nearly eight o'clock when Anna got home. She started upstairs, but the Prices' door was ajar and Bea put her head out and called her back. In their living-room she found Quex lolling in an armchair, a glass of red wine balanced on his knee. Selwyn was stretched out on the sofa looking hot and flushed.

Bea said, "I keep telling him it's heartburn but he won't have it. He insists on ulcers."

Quex unwound himself from the depth of his chair and poured Anna a glass of wine. "What about angina?" he suggested callously. "Got any pains in your left arm, mate?"

"You don't get ulcers in your left arm," Selwyn said, looking alarmed. "I haven't got a bad heart, have I, Leo?"

"No heart at all that I know of," Anna said. But he did look more flushed than usual for the time of night. She looked at the wine bottle and then raised her eyebrows questioningly to Bea. Bea shook her head and shrugged. "Not as much as usual, I'd say," she told her from behind Selwyn's back.

"It can't be my heart. I'm a fit man," Selwyn said worriedly. His hands were clasped protectively over his belly. "I may not look it, but I am. I'm just big for my age."

Anna put her glass down and laid her hand on Selwyn's forehead. It was hot and damp. "He feels a bit warm," she told Bea.

"It's a warm night," Bea said defensively.

"Has he had his appendix out?" Quex asked, towering over the sofa and looking curiously at the sufferer.

"That's what I was thinking," Anna said. "Has he, Bea?"

"Not that I know of," Bea said.

"There'll be a scar if he has," Quex said. "Is there a scar on his stomach?"

"I don't look at his stomach if I can help it," Bea said, beginning to be concerned. "Perhaps I should have."

"Excuse me!" Selwyn shouted. "I am here. I can talk for myself. Bloody marvellous, isn't it? As soon as you're not quite up to par they talk over you as if you don't exist."

"Well, have you had your bloody appendix out?" Bea shouted back. "It'd be just like you to pretend you had something classy like ulcers and then go and die of appendicitis because no one believed you had ulcers!"

Selwyn looked shocked. Even Quex and Anna were startled. Bea so rarely raised her voice. Selwyn said weakly, "Well, the pain's not that bad really."

"Have you had it out or haven't you?" Bea demanded.

"Not really," he confessed reluctantly. And with one of those switches characteristic of the Prices' marriage Bea was instantly alarmed about his health while he became unwilling to admit anything was wrong. She went immediately to the phone, saying, "I'm calling Dr. Jaffrey." And Selwyn said, "Not at this time of night, woman. It's only heartburn. He won't come anyway."

"It isn't a major operation," Quex said comfortably. "Not a long cut. Although in your case I'd say it'd have to be pretty deep."

"Cut?" Selwyn cried, sitting up abruptly and wincing. "No cutting! Nobody's slicing through my flesh."

"You can die of a ruptured appendix," Anna informed him kindly.

"There's only an answering service telling me where to get in touch with the locum," Bea exclaimed worriedly and started to dial again. The doorbell rang. Anna went to answer it.

She found David Rietz on the doorstep. He was wearing a light raincoat with the collar turned up. "Here's lookin' at you, private-eyes," he said in an affected drawl and with a mean stare that looked more like migraine than Bogey. "Mah gal says you want the dirt on Thea Hahn."

"No, let me guess," Anna said wearily. "Donald Duck! Brilliant."

"Fergit the wisecracks, sister." He was nothing if not a tryer. "I'm here now an' I aim to stay. Rietz's the name, sleuthing's the game."

"The mouth's the same," she said thoughtfully. She hadn't had supper yet, an omission that was liable to make her disagreeable.

"As who?"

"Donald Duck."

"Are you always this crabby? You said you wanted to see me, you know."

"The point is, have you anything to say—about Thea Hahn, I mean?"

"You'll never know unless you ask me in," he said cockily.

"All right." She let him in and took him upstairs. She turned on the lights and picked up the mail which Bea had thoughtfully pushed under the door. One from her sister and a gas bill. That was better than average.

David sat uninvited in an armchair by the fireplace. "Not bad," he said, giving the room the once over. "No handcuffs hanging from the picture rail, though. I'm disappointed."

"Sorry," she said absently. "Look, after that tutorial at George Stickle's, the Thursday she went missing, you and Thea left together. Where did you go?"

"Ah, my guilty secret's out. I can hide nothing from you, Sleuth-sayer. I weaved a circle round her thrice and when I had her in thrall I put her on a boat bound for Tangier or was it a bus to East Grinstead? Dear me, my memory."

Anna turned her back on him and went to open a window. The curtains were not drawn and she could both see out on to the dark street and the reflection of the room behind her. She kept her back to David and watched him watching her in the dark glass. After a while he said, "Come on, you don't really want to talk business tonight, do you? You know, you really fascinate me. You have a hard sort of charm, and I never could resist bitchy girls. After all, you did send for me."

Anna turned round. "One," she said sharply, "I am not a girl. Two: I left a business card because I want to talk business. Three: if you haven't anything to say about Thea, piss off."

"Well, congratulations, you can count." He got up and prowled over to the window, saying, "You want something from me, and you ought to ask me nicely." He reached out and hooked his fingers in her belt. She kicked him smartly in the kneecap. He sat down with a bump, letting go of her belt. Anna leaned back against the window and looked at him impassively.

"Thea Hahn?" she asked patiently. At the same moment Quex charged into the room. He bore down like a tank on David Rietz and jerked him to his feet saying, "All right, sonny, that's your lot."

Anna said, "Oy, just a minute."

Quex said, "Come on, out!" and hustled David out of the room like an earthmover shifting a molehill. Anna hurried to the door after them and shouted, "Quex, you bleeding berk! What the hell're you doing?"

Thumping and scuffling sounded from the stairs and the front door slammed. A moment or two later, Quex bounded back up two at a time, looking very pleased with himself. "Silly little pillock," he said complacently. "He won't be bothering you again."

"He wasn't bothering me, you steaming wally," Anna cried, furious. "Flaming Norah! He's a frigging witness.

Who do you think you are sticking your nose in like that?" She brushed past him and ran down the stairs. She opened the front door and stood in the street looking up and down. David Rietz had gone.

Quex came down too and said, "Of course he was bothering you. I heard him."

"That little pronk? What do you think he was doing on the floor, then? Assaulting my feet?" She started off towards Holland Park Avenue at a quick trot. Quex caught up and stopped her. "Where're you going now?" he asked. He was very annoyed too.

"I'm going to find him," she said. "He was the last person I know about who saw Thea before she went missing. He was going to tell me about it when you came barging in."

"Oh shit. I'll find him for you. Which way do you think he went?"

"I can do my own dirty work, thanks very much. You're more trouble than you're worth." She tried to sidestep him, but he kept moving in front of her. In the end he put both hands on her shoulders and bellowed, "Stop it, for Christ's sake. I said I'd find him so I'll find him."

A light went on in a window above them and a towsled head poked itself out. " 'Ere, what's your caper?" the head's owner said. "I'm on early shift and if you two don't shut your cake-holes I'm calling the Bill."

"Sorry," Quex yelled back. "Where does he live?" he hissed at Anna. "I can probably catch him."

"If he hasn't got wheels," Anna hissed back. "Towards the Gate then."

"Right," he said, letting go of her shoulders and turning on a shamefaced grin. "Oh, and Leo, you wouldn't have anything to eat upstairs, would you?" He turned swiftly before she could reply and loped away to the main road.

Anna kicked the lamp post and said, "Oh sod, sod, sod," partly because she was very angry and partly because the lamp post didn't have the same give in it as David's kneecap. She limped back to the house muttering slanders on Quex's parentage.

Upstairs, she searched ill-temperedly through the kitchen. A ruined weekend had given her no time to shop and all she could find was garlic, an onion, a green pepper, two tins of crabmeat, and a packet of spaghetti. She stamped downstairs and borrowed some mushrooms, half a bottle of red wine and a tin of tomato purée. Selwyn was in bed and Bea was nervously waiting for the doctor.

Back in the kitchen, Anna messily executed the vegetables, disembowelled the tins and drowned the lot in red wine. The result, simmering on a low heat, looked like the bloody aftermath of a massacre but smelled wonderful. She began to feel better. She put a Sadé record on the hi-fi, and with "Smooth Operator" rolling succulently out of the speakers went back to the kitchen and chopped up some of the new young basil. A large pan of salted water with a few drops of olive oil went on the stove too. Then she made a strong cup of tea and relaxed in her favourite chair.

Quex returned alone. "I found him," he said, rather grumpy. "And I invited him back, but he wouldn't come." Anna nearly laughed.

"He seems to have taken quite a dislike to you," he went on. "He's complaining of a permanently damaged patella."

"He was lucky," Anna said, trying not to smile.

"I think he probably was." He eyed her doubtfully, attempting to gauge her mood. "That's a terrible temper you've got there, Leo. I'm very sorry I interfered. Really. But having talked to the little bastard I honestly don't think he had anything to say. Apparently Thea and he went down to Chalk Farm station together, and at King's Cross he changed to the Circle Line. He doesn't know where she went after that. If you ask me he only came here on the make."

"That didn't escape my notice," she said drily. "So what? He's still connected with Thea."

"Hardly. He admits he made a pass at her at Kings Cross. But he says she got really frightened and ran away. He thought she was neurotic as hell. I must say, Leo, I believe him."

"Well, I'd've probably believed him too if I'd had the chance."

"I've said I'm sorry."

"It's *my* job to assess these things. It's what *I'm* paid for."

"Look, I apologize, fuck it."

"Oh never mind," she said, relenting. "Hungry?"

"Bloody starving," he said, a broad grin splitting beard from moustache.

"Do you really think Selwyn's got appendicitis?" she asked, going to the kitchen to test the spaghetti. The sauce had simmered down and now looked more like a sauce and less like a car crash. It still smelled delicious.

"Well, to begin with I was just kidding, like you." Quex filled the kitchen doorway, snuffing the air like a hound. "I don't know, though. Something seems wrong. I'd hate to be the lucky surgeon if he does need opening up. He's like a trick oyster, Selwyn is. You never know if you're going to find a pearl or a whoopee cushion till you prise him open. Is that ready?"

CHAPTER 20

Forewarned by Sunday's breakfast, Anna had cooked the whole packet of spaghetti. Quex ate three-quarters of it. On reflection she thought that it was a poor choice of food for a bearded man, but he twirled it dextrously round a fork that had assumed the size of a match in his massive fist and popped each load neatly into his mouth.

She got the impression it never touched the sides. Twirl, pop, swallow.

When he had slowed down enough to talk, Anna said, "That poem thing in Thea's notebook, who wrote it?"

"She did," he said with another twirl, pop and swallow.

"Never! Look, I've talked to loads of people about her, and she may've been brilliant but she was dreadfully inhibited and not at all imaginative."

"Don't judge her by what people said about her. She's different now. In fact, she's all sorts of different people—a kind of personality stew."

"But it wasn't even her handwriting."

"It was, though. I've seen her do it." He cleaned his plate with a piece of bread. "It was done with her left hand," he added, munching the bread. "She's normally right-handed. Odd, isn't it?"

When there was nothing left to eat he got up and cleared the table. Anna put the kettle on. She said, "Well, whichever hand she wrote with, I didn't understand a word of it. Was it nonsense?"

"Not exactly." He turned on the taps and filled the sink. "On one level it's about the destruction of a man."

"What man?"

"Someone disappointed by life. Someone who feels isolated." He whirled the washing-up mop over the plates at great speed. "Oh, and maybe he had written three books or had three kids—anyway produced three new things."

"Eh?"

"Yes. The 'three green shoots.' But the important thing is that he was destroyed by what Thea calls a 'spear of detached electricity.' Now that could be love or a flash of inspiration or . . ."

"Couldn't he have simply died in a thunderstorm?" Anna asked gloomily. She made the tea and put the pot on a tray with two mugs.

"Well, maybe. But the piece has a rather more mystical atmosphere than that." He picked up the scourer and got to work on the saucepan. "You can't take what she says too literally. Hold on, I can show you what I mean."

Anna took the tray into the living-room. After a few minutes Quex came and joined her. She poured the tea.

"Have you got something I can play this on?" He produced a cassette from the inside pocket of his jacket. "I taped one of her sessions with Tony Frank, and I think it'll demonstrate what I'm talking about."

Anna showed him how to work the tape-deck and he wound the tape back to the beginning. While it was spinning he explained, "Thea was looking at a print of Leonardo Da Vinci's 'Annunciation.' Do you know it? Well, it shows the Virgin Mary sitting on a terrace in a beautiful Italian garden. The Angel is kneeling in front of her in the grass, with one hand raised in a blessing. It's a gentle, civilized picture. Nothing wild or sinister about it at all. Now listen." He pressed the play button.

It started with Dr. Frank's voice, rather muffled, not close enough to the microphone. "Look at the picture, Thea. What do you see?"

Thea, clearly—"Well, it's Adam and Eve in the garden."

Dr. Frank—"Go on."

Thea—"Adam is giving Eve the apple."

"Yes?"

"Yes. The apple is knowledge. She shouldn't have taken it."

Pause.

"No?"

Thea, very forceful—"No! If you have knowledge you can't have faith. People say God expelled them from Eden, but actually they expelled God. It was Adam who expelled God."

"Not Eve?"

Thea, slowly and patiently—"How could she? Look.

The apple's got a horrible fat worm in it. A snake. Adam's giving it to Eve. It's quite clear. They'll say she tempted him. But how could she? She hasn't got a snake. He's giving her a snake. He knew. No wonder he had to expel God. Where's God?—" the sound of paper tearing—"God's dead. Adam's dead. Eve killed them—" more tearing.

Dr. Frank, calmly—"That's all right, Thea. We'll look at another one tomorrow."

Quex stopped the tape. "She ripped up his Leonardo book," he said with a wry smile. "And then she took her clothes off."

"Stripped?" Anna said, shocked. "What did you do?"

"Well, there was no point stopping her. I know that much. She'd have only got twice as upset. No, when she had finished I gave her my jacket. She was quite happy with that."

"So she was hot and she's not too keen on Leonardo. What of it?"

Quex looked disappointed. "Oh, wake up, Leo," he said. "Insanity is an escape from real life when it becomes too painful. So one way of gauging insanity is to test how far a patient strays from reality. Thea is shown a picture of the Annunciation, but what she describes is an upside down version of the Adam and Eve story."

"Why would she do that?" Anna was becoming confused. Quex was going too far, too fast, and for her purposes, in completely the wrong direction.

"Well, I suppose it's because something like the Adam and Eve story is on her mind. She's talking about a man who tempts a girl with knowledge, seduces her, takes away her innocence, and destroys her faith."

"Who's the man supposed to be?"

"There you go trying to be literal again," he said, impatiently. "Tony Frank says she's very upset whenever her father is mentioned, so it might even be him. It doesn't have to be a real seduction, you know. Suppose all she ever wanted was his love, but all he wanted from her was achievement. So to win his love she did everything he asked of her—learned everything she could. But still she gets no love as a result. All she's left with is knowledge."

"Hang about," Anna said, quite impatient too. "Just for once let's be literal. A real bloke calling himself Jones was shot in a Southampton hotel. A young woman, who could very well be Thea, was in a connecting room. She was passing herself off as his niece. When Jones' body was discovered in the morning, she had disappeared. The same day, Thea turned up in Britmouth, having got off a Southampton bus. She then more or less confessed to a helmet, of all people, that she'd killed her father."

"Well, there you are then!" Quex interrupted excitedly. "That's an even more interesting interpretation, isn't it? Jones was her lover. He was the father figure. Someone else whose love she tried to win. The seduction is a real one. The knowledge is carnal knowledge."

"Oh lovely," Anna said, feeling more and more depressed. "So what about Eve killing Adam and God?"

"Quite obviously she feels responsible for someone's death." Quex poured more tea into his mug. "Or destruction," he added eagerly. "It could be a spiritual or moral death she's talking about."

"Well, it isn't a spiritual corpse in the Southampton morgue," Anna said angrily. "Am I ever going to get anything but metaphors out of her? Is she going to be able to give a straight answer to a straight question?"

"Not in the short term," Quex said, considering. "I'm afraid metaphor is the best she can do. But it's a hot-line direct to her subconscious, which in a way is better than straight answers."

"Not to me it isn't. And it won't look too clever in court either. The law doesn't like insanity. The law likes people to be responsible for their crimes. Take a mass murderer—you know who I mean—nutty as a fruitcake, but because there's only an ill-defined line between justice and revenge, he has to stand trial and go to prison. All because the law and the public can't bear to see him take what they think is the soft option. As if Rampton or Broadmoor are soft options! Think of the time and money and man hours they wasted proving he was sane. And then a few months later they had to transfer him anyway."

"No one would try to prove Thea was sane, surely?" Quex was beginning to look worried.

"They wouldn't have to. The way the law stands it's up to her to prove she's of unsound mind."

"But that'd be easy."

"Not necessarily. If it was important enough the Crown could find any number of tame shrinks to say the reverse of anything Dr. Frank said about her."

Quex ran his hands over his face and then sat forward, his elbows on his knees. He said, "So how serious is it?"

"I don't know. If the police put two and two together they might be able to prove she was in the next room to Jones at the Gateway Hotel. Plenty of people saw someone like her. What they can prove after that is anyone's guess. No one's found the weapon yet. But suppose they found it conveniently along the bus route between Britmouth and Southampton? And then of course she's already told one of them she killed a man.

"If the police think they've got a case they'll take it all the way. Trouble is, I don't think they'll have much bother making a case once they start."

"Bad," he said moodily. "In fact tragic. I mean, when you look at Thea herself, you can't see her doing harm to anyone, can you? She's more the type who'd do harm to herself."

"Yes. But she thinks she's responsible for someone's death. You said so yourself."

"I know, I know. But I haven't been looking at it the way you have. I've been fascinated by her state of mind. You've been looking at the practical implications.

Take this evening, with the tape and everything I've said: I've been making her look as guilty as hell."

"Well, it doesn't matter," Anna said. "It's only to me and I'm on her side too."

"But can you be? If she's really killed someone, I mean."

"Yes. Because she's very young and helpless. Whatever she's actually done, I've convinced myself she's not to blame."

"Convinced yourself?"

"Well, it's only a personal viewpoint. I'm not defending it. But she isn't malicious, she isn't greedy, she isn't cold or calculating. She's only mad. So I can't really hold her responsible."

"I don't know about you, Leo," he said, leaning back on the cushions again and regarding her curiously. "You seem to reduce complicated subects to such a simple level."

"Oh I try, I try. It's a lot easier than being intelligent." She yawned and put the mugs back on the tray.

Quex took the cassette out of the machine and slipped it into his pocket. He yawned too. "I give up," he said despairingly. "Can I stay here again? I'm dead tired."

"All right, but the sofa's still only six foot eight and there's nothing for breakfast except coffee."

CHAPTER 21

In the morning, as it turned out, there wasn't time for coffee. Anna overslept and was woken by the telephone. She had been dreaming about a wide street in a university town. On both sides were buildings, with towers and turrets and baroque curlicues, rising like cliffs and blocking the sky. Someone told her it was the City of the Mind. As she walked down the street it branched into smaller and smaller roads until the roads became mere alleyways. But however small the alleys, the buildings grew ever taller and more complex.

There were no people out in the streets, but the buildings were humming with life, and the nearer she drew to the heart of the city the louder the noise became. At last she found an alley that led to the city centre. But it was too narrow to walk down. Try as she would she could not squeeze herself between the buildings, and the noise became so loud it hurt her ears. At last she gave up. But now she found it impossible to leave. She ran this way and that, her hands covering her ears to shut out the cacophony, but she could neither escape the city nor could she get into any of the buildings.

As she tumbled out of bed the demands of the telephone were joined by a knocking on the door. Quex went to the door in his underwear. Anna answered the phone in her nightdress.

Beryl said, "You were supposed to be in Southampton. I've wasted three phone calls there because I thought they were being incompetent and couldn't find you."

Bea said, "Quex. What're you doing here?" Quex pointed to the phone and placed his finger on his lips.

Beryl said, "So if you're in London you're late for work. You should've been in the office ten minutes ago."

Bea said, "It's Selwyn. He's got to go to hospital."

Beryl said, "There've been developments to the Hahn account. The Commander wants you here as soon as possible."

"Hospital?" Anna said.

"What are you talking about?" Beryl snapped. "Here! I'll expect you here in fifteen minutes."

Anna put the receiver down. "What's this about Selwyn?" she asked.

"Oh Anna, you were quite right," Bea said tremulously. "It is appendicitis. The doctor came last night. She said it was a grumbling appendix. It isn't urgent but it ought to come out now. She booked him into St. Mary's this morning."

"What the hell's a grumbling appendix?" Quex asked. Anna said, "If it's Selwyn's, it's bound to be grumbling."

"The trouble is, he says he won't go," Bea said helplessly. "He says he'd rather die of natural causes than perish under a surgeon's blade. So I was wondering, Anna, if you'd come down and shout at him. You're better at shouting than I am."

"I'll say," said Quex.

"And then perhaps you could take him to St. Mary's in your car," Bea went on, ignoring him. "He just wants fussing over, really."

"Give me a minute to dress," Anna said. "I'll be right down."

There was so little time. She flew from bedroom to bathroom and back, throwing on clothes, giving face and teeth a lick and a promise, brushing hair.

Downstairs in the Prices' bedroom Selwyn, a picture of sartorial disorder in only a T-shirt, pyjama bottoms, and white nylon socks, clung stubbornly to his sheet as if they were going to wrench him forcibly from his bed and carry him kicking and screaming to the abattoir.

"Body snatchers," he cried, as Anna, Bea and Quex approached his stronghold. "No one's slicing me. It's butchers they are at St. Mary's," he exclaimed, hugging a pillow to his threatened gut, and waxing very Welsh in his hysteria. "Why can't you let me die peaceful in my own bed?"

"Peaceful?" Anna shouted, shooting a sidelong glance at Bea, who nodded encouragingly. She then gave him a vivid though not entirely accurate account of the horrible agonies suffered by cretinous Welsh poets who died of peritonitis. Bea punctuated the harangue with approving nods and whispered comments like, "Lovely; stinking, yellow pus in the bloodstream, gangrene. I'd never've thought of that. Go on. You're doing lovely."

When Anna got to the wormy fate of his green and putrefied carcase shovelled hastily into a pauper's grave, Selwyn surrendered. And when Quex took over the

Mr. Nice Guy role, and promised to drive him in state to the hospital in his Jaguar, Anna was able to escape.

She scampered at top speed across Holland Park, scattering pigeons, joggers, and early strollers alike, and arrived panting at Brierly Security.

"At last," Martin Brierly said, turning away from his lofty scrutiny of Kensington High Street and glancing at her peevishly.

"Yes. Sorry," Anna said quickly. "An emergency. A neighbour had to be rushed to hospital. I couldn't refuse." She had already practised this half-truth on Beryl and it came out pat.

"Well, that aside, you're late. So now perhaps you'd devote your energy to relevant circumstances. There is a lot to do. The Hampshire police have been in touch with Mr. Embury and require some sort of statement from Miss Hahn. Mr. Embury and Mr. Hahn are due here at midday. Is there anything I should know?"

"Yes," Anna said, and told him what her inquiries in Britmouth and Southampton had uncovered. He was silent for a while, rotating his thumbs like a waterwheel and fidgeting with his pen. At last he said, "Well, it looks as if it's Mr. Embury's turn to earn his money, doesn't it? Meanwhile I want everything you've told me on paper. You'd better dictate directly to Miss Doyle for once, because I want it fast and I want it well presented. Be ready by twelve."

Beryl would be extremely unhappy with this arrangement, so Anna left the breaking of it to Mr. Brierly and went off to the rec-room to make coffee. She found Bernie and Johnny in the report room. Bernie was actually writing. Johnny was replacing the batteries in his pocket dictaphone. He never took notes.

Bernie said, " 'Morning, love," and placidly continued writing. Johnny, eager for any distraction, jumped to his feet saying, "Come for your quartz rotary? That'll be fifteen quid."

"You told me twelve-fifty," Anna said, going on to the rec-room. Johnny followed her. "You're a hard woman," he complained. "All right, say no more, twelve and a half, cash. I must be mad."

Anna filled the kettle and lit the gas. "I'm not paying for anything sight unseen," she said. "Where is it?"

"Make us a cuppa and I'll show you." He opened his locker. His was next to Anna's and was decorated with pinups of racehorses and greyhounds. It was a source of amusement to everyone that he should want to be reminded of the animals that, on most occasions, let him down so badly. Most of his money went to boost the odds on otherwise unfancied contenders.

"Now there's an elegant timepiece," Johnny said, displaying it like a conjuror, dangled from thumb and forefinger.

"It seems to be working," Anna said, surprised. It showed the correct time and the sweep hand swept reassuringly.

" 'Course it's working," Johnny said indignantly. "Genuine Japanese precision technology, this is. Would I give you rubbish?"

Anna snorted and made three cups of coffee. She took one in to Bernie.

"It's a once in a lifetime offer," Johnny said persuasively. "They're selling like hot cakes. If you don't take this one you'll regret it. They'll be all gone by Friday."

"What do you think?" Anna asked, giving Bernie his coffee.

"Ta, love. Well, it seems to be working," Bernie said, surprised.

"Genuine Japanese precision technology," Anna told him. He snorted. Johnny said, "Go on, Anna. You won't do better."

"Give him ten," Bernie said. "Not a penny more. Remember the toasters?" Anna did. Both Tim and Phil had bought one and neither had got more than a week's work out of them.

"Ten?" cried Johnny. "Where's your heart? That's hardly more than cost."

"Ten," said Anna, taking the money out of her bag. "Take it or leave it."

Johnny took the ten and Anna took the watch.

"Anna!" Beryl shouted from the other end of the corridor. "Where are you? I haven't got all day."

"A nightingale sang in Berkeley Square," Bernie murmured as Anna picked up her cup and left the room.

At twelve Anna was ready with four neatly typed and photocopied reports clipped into four identical blue folders. She was admitted to the front office where she shook hands with Mr. Hahn, nodded to Mr. Embury, and distributed the reports.

Mr. Embury had obviously mastered the technique of speed-reading. His eyes flicked over the pages like a snake's tongue, and before Mr. Hahn had read half of the first page he turned back to the beginning and said, "I see that Miss Lee thinks we have cause for concern." There was silence for a few minutes while Mr. Hahn caught up. He said, "I don't see that there is too much cause for concern. My daughter has not been positively identified at the hotel, and until she is I refuse to believe that she could in any way be involved."

"Miss Lee could hardly show your daughter's photograph to the hotel staff," Mr. Brierly said. "But circumstantial or not, I think we should take both her findings and her suppositions seriously."

"Did you tell Police Constable Mason you had found Miss Hahn's luggage at the Britmouth bus station or that it had been left on a Southampton bus?" Mr. Embury asked.

"Of course not," Anna said. "At the time I didn't know she had any. I only told him I was looking for it because it seemed the most innocuous reason for me to be . . ."

"Well, however innocuous it seemed, Miss Lee, the police now know you have the luggage and where it was found. Did it also seem innocuous to tell the police where to contact me?"

"Mr. Embury, please," Mr. Brierly said quickly, darting a warning frown at Anna. "In our profession we depend a lot on police cooperation. We cannot be seen to be hindering them. They knew Miss Hahn's name already. They knew her passport number and could easily have asked Britmouth General her present whereabouts. In giving the police your telephone number Miss Lee was protecting Miss Hahn and her parents. An act I would have thought you might applaud."

"She might have played for time," said Mr. Embury coldly. "Now the police wish to interview Miss Hahn, and I, like yourselves, cannot be seen to be obstructing them."

"Surely she is unfit to be interviewed," Mr. Hahn said. "She's in hospital."

"That's neither here nor there," Mr. Embury told him. "The police can question whom they like, where they like. Neither Dr. Frank nor I can stop them."

"As to her fitness," Mr. Brierly added. "They don't consider anyone but a judge and jury competent to decide whether or not she's sane; not even a psychiatrist. They would simply proceed as if she were fit until a judge instructed them otherwise."

"That is monstrous," Mr. Hahn said. He looked tired and anxious. Anna noticed that bruised pouches had appeared beneath his eyes in the last few days.

"It's merely to prevent insanity from becoming too easy a defence," Mr. Brierly said, himself an old policeman with many old police sympathies.

"Be that as it may, we ought to decide how best to proceed," Mr. Embury said. "Obviously, I will put the police off for as long as I reasonably can. But I feel we should also prepare some sort of defence. If the police do have evidence to prove Miss Hahn was with Mr. Jones at the Gateway Hotel, they may well charge her with his murder and we should be ready for that."

"It must never come to that." Mr. Hahn's voice cracked fretfully. "Miss Lee must find evidence to counter theirs. She must prove that my daughter was never at the hotel."

"That may not be possible," Mr. Brierly said clearly. "However, there are two possibilities. The first is that someone as yet unknown shot Mr. Jones. The second is that Mr. Jones committed suicide."

"Of course," Mr. Hahn said eagerly. "Miss Lee must show that he shot himself."

"That may not be possible either," Mr. Embury said. "But it might be useful if Miss Lee turned her attention to Mr. Jones. It might be possible to throw doubt in that area."

"No gun . . ." Anna began, but Mr. Brierly held up his hand and said, "We might reasonably query how or even if Miss Hahn was connected with Mr. Jones. Mr. Jones is an enigma but it might be fruitful to research into his background."

Mr. Embury said, "Hm, you mean the possibility of self-defence or something of that nature? Yes, investigating Mr. Jones might well be to our advantage."

"I'll need some help," Anna said quickly, before she could be interrupted again.

"She should have all the help she needs," Mr. Hahn said to Mr. Brierly.

"Very well," said Mr. Brierly. "I'll see what can be arranged."

CHAPTER 22

Mr. Brierly arranged for Bernie to be free for the rest of the week; but not until he had finished his current report. To fill in time, Anna looked up the section called "Insanity on Arraignment or During Trial" in the ancient office edition of *Criminal Law*. It did not look encouraging.

If the only chance of redemption for Thea was to remain in Dr. Frank's care, it was imperative that she should be able to pull something out of the hat before the police really got their teeth into the case. The alternative would seem to be prison hospital, with prison officers sending their own assessments to the Director of Public Prosecutions and through him to judge and jury who would in their turn decide if she was fit to plead.

The thought of Thea questioned by police in police cells, or prison hospital made Anna very uneasy. Adam House, with its cosy rooms and sunny garden seemed the only place that might soothe Thea's troubled mind. And Dr. Frank looked a much better option for her than officials who didn't know her or who might not care about her.

Anna felt Thea was safe with Dr. Frank. What was less realistic, but a hope none the less, she wanted him to cure her. As far as she could see Dr. Frank didn't think of Thea's treatment in those terms. In fact Anna didn't know at all how he thought about Thea's treatment. He might in the end resort to drugs and ECT. But Anna thought not.

"How can you possibly know where a girl in her state would be happiest?" Bernie argued when she told him of her unease. They were having a late lunch in Scoffs, next to the Odeon.

"I saw her all drugged up and zombieish at Britmouth General," Anna said, washing down the last of a tasty mushroom omelette with some good strong coffee. "And I've seen her looking a lot better since."

"But how's she feeling?" Bernie asked, reasonably. "It might be best for a girl in her state not to feel at all. Maybe zombie feels better. Maybe Adam House is just a better class of bin and you're taken in by appearances." He signalled to the waitress for the bill.

"I can't believe it's better to drag around more dead than alive," Anna said stubbornly. "The drugs only suppress the weird behaviour. They don't do anything to help what's wrong. And I think it's the weird behaviour that'll tell Dr. Frank what's wrong, in the end."

"So now you're the expert in psychiatry," Bernie said with a soothing grin. "Well maybe you're right and the poor child should stay at Adam House, but if that's so we'd better get our skates on. You haven't filled me in on anything but your own opinions so far."

They paid for lunch and went out into the warm, dusty High Street. The park looked green and inviting and Anna thought they could talk there as well as anywhere. But Bernie had a better idea. He drove them to his house in Finchley where they caught his wife, Syl, in the act of taking her own secret version of a Sacher Torte out of the oven. The kitchen windows were open and the buttery yellow curtains stirred fitfully, wafting chocolate perfume out into the garden.

They went out and sat under Bernie's precious plum tree, he in a creaking old bamboo chair and she lolling on the grass at his feet, with glasses of lemon tea beside them. If you had to work on such a pleasant afternoon, Anna thought, what better place to do it? The Schillers' garden, with its three fruit trees, plum, and two apples, had the feeling of a small orchard. And at the end furthest from the house there was room for a few rows of vegetables. Just one or two lettuce seedlings, carefully pricked out, showed their heads. Otherwise the only evidence was the finely dug soil mounded over seed potatoes, carrots, and french beans. Nearer the house the old-fashioned flowerbeds were planted with scarlet geraniums, sweet williams, foxgloves, and hollyhocks.

Anna sighed and closed her eyes. There were no two people in all the world, she thought, as effortlessly comfortable as Bernie and Syl.

Bernie said, "Wake up, dozey. I didn't bring you here to kip," and nudged her with his foot. She sighed again and then sat up and began to tell him what had happened so far. After a while, Syl came out with a plate of Sacher Torte, still warm and moist from baking. She brought her knitting with her and sat beside them under the trees, fleet-fingered and pretty, the way only a truly happy woman can be. While Anna talked she watched her. Syl was a mystery. Beside her Anna felt rootless and unquiet, lacking any gift for peace. It wasn't that Syl hadn't known trouble. It wasn't that she hadn't worked hard, because Anna knew she had—first to help keep her ailing refugee parents after the war, and later when Bernie couldn't earn enough for his young family. And she still did. She was always busy, and all her work was useful. But Syl had the attitude that if you had to cook a meal, let it be absolutely delicious. If you cleaned the windows, make them really sparkle. And if you upholstered an old chair, make it the snuggest one in the house. Yet there wasn't an ounce of complacency in her. She knew she was lucky but treasured her luck and built on it.

Anna didn't understand at all how anyone could get so much pleasure out of such small and ordinary things, but she was glad Syl could. It proved, sometimes, when she was at her moodiest, that you could find gold in the blackest hills if you knew how to look. Anna didn't know how to look; but Syl did and mostly it was enough for Anna to know that someone, somewhere had the secret.

Meanwhile, Bernie reclined, grizzled head leaning against the back of his chair, eyelids drooping Buddha-like, and fingers laced across his ample waistline. "Got any ideas?" he said at last crossing his ankles and stretching out his legs in the patchy sun.

"Well, um, there was this, um, sort of voyeur," Anna mumbled. It was the bit she hadn't related yet. "One of the porters at the Continental Gateway. Goes through people's luggage and, well, sort of spies on them."

"So what did he say?" Bernie asked.

"Ah well, he didn't actually say anything. I didn't sort of ask."

Bernie stared at her. Syl caught on quicker and said, "Oh Anna. It could only happen to you."

Bernie said, "You mean . . . ? Go on—pull the other one." He let out a yelp of laughter. Anna plucked a daisy out of the grass and studied it with great interest. Syl dug Bernie reprovingly in the ribs and he, struggling to keep a straight face, said, "Not called Tom by any chance, is he?"

"Miles," Anna said stiffly. "Miles Gancitano. And if you so much as breathe a hint of this in the rec-room I'll pepper your tuna sarnies with powdered glass. So help me."

"So all right, all right." Bernie raised a placatory hand. "But this schmuck needs talking to, obviously. Lord knows what he might've seen. Present company excepted," he added hastily. "If you're that squeamish I'll do the talking. But our real brief as I see it is getting a make on this Jones character."

"Which so far even Plod hasn't been able to do," Anna put in.

"Right. Not that we know what Plod's been up to in Hampshire."

"Know anyone in Hampshire?"

"Don't think so," Bernie said thoughtfully. "But I'll ring round tonight and see if anyone else does." His countless years on the Metropolitan force had given him a network of people who knew people who knew people, whereas Anna's time in uniform had been comparatively short and her contemporaries there were still in quite junior positions. Anna said, "In some ways, it'll make things a bit easier now they've tumbled Thea."

"Right. At least we can work out in the open. So what I'll do is wait till morning and then get on the trumpet to your Mr. Embury and see if they've had their interview and find out what they know and what they don't know and then we'll take it from there."

"Okay," she said. "And then down to the South Coast?"

"Yes. Shall I pick you up or do you want your own motor?"

"My own."

"Then I'll ring you in the morning too."

Syl broke in and said, "If that's all settled, Anna, why don't you stay to supper?" But Anna regretfully refused. She had to restock her plundered kitchen and she wanted an early night. Bea would be on her own and anxious, and Selwyn might want visiting in hospital.

Bernie dropped her at Finchley Central and she went home by tube to find the house deserted. The silence was unnatural. She was so used to the faint sounds of Selwyn's typewriter, the television, running water, that without them her flat felt like a vacuum. She put a Free Key record on the hi-fi and cleared away Quex's bedding. The phone rang.

A loud voice with a distinct Edinburgh accent said, "This is Samuel Tulloch. Are you the young lady my grandson's been visiting?"

"Sam?" Anna said, surprised. "I suppose so, but I haven't seen him since Saturday."

"Outrageous," the old voice stated. "His mother told me he came home drunk at three in the morning. I don't know if you're aware of the family circumstances, young lady, but it's a cruel thing to worry the life out of the boy's mother only a few short weeks after her husband passes away."

"It was not intended, Mr. Tulloch," Anna said, doing her best to sound like a responsible adult. "There was a party at a neighbour's and Sam was already there when I arrived. I'm very sorry his mother was worried."

"As an older woman you should show more concern for the welfare of a young lad," Samuel Tulloch senior went on implacably. "The boy's vulnerable now and I'll not see him come under a poor influence. So I'll ask you to send him home now, if you don't mind."

"He's not here, Mr. Tulloch," Anna said, edging across the room, with the phone to her ear, to turn down the blare of the record. With Mr. Tulloch grating in one ear like a bad-tempered schoolmaster and Free Key pouring heavy blues into the other there was not much room left for thought.

"There's no need to cover up for him, young lady," the old man said. "If he's home within the hour we'll say no more about it."

By stretching she could just reach the volume knob. She turned it quickly and in the blessed quiet said, "I'm not covering for him. He isn't here. I've only just got back myself. I'm not expecting him but if he does turn up I'll send him home immediately."

"The boy's not there, y'say?" There was a quaver in the old voice. "But he said he was going to see you and that was two hours since. We had words, the boy and me, and he said he'd see who he pleased. I told him to go straight home to his mother but she has'na seen him."

"I shouldn't worry about him," Anna said, feeling a little uneasy. "He probably just lost his temper. I expect he's on his way home now."

"But I am worried about him." Mr. Tulloch paused to clear his throat. "Especially if he's not in control of himself. Y'see he's taken a piece of my property . . ."

Anna said, "What's that, Mr. Tulloch? I can't hear you." The old voice had died away to a whisper.

"My gun," Mr. Tulloch said, loudly. "The boy's taken my pistol."

"Frigging Ada! He hasn't."

"He has, and I'll thank you not to blaspheme." The gritty voice seemed to recover strength with a reprimand. "It's only a souvenir from the war. I don't even know if it works. But it's loaded and . . ."

"Oh no," Anna groaned. "What on earth were you doing keeping a gun where a boy could find it?"

"I captured it myself during the war, and I'll have

you know it's been under lock and key ever since. D'y'think, young lady, I'm the kind of man to let children play with a Luger?"

"A what?" She sounded a little shrill even to her own ears. "Give me your address, Mr. Tulloch. I'm coming right over."

CHAPTER 23

Street lamps were just beginning to flicker on when she arrived at the house in Dulwich. Samuel Tulloch senior had a second-floor flat in a building that had long ago ceased to be a respectable Edwardian home. Now it was hemmed in on both sides by flat-fronted blocks of council flats and itself divided up into a small warren of bedsitters and communal bathrooms.

Mr. Tulloch had the comparative luxury of two rooms with a kitchen and bathroom of his own. He met her at the door and showed her into a front-facing room made gloomy by black mahogany furniture which ate up the mean light from a single sixty-watt bulb in the ceiling. He was a lean, spare man buckled by the invisible weight of arthritis. The hand he extended was disfigured by swollen, stony knuckles and the fingers clawed sideways. Anna shook it tentatively. If she had owned a hand so obviously painful, she thought she would avoid offering it to strangers.

"Miss Lee, is it?" he said, looking at her with glittering, heavy-lidded eyes set close together over a nose like a shark's dorsal fin. "My grandson says you're some sort of detective. I must say you don't look like one to me, but he's an impressionable boy. He'll be looking for heroes now my son's gone. It's a dangerous time for a boy that age. I told him to look no further than the minister but he's a stubborn child and this is a godless age, I'm sorry to say."

"The gun," Anna interrupted. "Where did you keep it, Mr. Tulloch?"

"Aye, the gun." The old man sighed. "It was where I always kept it—locked in the cabinet beside my bed. I'll show you." He shuffled slowly towards the bedroom door. Anna followed. She said, "How do you know Sam took it? Did you see him take it?"

"Of course I didn't," he said angrily, stopping with his hand on the doorknob. "Would I have allowed it? But I was away for a few minutes to the bathroom. He'd been at me to give him my picture of his father and mother on their wedding day. But I refused. His mother has one like it anyway. Let her give it to him, I said. But when he'd gone I noticed the picture was missing. It shocked me to think the boy'd stoop to steal from his own grandfather so I looked around to see what else he might've taken."

"The picture was in the bedroom too?" Anna asked.

"Aye, it was." He opened the door and turned on the light. A tall black wardrobe loomed out of the shadows with its companion piece, a heavy chest of drawers, by its side. The bed was a narrow, spartan divan with a brown blanket stretched tight over it. A cabinet stood next to it, covered by a white lace doily. On top of that was a large Bible, and a pair of bifocals. There was no lamp. Old Mr. Tulloch would have to get out of bed to turn out the light when he had finished his nightly reading.

"The gun was here," he said, rattling the door to the cabinet. It was well and truly locked.

"And the key?"

"Here." He opened the cabinet drawer and took out an old leather spectacle case. Several keys were inside the case. He chose one and unlocked the little cupboard. Inside was a plain white chamber pot with a chipped tin cash box sitting on top. He reached behind the pot and brought out a stiff leather holster with the letters K. H. W. embossed on the flap. He said, "I took it from a German officer in 1944. I should have turned it in but I did'na. I wanted something to remember the day by." Gun or no gun, his thin lips stretched in grim satisfaction and he rubbed his twisted thumb possessively over the leather.

"Who knew it was there?" Anna asked. "And where to find the key?"

"My family knew. No one else." He stooped and put the holster back behind the pot. "Who can you trust if not your own family?" He relocked the cupboard and held the key up for Anna to see. "And for your information," he went on, giving her a hard, suspicious glare, "I'll be finding somewhere new to put the key."

"Very wise," she said, ignoring the glare. "When did you last check to see the gun was in place?"

"I had no call to before today when I discovered the boy had stolen my picture."

"And where did you keep that?"

He pointed to the chest of drawers. Two other photographs stood on it and Anna went over to look. One was of two women, the elder sitting stiff as a post in a straight chair, the younger like a guardsman behind her. They both had chests like bow windows.

The second was a family photograph. She had to hold it up to the light to see it properly. She recognized Sam, a few years younger, skinny and eager, but what startled her was the man standing next to him. He had a hand on Sam's shoulder and an arm round a girl a little taller than Sam. A woman stood beside her with an even smaller child.

Anna swung round and held the picture out to Mr. Tulloch. She said, "Is this your son and his family?"

"It is," he replied stiffly and turned his head away.

Anna felt as if she had pins and needles in her spine. Her first impression was that the man in the photograph might have been Rodney Hahn's younger brother: a thinner man to be sure, and not so prosperous, but resembling him none the less.

Her next and more forceful thought was that this was the man whose face she had seen on a police poster at the Continental Gateway.

She put the picture down very gently and said, "Tell me about your son, Mr. Tulloch."

"I never discuss family matters with strangers." He turned his back on her and went into the living-room. Anna followed, softly closing the door behind her. She felt as if she was walking on a paper roof. She said, "You disclosed the fact that your grandson's a thief. How about your souvenir, Mr. Tulloch? Was it registered?"

"Don't try to intimidate me, young lady," he grated, glowering at her. "I'm a law-abiding man, and it's only a memento after all. An antique probably. It'd never fire. Not after all these years."

"It's still an unlicensed firearm. And it wasn't kept in a safe place. The police'd take a dim view of that." She took a dim view of people who bullied poor old men, but she wasn't going to stop.

His shoulders slumped. "If you were anything of a detective you'd find my grandson and get the thing back for me before there was any trouble," he said, unwilling to be browbeaten.

"It may be too late for that, but I'll try." She looked at the threadbare old carpet, unable to meet his eyes. "First, tell me about your son."

"I don't know what you'd want to know about him for," he said. He sat down massaging one of his crooked shoulders painfully. "I never had much to give him, but he was a good, upright boy—even living in this concupiscent city. I was a poor man. I would never have come but for the Depression when there was no work at home. My son was born down here. I remember telling his mother this was no place to bring up a family, but he proved me wrong. He won his scholarships and never cost me a penny I couldn't afford, and he never took his foot off the path—honest, hardworking, a son to be proud of.

"I only wish his mother'd lived to see—him a teacher at the university, you know. I thought he was reaching too high, but he passed all his exams, never brought me a moment's grief till now." The old man blinked and frowned hard at Anna. She waited patiently for him to go on.

"You hear all kinds of goings-on at the university— the drinking and cards and other sorts of shamelessness. And there was a time when he was a young lad just off to Oxford when . . . but I told him, 'There's always two pairs of eyes watching you: God's eyes and your own. If you're tempted, remember that; and ask yourself is this something I could tell my father without shame.' I'd brought him up to fear the Lord, you see. And he always listened to me after that.

"So when he was courting Margaret it was all open and above board. Night after night he'd bring her here. And after he'd taken her home he'd come straight back. I know because I'd look at my watch. I knew he'd pick a good woman. And he did. Like his mother, she was—a plain, honest, good sort. None of those flighty young things always showing their legs and telling you lies.

"Margaret was a good wife to him, and you can't say that about many women these days.

"He was a good husband to her too. She never had cause to complain. And they won't be short of a penny now he's gone neither. He looked after his family."

Anna waited but he had run out of things to say, so she asked, "When did you see him last, Mr. Tulloch?"

The old man shook his head wearily. "He always came with the family on a Sunday to take me to church. But the last time he came was the Thursday before he died. He came to tell me he'd be away for the weekend, working. He was a hard worker. I was at the library. I always go to the library of a morning. He didn't leave a note like some would. He came to find me. He knew I'd be annoyed, but he came anyway."

Anna said, "Did he have the key to this place?"

"Of course he had," Mr. Tulloch said. "He could've left a note on the table, but he did'na. I'll always be grateful for that." He shook his head again and started to rub some life into his twisted hands.

Anna said, "I ought to be off now, Mr. Tulloch. Can I make you a pot of tea or something before I go?"

"I'm not sick, am I?" he snapped with something like his old spark. "I'm quite capable of making my own tea, thank you very much. Just you find the boy and tell him to bring my property back. I'll not want for anything else. And after that, you can leave him to his mother's care. She doesn't want him gadding around till all hours if you don't mind." He showed her out and waited mistrustfully on the stairs till she had left the house.

CHAPTER 24

"Trouble, trouble, trouble," she muttered out loud, drumming her fingers impatiently on the steering-wheel. She was stuck at the traffic lights at Earl's Court waiting to cross the Cromwell Road. Where was everyone going? A river of cars flowed west and east, in and out of inner London: six never-ending lanes of headlights, an inexhaustible pool of people travelling one way being replaced by an inexhaustible supply going in the opposite direction.

" 'How many deaths does the Saviour die?' " she whispered to herself. "Thank you very much, Thea Hahn. 'A self-made man.' Isolated, disappointed, and with three kids. Good work, Quex. Good work but not specific enough."

She watched the nightly traffic exchange and wondered why the traffic planners didn't simply admit the Cromwell Road was a river and build a few bridges over it for the people unfortunate enough to be travelling north or south.

"Frigging trouble," she muttered, still drumming as she waited in Warwick Road to cross Kensington High Street. She rolled down the window and took a lungful of pure warm carbon monoxide. Someone was going to have to visit Sam Tulloch's house. She didn't want it to be her, and she didn't want it to be now, and she certainly didn't want it to be alone. She wanted to be at home, talking to Bernie on the phone, halving the trouble.

When she got home, she found Bea and Quex in the Prices' flat. Bea was worried about Selwyn. Quex was worried about Thea. They both wanted to talk to her. Everyone wanted to halve their troubles that night. Even if she halved her own she'd end up with more than she started off with.

She hared upstairs, promising to be back in a minute, and dialled Bernie's number. "Naffing trouble," she whispered, drumming on the phone books while she waited for him to answer. When he did, she said, "I'm pretty certain I know who bloody Mr. Jones is. It's one of Thea's tutors, Joseph Tulloch. Only it can't be."

"Hold everything," Bernie said calmly. "Isn't he the one found drowned off the North Devon coast a few weeks ago?"

"Not found," Anna said. "Presumed. But they've had a memorial service for him."

"Never mind that," Bernie said. "Just give me the timetable and slow down. You're gabbling."

"Yes, sorry," she said, getting her breathing under control. "Well, Thea went walkabout on Thursday the 12th. Tulloch drowned or whatever on Friday the 13th. Then nothing for twelve days when someone called

Jones is found shot on Wednesday the 25th. Thea turned up bonkers on the same afternoon."

"All right." He hesitated for a minute. Then he said, "So supposing Tulloch is Jones, what's the drowning chicane all about? How's the family off for insurance?"

"Nicely. The point is, someone's going to have to tell them. One of them's going to have to identify the body. They're going to be bleeding destroyed about it."

"That's not the point at all," Bernie broke in. "At least not yet. You're getting all base over apex. Just calm down and tell me why you think Tulloch's Jones."

"I saw his picture at his father's drum down in Dulwich. He's the same face on a police poster in Southampton. Oh shit, and I almost forgot the worst bit—his father had a Luger he always kept by the bed, the silly old fool. The Luger's gone. He thinks young Sam took it today, but it could've been gone for ages because he never looked till now."

Bernie sighed. "I see. Well, first you'd better ask young Sam if he nicked the gun. After that we'll worry."

"Sam's missing. That's why his grandad called me. They had some sort of ruck."

"Phone his home and see if he's back," Bernie told her. "Then phone me."

Anna hung up and leafed through the directory till she found J. S. Tulloch's number. A woman's voice, flat and dreary, answered. Anna asked for Sam and to her mixed reaction of relief and concern Sam's voice came on the line a few minutes later. She took a deep breath and said, "Hello, Pilgrim, what've you been up to? Your grandad just gave me an earful for leading you astray."

"He didn't!" Sam said, sounding shocked. "I'm awfully sorry. We had a bit of a row, that's all."

"Easily done, I should think," Anna said casually. "He seemed like a stroppy old chap."

"You can say that again," Sam said with feeling. "It's all 'God's will be done' with him. Only God's will and Grandpa's always seem to be the same. He's got more 'Thou shalt nots' than you'll ever find in *Leviticus*."

Anna laughed. "Speaking of which," she said lightly, "you didn't happen to covet anything of his when you were there today?"

A guilty silence followed. Then Sam said, "Well, you see Mum's lost her wedding photograph. She was really going up the wall about it. We all looked everywhere but no one could find it. So when I saw Grandpa today I asked if he'd give me his. But all I got was a lecture about the sanctity of property. So I got a bit wild, and when he went to the loo for a minute I stuffed it up my blazer and went home. I know I shouldn't have."

"He thinks you've half-inched his war souvenir as well."

"You're kidding," Sam cried indignantly. "The German gun fearless Corporal Tulloch captured single-handed? I wouldn't dare. He kept it next to his money box, you know. He's not claiming I pinched his savings too?"

"Just the gun."

"He must be getting senile. I wouldn't touch it with a barge pole. It'd look pretty silly, wouldn't it—me campaigning for nuclear disarmament one day and pinching his stupid gun the next."

"Pretty silly," Anna agreed. "Well, I thought I'd let you know. You'd best ring the old boy up and smooth things out before he does something really daft like calling the fuzz."

"He would too," Sam said. "I'll do it now. And I'd better take his rotten photo back. When can I come and see you?"

"I'm going to be out of town for a couple of days," Anna said cravenly. "I'll drop in when I come back." She hung up and then rang Bernie's number again.

"He hasn't got it" she said when Bernie answered. "What're we going to do?"

"Well, you aren't going to do anything," he told her

placidly. "I'll get on to the governor and tell him what you've said. Any decision about telling the Tullochs or the police or the client we'll leave to him. That's his job. What the Tullochs don't know won't hurt them, for a few days anyway. You and me'll go down to the south coast as arranged. As I see it this new stuff doesn't alter what we've got to do. We're still looking for our old friend, extenuating circumstances, for Miss Hahn. Right?"

"All right. But Bernie, it's getting messier and messier, and Thea's in it right up to her eyeballs."

"Don't worry so much," he said, sounding as peaceful as custard. "You'll do yourself an injury. Get a good night's sleep and I'll see you in the morning. Your trouble is you take it all so personally. What's done's done and it all happened long before you got involved. You can't change it now. So don't get all of a tiz-woz."

With Bernie's good advice ringing in her ears Anna dashed straight downstairs to join in the tiz-woz surrounding the absent Selwyn. Bea had poured herself a generous tumblerful of vodka and tonic and was nesting in her accustomed armchair looking drained. She said, "Honestly, Anna, if that man snuffs it under the anæsthetic tomorrow morning, it'll save me swinging for him."

"He only sneaked himself a bracer," Quex said. He was leaning with his back against the mantelshelf, arms outstretched, looking colossal and amused.

"Dutch courage at nine in the morning—I ask you!" Bea exclaimed furiously. "So of course they couldn't operate, could they, Quex?"

"They could not," Quex said, grinning. "They were also somewhat miffed."

"Miffed wasn't the word. He'd thrown their whole schedule out the window. So he only says—'Well, I'll be off home if you can't fit me in.' As if they'd messed things up. 'Same time tomorrow?' he says, bold as brass. I'm telling you, Anna, I didn't know where to put myself, did I, Quex?"

"It was a bit embarrassing," he said. "The poor old thing had to stay in the ward the whole day to keep Selwyn from coming home. Can you imagine?"

"Vividly," said Anna sympathetically.

"It was murder," Bea went on. "Anyone'd think he was having his brain transplanted, the fuss he made. Do you know, I wish he would. If they gave him Attila the Hun's I'd get more peace. I'm worn out."

"I'm hungry," Quex said hopefully. Both Bea and Anna said nothing and looked with great concentration at the ceiling, so after a long pause he said, "I'll cook of course, if someone'll just lend me the food."

"Help yourself," Bea offered sweetly. "Just don't ask me to move."

Listening to Quex cooking was like hearing the percussion section of the Royal Philharmonic warming up for *The Rite of Spring*. Bea and Anna sat with their hearts in their mouths waiting for the final crash that would signal catastrophe. But after a while he emerged rumpled and triumphant with three overflowing plates. "I'm famous for my omelettes," he declared, distributing plates like loaded frisbees.

"Don't you mean notorious?" Anna murmured.

"How many eggs did you use?" Bea asked faintly.

"You only had ten," he said with mild reproach. "It's a little singed on the bottom," he pointed out, confirming what their noses had already told them. "But I think it'll add to the texture."

The texture didn't need much addition, Anna thought as she stared with disbelief at her unmanageable plateful. Into the eggs he had tipped chopped apple, bacon, tomatoes, onion, cooked potato, frozen peas and a tin of sweet corn. The garnish was grated cheddar. She felt an uncontrollable urge to giggle and glanced quickly at Bea who met her gaze with a panic-stricken expression.

"Glass of water," Anna squeaked and fled from the room. When she got back Quex said, "The police came to Adam House this afternoon." And the urge to laugh vanished entirely.

"What happened?" she asked, sampling the omelette with great caution. It wasn't quite as awful as it looked, provided the apple and bacon could be kept separate. All the same it gave her an insight into his enthusiasm for her spaghetti.

Quex munched vigorously and said, "They sent me packing so I can't give you a blow by blow account. But I waited around to talk to Tony Frank afterwards and he gave me the gist of it. In fact he specifically asked me to pass it on to you. Incidentally, I've been considering myself something of a conduit here: I've passed everything you've told me back to him. I assumed that was what you wanted."

"More or less," Anna said, surreptitiously discarding a pebble-hard, still frosted pea. "Who came? Do you know the names?"

"Two of them in plain clothes, I think from Southampton. The older one introduced himself as Detective-Inspector Fuller. I don't know about the other one. Then there was a very smooth solicitor for the home team and of course, Tony Frank. They all disappeared with Thea into one of the occupational therapy rooms. They stayed there for about three-quarters of an hour. Then a nurse fetched Thea away, very disturbed I might add. And after another twenty minutes the police and the solicitor left. Nobody looked happy, least of all Tony who was in a very bad mood."

Quex had been punctuating his story with giant mouthfuls and had now finished his food. Bea, who had struggled heroically with hers, mutely passed her plate to him and he continued eating scarcely noticing the change. He went on, "Apparently at first Thea was at her most withdrawn and sat rocking, you know the way she does, and ignored all their questions. And then she got overexcited and started gabbling. She said she had swung on a gate and crushed her father. She said he couldn't bear the weight so he died. When he was dead, she said she folded him up and hid him in her head, and she had scars on her brain to prove it. The scars were caused by the fact that she'd buried him alive and he had tried to bite his way out. He had teeth like a wolf and at night she could feel him tearing at her brain with his teeth. Something like that."

"I think I'll make a start on the washing-up," Bea said, getting up and leaving the room.

"She said this wolf-stroke-father is eating away at the inside of her head." Quex continued without noticing Bea's defection. "He's eaten most of her cerebrum and lies curled around what's left sucking his own tail. Sometimes he hears through her ears and sees through her eyes. Sometimes he even speaks through her mouth. Tony said she treated them to a demonstration: howling and snarling."

Anna put her fork down and pushed her plate away. Quex said, "Did I put you off your food? Sorry; but I find it fascinating. Can I finish it for you?"

Anna passed him the third plate. "I think it'd be more helpful if you tell me what the police were particularly interested in," she said queasily.

"Oh, that. Well, I suppose it was very much what you'd expect—where had she been in the last few weeks, what had she been doing. They were most interested in the gun: had she seen it, where did she get it, what had happened to it; and also, apparently, the identity of her companion. Tony said they wanted to take her to Southampton to attend an identity parade but both he and the solicitor protested. I think though that the solicitor might've agreed to provide photos, in return for which she could stay where she was."

"Did she answer any questions directly?"

"Fortunately, no." Quex at last stopped eating, but only for want of anything else that was edible. "But there was one bit that might amuse you," he went on, giving her a lop-sided smile. "When she was asked

about her companion, she said it was a cat and went on
to give a perilously close description of you. That was
just before the wolf-man outburst, after which she got a
bit incoherent."

Anna got up and started to stack the plates. It was a
relief to know that Thea hadn't made things any worse
for herself. She juggled with the notion of telling Anthony Frank, through Quex, who Mr. Jones really was,
but decided it was too risky. So she went out to the
kitchen to find Bea, perched on a high stool, trying to
scrape egg splashes off the ceiling.

"He's very good-natured," Bea whispered, looking
doubtful. "But a little on the excessive side, wouldn't
you say? I can't think where Selwyn finds these friends
of his. Do you remember the one who painted blue
elephants mating and worked as a fairground barker?"

"And that one with the albino gerbils who helped
gun-run to Basque Spain?"

They both sighed and Bea said, "I hope they've given
him something to make him sleep. It'd be just like him
to turn up at midnight in that white nightie thing they
put him in."

CHAPTER 25

The next morning, with rain beating sharp tattoos on
the roof of the car, she drove back to Southampton.
Yesterday's fine clear sky had given way to black-bellied
clouds that emptied themselves viciously all over the
south of England.

She followed Bernie's Austin Maxi, comforted by his
presence in the rain. When the sun shone she could
keep Thea's nightmare world at bay. But last night she
had dreamed about sitting down to breakfast with Quex.
She had a boiled egg in an ornate silver cup and when
she sliced the top off the egg she found thousands of

grey maggots squirming in the eggshell. "Embryo wolves," Quex said, leaning over with a magnifying glass. "How very interesting." But when she looked down at her plate the maggots had grown and were overflowing the eggcup, on to the plate, on to the table, and were crawling over her hands and up her sleeves.

If it had been a bright clear morning she might have shaken off the dream and forgotten it before her first cup of coffee was cool enough to drink. But it was a sombre day she woke up to, and the chill and wet made the dark side of life almost tangible. The morning paper was dominated by the failure of the peace summit. An Ulster man had been knee-capped in front of his three-year-old daughter, and the anti-vivisection league had published a horrible report about what scientists did to baby rabbits on behalf of women who wanted to cream the hair off their legs. Nightmares everywhere you looked.

Ordinary people could get by in such a world only by not looking too closely at what happened in it. Anna was an ordinary person who normally avoided thinking about the monstrosities she knew she couldn't possibly change. But every now and then her sensitivity was sharpened to a point where she couldn't avoid them. And then the world seemed an alien place and ordinary people seemed too small and weak to cope. Today Thea's delusions seemed more like an appropriate response to everyday life.

A truck cut in front of her, blanketing her windscreen with dirty spray. She gripped the wheel tightly and steadied her small car. Then she dropped back and recited out loud, "There was an old man from Dundee, who once found a wart on his knee. His doctor said, 'Simple, this isn't a pimple, it's an allergic reaction to me,'" which made her feel a little better.

She saw Bernie's Maxi dwarfed by three container lorries in the car park of a roadside café. She dashed inside shaking water off her hair to find he had already ordered a fried egg sandwich and tea for her. He still had his coat on, but it was unbuttoned and his wet hat was decorating the plastic table next to the sauce bottle. He said, "So let's get this straight—you've already talked to a porter called Des, Jacqueline Powis and Carmen Ockney, right? And they'll take money right?"

"Not half!" She drank some tea—hot and wet was the kindest description. The egg sandwich was better— hot and wet too. Bernie took his notebook out of an inside pocket. He tore out a page and put it on the table between them.

"This is what I've got for you," he said. "Ring that number, ask for extension 19. Mary Marks. She's a nice girl. Not too bright, but reliable. Give her my love."

There was a phone on the wall next to the entrance to the gents. Anna went over and rang the number. Mary Marks, when she finally came on the line, simply identified herself and said, "Yes?"

"Anna Lee," Anna said. "I'm a friend of Bernie Schiller. He said you might be able to help me out a little."

"I got his message. How is Mr. Schiller? It's been ages . . . I heard he'd taken up security work."

"He's fine," Anna said, looking over at Bernie who was watching from the table. "He said to send his love."

"He always was a sweet old thing," Mary said as if she'd known him as sweet and old since he was a baby. "I can't talk on this line, but I can meet you in an hour."

They arranged to meet in a coffee bar well away from Mary's station, and Anna rang off.

"Bingo," she said, rejoining Bernie. "The old charm's still working, you sweet old thing, you."

Bernie grinned. "She's all right," he said, pouring sugar in his tea. "The sort you always stick on the phones: absolutely unflappable and knows procedure backwards. Isn't much cop on the artwork though."

"She'll have to do," Anna said. "We don't know anyone else on the Hampshire force."

Outside, it had stopped raining and the grime on her rear window had dried, providing a blackboard on which someone had written, "Say it with flowers: give her a Venus flytrap." She wiped it off. Bernie tooted and waved as he drove out of the car park and headed towards the docks. Anna took a different route into the town centre and twice around the one-way system until she found a place to park.

The coffee bar was called the Trawler, and it was a narrow-fronted place with false planking under the window. Anna peered through the fishnet curtains and then at her watch. She was a couple of minutes early so she waited outside. On her left was a shoe shop which had wire baskets of cut-price sandals and slippers on the pavement. On the other side, in the electrical goods shop window, were vacuum cleaners, TV sets and tumble dryers. Shoppers in raincoats paused and looked in both windows. She was the only one waiting outside the Trawler. She hoped there would be no difficulty recognizing Mary Marks—waiting for a stranger was always tricky.

But when she saw a woman in black shoes and stockings, a powder-blue mackintosh hiding the uniform, striding towards her like a games teacher crossing a hockey field, she knew instantly who it was. They greeted each other cautiously, and went inside where gloomy concealed lighting obscured the shelves of tired cheesecakes and Black Forest gateaux.

"Cosy, isn't it?" Mary Marks said. She was tall enough for the festoons of decorative fishnet to brush the top of her head. She ordered coffee and a slice of strawberry cheesecake. They went and sat in a cramped little booth; a table, formica pretending to be mahogany, between them.

"Romantic," Mary commented. "I should bring Harry here. Harry thinks the world of Mr. Schiller. He was sarge when Harry and I were probationers in London. Treated Harry like a son, Harry always says." She fingered her wedding ring and smiled, pink cheeks shining like polished apples. "Those were the days. I sometimes wish we hadn't moved." She sighed. "Never mind. You want to know about the hotel incident, don't you? Mr. Schiller says you've got a client involved."

"That's right," Anna said. "It's all out in the open. One of your lot, Detective-Inspector Fuller, spoke to her yesterday. We don't want to get in your hair, obviously, but we would like to know what you've got."

"Well, I can't tell you much," Mary said, sipping coffee and wrinkling her brow. "And I shouldn't tell you anything really. But I was on one of the telephones in the Incident Room in the first few days till the excitement died down. I haven't had anything to do with it since. But of course you do hear odds and ends."

"Mr. Schiller said he'd be grateful for anything," Anna said, shamelessly trading on his popularity. "Did you see the post mortem report, for instance?"

Mary shook her head. "Heard about it, of course," she said. "The man was shot in the neck and the bullet tore out the front of his trachea. Not a very good shot, Harry says. It made an awful mess but missed the great arteries and spinal column. Close range. Not more than three or four inches, the boys in the backroom said. There were extensive powder burns."

"Was death immediate?" Anna asked. She was conscious of slipping into the half-scientific circumlocution that removed her a couple of steps from the morbid details. She could have said, "How long did it take him to die?" but that would have made the question too personal.

Mary shook her head again. She said, "It could have taken a good two or three minutes. There was blood in the lungs and froth in the right side of the heart. Officially the cause of death was embolism."

"Did anyone consider suicide? Were the hands swabbed?"

"I don't know. The hands were bagged, of course.

But whether they were swabbed for nitrates . . . well, I wasn't told. But then, you see, the weapon was missing. The doors to the corridor were locked, but the connecting door between the two rooms wasn't. Scene of Crime Officers say there was someone in his room—in his bed, in fact. They found a few hairs on his pillow that matched hair found in the waste pipe under the sink in the next room and semen stains on the sheets, that sort of thing. And there were some signs of a struggle. The woman in the next room's your client, I take it?"

Anna agreed that it was and went to the counter to get some more coffee. When she got back Mary said, "Well, bad luck. I don't think you've got a hope of clearing her, you know."

Anna passed her the fresh coffee and sat down. "We aren't thinking about clearing her so much," she said rather vaguely. "It's more a question of extenuating circumstances. The struggle, for instance, what did SOCO say about that?"

"Well, the bedding on both beds in the room had been disturbed. The lamp on the night table was knocked over and a glass broken. Not much. But the victim probably knew the assailant well enough to let her close to him. He was on the bed when he was shot. We know that because they found the bullet in the wall along with bits of his windpipe. He was probably sitting on the bed, facing the window and she shot him from the side. She must've been beside him on the bed or kneeling on the floor because the path of the bullet was angled slightly upwards. Or she could've been in front of him, I suppose, if she'd shot him left-handed. But there was a bit of a scrap: he had some bruising and scratches on his chest and right arm. What does your client say? She must've said something."

Anna shrugged. "What she says doesn't make any sense. She's off her head in a private bin."

"Oh yes?" Mary said sceptically.

"Had the victim been drinking?" Anna asked quickly.

Mary smiled at the abrupt change of subject. "Some," she said. "We know he had half a bottle of wine with his meal, and the broken glass had contained whisky. I expect you mean he might've become violent and she was defending herself in the struggle and the gun went off?"

"It's a thought," Anna said. "Where would a sixteen-year-old get a Luger anyway?"

"Well, it's certainly a possibility," Mary conceded generously. She glanced at her watch, and added in a kindly but superior tone, "Look, you want to be a bit careful about insanity. If her brief wants to get her off that way he has to prove she was insane when she committed the act, and there were some signs that she wasn't, you know."

"How d'you mean?"

"Well, some of the surfaces in his room, doorknobs, another glass, the night table, for instance, were wiped clean. And she washed in his bathroom afterwards. And cleaned the bath after that. She knew what she was doing all right."

"What about her room?" Anna asked. "Did she clean that too?"

"Prints all over the place," Mary admitted, looking at her watch again.

"Blood?"

"She must've been covered in it," Mary said, "but there were only a couple of stains on the carpet in her room. But then we know she washed afterwards, as I said. Traces of blood were found in the shower and the plumbing under it. That doesn't look like insanity either, if you ask me."

Anna sighed. She didn't want to argue with someone who had been so helpful. Mary said, "Look, I've got to go now. You tell Mr. Schiller to get in touch next time he's in Southampton. Harry'd love to see him again. He's away on a course now and he'll be really sorry to've missed him."

It was all very well, Anna thought sitting alone after
Mary had gone, to talk objectively about the victim and
the assailant. But if you gave victim and assailant names,
it came down to Thea in a bloody struggle with her
tutor, Joseph Tulloch; Thea shooting off his Adam's
apple; Joseph falling off the bed and lying in a pool of
blood; and Thea washing blood off herself in the bathroom. It was impossible to imagine. She got up, paid
for the coffee and cheesecake, and went out to meet
Bernie.

CHAPTER 26

"Leave yours here and hop in," Bernie shouted, and
leaned over to unlock the passenger side door. Anna
found a space, parked, and walked back to the Austin
Maxi. The dull yellow light, the smell of exhaust fumes,
the sound of slammed car doors echoing off concrete
combined to give the place the feel of a twentieth-
century limbo. They were in the car park deep under
the foundations of the Continental Gateway.

"Your Tom's done a flit," Bernie told her as she got
in beside him. "I've already had a shufti round his
lodgings and he isn't in. Want to go there and wait?"

"Might as well." Anna buckled the seat-belt across
her lap. Bernie started his motor and slowly spiralled
up past ranks of abandoned cars to daylight.

"Lives with his mum in a block of flats north of here,"
Bernie said, and edged out into the traffic. "Just one
entrance—easy to watch." He stopped outside a sandwich bar. "Cheese and pickle for me. We'd better have
something to keep us going. Lord knows how long he'll
be."

Anna bought sandwiches and coffee in styrofoam
cups and settled back in the passenger seat. She said,
"You know, Bernie, I don't really believe any of this."

"What?" He was driving through the commercial part of town to where shops and businesses thinned out and family homes began.

"Well, Joseph Tulloch was supposed to be such a *good* man. He went to church. He's brought his son up to be a nice lad with his heart in the right place. He spent more time on his students than he had to. Anyone who needed help went to him. What the hell's he doing dying in a sordid bloody hotel like that?"

"The wildest boy I knew when I was at school was a Church of England vicar's son," Bernie said, glancing in his mirror and indicating left. "My Mum'd never let him come round our house he was such a tearaway. But one day I went to his place without telling her. I was really looking forward to it because he seemed to have all the fun in spite of always being in lumber at school. And, you know, when I got there I was bored witless. He was a little angel—almost a prig, you might say. Talk about disappointing."

Anna laughed. "Yes, but this bloke's been doing the right thing all his life," she said. "He's not a rebellious boy, is he? He's based his whole life on the assumption that he's a good man with a moral outlook, married to a good wife, bringing up decent children. What happened to him?"

"Thea Hahn?" Bernie mused. "There's no law says you can't suddenly fall for the wrong one at the wrong time. People don't have a lot of control about who they fall for. You know that. Most people'd just lie back and enjoy it. But he'd be tortured. It must be terrible, if you're accustomed to seeing yourself on the side of the angels, to wake up one day and find yourself doing something you'd previously thought of as disgusting. With no excuses."

"Is that why he nicked his dad's gun?" she asked after a couple of minutes' thought.

"I don't know. Maybe he had some stupid fantasy about sin and death. If he'd had other affairs before he'd've probably been all right. But if what you say's true, he wasn't like that. So he'd've thought his moral life was over. And what about the fake drowning? He'd rather his family thought he was dead than know he'd been a bad boy and left them."

"Well, there was the insurance money too."

"Yes, but I bet the impulse to keep their love and good opinion was just as strong. He must've been a wreck those last few days."

"It's got to be suicide," Anna said. "It doesn't make sense if it's not."

"What law says it's got to make sense?" Bernie said, pulling the car over to the kerb and braking. Across the road a bare stretch of grass separated a block of flats from the pavement. It was a featureless, yellow-brick oblong. Bernie opened his door and said, "I'll just check if he's back yet."

In a few minutes he was back, shaking his head. "It's the old job again," he sighed. "Watch and wait, wait and watch. Pass us the coffee before it goes cold."

After a while Anna shifted restlessly and said, "I hope old Mr. B. bucks up and tells the Hampshire squad about Joseph Tulloch and his sodding gun. The quicker they know about that, the quicker they'll work it out what state he was in. It'll take the pressure off Thea."

"I don't know about that." Bernie crumpled his cup and put it in an empty paper bag. "If they work out the relationship between those two they might conclude it's even more likely she pulled the trigger. What did Mary Marks have to say?"

"Nothing wonderful from our point of view. The good news is he lived a couple of minutes after the shot, so he could've chucked the gun or something."

"Oh really?" he said, raising an eyebrow and looking a her intently.

"No, all right. Too much blood and no sign of him moving about much, unless it all went inside his clothes."

"So what's the bad news?"

"Room 627 was wiped for prints. Someone washed blood off in the bathroom. A woman's hair was found in his bed. The connecting door between Thea's and Tulloch's rooms was unlocked. But the doors to the corridor were locked. And your Mary doesn't think nutters scrub up after killings. She's a typical fuzz know-it-all."

"You are in a paddy, aren't you?" Bernie murmured. He collected the rubbish from the sandwiches and gave it to her. "There's a bin over there." He pointed through the windscreen. "Why don't you throw this stuff away and stretch your legs. A breath of fresh air might sweeten your temper."

Anna walked the twenty paces to the rubbish bin reminding herself that none of this was Bernie's fault and she really ought to keep her moods to herself. She dumped the sandwich papers and cups and started back to the car. Then she stopped abruptly.

About fifteen feet away from her and about to cross the road to the flats was Miles Gancitano. He turned his head and saw her. He hesitated. For a second it looked as if he was going to brazen it out. But suddenly he spun on his toes and started running.

Anna ran in pursuit. He looked over his shoulder and lengthened his stride. As she sprinted past the Austin Maxi she saw Bernie fling the door open and get out. It didn't matter. Bernie's running days were well behind him.

She had a sudden rush of exhilaration. She filled her lungs and felt the blood pounding in her ears. Miles Gancitano was about five yards ahead and she was catching him. He swerved to avoid an old lady, swung right into a building site, past a hut where several workmen were packing up their tools. Anna raced after him. Someone yelled, "If you want a man, take me! I won't run away."

Miles dodged through the entrance to a half built building, ran through rooms with knee high walls and out the other side. He turned right again. He was curling back towards his home. Anna hurdled the last wall, cutting the distance between them to a couple of strides. He turned again, saw her close behind him, panicked and tripped headlong over a heap of loose timber. Anna put all the frustration of the last few days into launching herself at him.

CHAPTER 27

She landed with both knees in the middle of his back. For a second he lay stunned. Then he gasped air into his lungs and began to shake her off his back.

With one hand she grabbed a handful of his hair and pushed his head down so that his forehead struck the concrete. The other hand searched frantically in her pocket. She wasn't strong enough to hold him for long. The only thing in her pocket was a felt-tipped pen. She rammed it hard behind his ear and said, "Move a muscle and I'll shoot your ear off."

He went suddenly limp, but she could feel him gathering himself for another effort. She hissed, "Don't try. You could live without your ear but the bullet might ricochet off the floor and take your eye out."

"That's no gun!"

"Oh yeah? Want to risk it?"

"You ain't shooting me."

She gripped his hair even tighter and leant on the pen. Bernie panted round the corner, his face scarlet and streaming with sweat. He flopped down hard on a pile of breezeblocks and fought for breath. After a moment or two he said in something like his normal voice, "Miles Gancitano? That wasn't too clever, sunshine. You don't want to add resisting arrest to the list, do you?"

"What list?" Miles said, his mouth pressed against the concrete. "I didn't know she was fuzz."

"He resisted all right, Governor," Anna said briskly.

"Dear, dear, dear. Theft, obscene exposure, *and* resisting arrest. Your old mum's not going to like that when she comes to bail you out."

"I didn't take nothing. If she says I did she's lying."

"I feel quite sorry for him really," Anna said. "They're a bit hard on sex offenders inside, aren't they, Governor?" She let go of his hair and put the pen back in her pocket. He was lying quite still now, so she caught his arm and twisted it into a conventional arm lock and allowed him to sit up.

"I never touched her," Miles said, shaking his head. "I never touch no one."

"A pervert's a pervert to a con," Bernie explained in a very reasonable voice. The sound of footsteps and men talking came from the other side of the unfinished building. Bernie cocked his head. The footsteps approached.

"Don't say nothing," Miles pleaded in a whisper. "Don't! My mum lives just round the corner. It'd kill her if this got out."

A big man in blue overalls appeared round the corner of the site followed by a smaller one. Bernie half turned in his seat on the breezeblocks and said, "Can I help you, gentlemen?" very politely.

The big man settled his cap more firmly on his head and said uncertainly, "I'm the foreman here. I saw you three come through." He turned to his friend and muttered, "That's Mrs. Gancitano's boy, ain't it? Is everything all right, lad?"

"Everything's OK, really," Miles said urgently. "It's mistaken identity. Isn't it?" He appealed to Bernie.

"I could find your mum for you," the big man offered. "You in trouble?"

"No, no. I'm not. Honestly I'm not."

The big man turned to Bernie. "You from the Down

Street nick?" he asked, and when Bernie shook his head he went on, "I didn't think you was. I know most of them at Down Street."

Bernie said, "I'm glad to see someone keeps his eyes open round here." And Anna, who had unobtrusively released Miles Gancitano's arm when the two men first appeared, now said, "It's amazing how few people ask to see your warrant card, isn't it Sarge?"

"Well, if you're sure it's all right, lad . . ." the big man said, looking to his friend for confirmation. His friend was already backing away. The foreman straightened his cap again. "You shouldn't be on this site really. It's not safe."

"That's all right." Bernie didn't move an inch. "We'll not be more than a couple of minutes. You don't have to worry about us."

When the sound of the two men had died away he turned to Miles again and said, "You'd better start getting used to it, sunshine. It'll be in all the papers soon. What did you leave your job for? The manager said you've not been in since Monday."

"It was her, really." Miles jerked his thumb at Anna. "No one's ever caught me at it before, see. She came back unexpectedly so I hid in the bathroom. And then when she came in to wash I couldn't help myself. I didn't mean anything, honest, but I thought she was bound to complain and I couldn't face them at work. But I didn't take anything. I hardly ever take anything. I just wanted to see what she was wearing, what she had in her case. I don't do any harm."

"That's a matter of opinion," Anna said from behind him. She wanted to be where she could see him but he couldn't see her. "All the same, Guv, I might be prepared to forget it if he was any help with the Jones killing. He could chalk up a lot of brownie points there."

"No chance," Bernie said indifferently. "That's all settled. If he'd seen anything there he'd've already made a statement."

"Not necessarily. If he saw anything it means he'd've had to use a pass key illegally. He wouldn't've admitted that."

"Forget it. A collar's what we wanted and a collar's what we've got. This lad'll do us."

"Too bad. I'd've given a lot to know what happened to that gun." Anna watched Miles's shoulders squirm uneasily under his jacket. "Still, a bird in the hand . . ." she went on brightly. "Think Vice'll want to talk to him? There've been a few assaults against minors they want to pin to someone. They need a collar too."

"Hey, listen—I seen the gun," Miles said desperately. "I never touched no little girls in my life, I swear."

"What gun, sunshine?" Bernie was very quiet. He almost sounded bored.

"The Luger . . . killed that bloke in 627. I seen it." Miles was very excited. Bernie got up and put his hands in his pockets. Turning away he said, "Don't start, son. We aren't interested. You'd say any old thing now."

"I tell you, I seen it," Miles insisted. "Straight. It was there next to him. He was lying between the twin beds and it was there, sort of under the one by the window."

"You were in room 627 on the morning of Wednesday the 25th?" Bernie's face was innocent of any expression. "You didn't mention that little fact in your statement."

"I couldn't, could I?"

"You got in with a pass key?"

"I didn't have to. The room next door was open. I thought she'd forgot to lock it, see. I only wanted a look. Only she weren't there, was she? So I thought, well, I thought she was next door with him. The connecting door was ajar and I just wanted a quick look. I didn't hear anything so I just sort of put my eye to the crack and I seen him on the floor."

"I don't think so," Anna said. "The report said when the body was found the light was off and the curtains drawn. It would've been pitch black in there."

"We're wasting time," Bernie said. "Let's get this body down the station before he starts seeing little green men."

"No, honest," Miles cried. "She's right, but I could see because someone'd left the bathroom light on. He was on the floor and the gun was half under the bed."

Unable to see Miles's expression, Anna was watching Bernie. Sometimes he looked at the sky, sometimes at the ground. Only occasionally he shot a penetrating glance at Miles. Even knowing him as well as she did, she couldn't tell what he was thinking. He was very good, she thought. He didn't even look interested. Now he said, "What time's this supposed to have taken place?"

"I can't say exactly." Miles moved a step forward, clamouring for Bernie's attention. "But at about three that morning someone on the fifth floor rang down for a bottle of Perrier. We'd been really busy all night because of the convention. Those blokes drink a lot, see, and there's a lot of coming and going. And they're always asking for this and that. Well, things quiet down a bit after midnight but with the hotel full like it was we're on the go till morning."

"So you take the Perrier up to the fifth and then you wander on up to 627. Just like that, eh?"

"No, not like that. Look, like I said, there was a lot of drinking. People get careless—forget to lock their doors, some of them. Well, there's a lot of things going on at night, know what I mean? Des and one or two others have this arrangement with some women in the town, and when there's a lot of blokes in, well, you know, some of them're willing to pay for an introduction, and then Des or whoever'd just sort of help them out."

"And you sort of like to keep an eye on what's happening."

"I don't know what it is." Miles shifted unhappily. "I think I need help, really."

A dog with black and white paws nosed round the bare wooden uprights of an empty doorway. Bernie watched it and said, "You do, son, you do. So now you're on the sixth, trying doors, are you?"

"I didn't have to try hers. It wasn't even shut."

"Well, go on."

"That's all, honest. I told you everything, didn't I? After I seen him on the floor, I went back down and I didn't move from the staff room unless I was rang for. It was a girl off the morning shift found him, and I'd gone home by then."

CHAPTER 28

A car hooting in the road broke the silence. Anna looked up to find Bernie's eyes on her. She moved a few steps to where she could see Miles in profile, and said, "Rubbish, Guv, absolute rubbish. He's saying he touched nothing, he did nothing, he just stole away like a ghost in the night—rubbish."

Miles hung his head. She was interested to see that he was unwilling to look her full in the face. Bernie said, "Ah well. You can't help those who won't help themselves. Well, back to the motor, son. We're parked just outside where you live. We'll put the cuffs on there." He went close to Miles and laid a big hand on his arm in the symbolic gesture of an arresting officer. "Miles Gancitano," he began. "I arrest . . ."

"Wait," Miles shouted. "I haven't finished yet."

"He hasn't finished, Guv," Anna urged. Bernie let his hand drop slowly. Miles said, "I don't understand what you want. I said I seen the gun, didn't I?"

"We don't give a toss what you said you saw," Anna

told him. "What we've got is a forensic report which tells us all sorts of other things. When you say something that matches the facts we'll believe you. We don't want a load of rubbish you think we want to hear. Start with the door. When you went out, you didn't leave that as you found it, did you?"

"I locked it," Miles said reluctantly. "I didn't want no one else nosing around."

"Why?"

"I dunno."

"Yes you do. Guv, he took something. He locked the doors because he didn't want anyone else discovering the body before his shift ended when he could get whatever it was out of the hotel."

"Well I never." Bernie looked almost happy. "Is that right, sunshine? What did you take?"

Miles mumbled something and Bernie said, "Speak up. I can't hear."

"His money," Miles shouted. "I said, I took his money. He wasn't going to want it, was he? Is that right?" He looked directly at Anna for the first time. She narrowed her eyes and stared back, saying, "Carry on—every little movement from when you first went in to when you locked the door on the way out."

"Oh Christ." He looked away and then back to Bernie. "I'll try. I pushed the door open. It was dark in there, but I could see from the light in the passage. There was no one there, no bags, no clothes, nothing. Nothing in the bathroom neither. Then I saw the light through the connecting door. So I went over there and looked, and there he was, like I told you. I stood there a couple of minutes. I'd never seen a dead'un before and I didn't know what to do.

"It was really quiet, and after a bit I realized there was no one else around and I was the only one who knew about it. So I went in. First I went to his door and I locked it in case someone else was doing that corridor too. Then I looked in the bathroom. I told you the light was on there. He had a brand-new electric razor which I thought he wouldn't need, so I put it in my pocket.

"I know it sounds bad, but he was dead, right? Once I'd took the razor, I thought, well, why not? What else don't he need? There's a pub I go to where you can get rid of all sorts of things and nobody asks no awkward questions. Well, in his case was a brand-new pair of leather shoes. Everything he had was brand-new. Some of the shirts was still in their wrappers even. I didn't take everything, mind, just one pair of shoes and a couple of shirts. If I'd took it all someone would of noticed, right?"

Bernie nodded encouragement, and Miles continued, "His money was all out on the dressing-table. There was francs and pounds, both. I put most of the English in my pocket. Not all."

"How much?"

"Must of been about three hundred nicker. I was amazed him leaving all that out on the dressing-table. I left about fifty to make it look right."

"What else?"

"There was a nice silver frame with a photo in. Right at the bottom of his case. I took that too. I put everything I couldn't put in my pockets in a carrier bag and went out through the connecting door and back the way I come. Then I locked that room and went downstairs. I was sweating blood I'd meet someone and they'd want to know what I got. I went straight outside by the kitchen door and hid the bag behind the rubbish. It was a risk, but sometimes they do spot-checks and search everyone coming off a shift. Anyway, they didn't that morning, and the bag was still there when I went home."

Anna wanted one piece of confirmation before she took on the big question. She said, "Describe the photo."

"A wedding photo. Bride and groom. Old-fashioned.

I suppose it was of him on the floor. I didn't look too closely. I chucked it—only wanted the frame."

Anna sighed. She was suddenly very tired, as if his last answer had pricked a balloon and let all her energy escape. She met Bernie's eyes and nodded. Bernie yawned. "You haven't said anything about the gun yet, sunshine."

It was as if tiredness had infected all three of them. "I don't know why you bother asking," Miles said wearily. "I put it in the bag with the rest of the stuff. Don't ask me why. I wish I never touched it but I was going round just picking up things I thought I could sell, and once I touched it I thought well I can't just put it back. It would of had my prints on it, see."

"Still got it?"

"I let the whole lot go for a ton, down the boozer. Except the cash of course," Miles explained. "I don't know what a shooter's worth. I never had one before. This guy I do business with said it wasn't up to much but he knew an Irishman he could shift it on to. I was glad to see the back of it."

Bernie said, "We'll need a name."

Miles shook his head and Bernie went on, "Well, leave that aside for a bit. Did you wipe your prints off the room before you left?"

"Yes." Miles thought about it for a while. "The case, the dressing-table, the doorknobs. I don't think I touched nothing more."

"What about the night table?" Anna asked.

"No way! He could've had the crown jewels on that and I wouldn't of touched 'em. He was lying right in front of there, see." He looked at Bernie. "If there's anything else gone, someone else took it. That's the truth I've told you. There's no more."

"Did you sell his passport?" Anna asked.

"There wasn't no passport," Miles said earnestly. "Unless it was on the bedside table and I never seen it."

"All right," Bernie said quietly. "Just the one name. Give us that and we'll let you go home."

"Home?"

"That's right. We'll put in a good word for you, and my colleague'll keep stumm about the business the other day. All for one name."

"It never ends, does it?" Miles complained. "Allan Worthing. The pub is the Lamb and Flag. Is it over? Can I go now?"

"Don't leave town," Bernie said. "You'll be tempted, but don't. All the promises we made'll mean nothing if you're not at home waiting when we come round next. Got it?"

It was hard for Anna to convince herself they had achieved what they had come for. With relief she watched Miles go. Bringing off a successful con brought dissatisfaction too: feelings of shabbiness and squalor. She wondered what Bernie was thinking. He sat again on his breezeblocks, elbows on knees, hands dangling loosely. The dog with black and white paws sidled up and pushed its nose under his fingers. Bernie stroked it abstractedly and gazed at the lengthening shadows across the site. At last he said, "Ah well, this won't buy any spuds for Sunday lunch. Better find a phone and see if his nibs wants this lad shopped now or next week."

They picked their way carefully over bricks and timber back to the road and Bernie's car. There was a phone box two streets away and Anna, watching from the passenger seat, thought Bernie was doing more talking than listening. When he came back he said, "Panic stations back at the shop. I've got to stay here till the Old Man's checked with the client, but he wants you back on the double. He wasn't too clear but it seems young Thea's pulled some sort of stroke."

The drive back to the hotel was completed in silence. Bernie took Anna all the way into the depths of the car park and waited till she started her motor. When she had backed out, he took over the space she left and after locking up he came to stand by her window. "Not to worry, love," he said by way of leave-taking. "Those Hahns are panicky people. It's probably nothing. And by the way, what were you doing with your pen in Gancitano's ear?"

Anna grinned morosely. "Just taking his statement, Sarge," she said as she drove away.

CHAPTER 29

It was lighting up time on Kensington High Street and Martin Brierly let the venetian blinds run down like a portcullis against the evening. His office was lit by a single desk lamp which cast its pool of light on his blotter and left Anna sitting almost in the dark. He sat down, leaning forward on the desk, his hands floodlit but his eyes in shadow.

"Thank God I don't have daughters," he said. "Apparently the silly girl broke a window and tried to cut her wrists on the glass. God knows why. Her father seemed to think she had been progressing nicely until then."

"Her father's too optimistic. Besides, he hasn't seen her for a while. No one else thinks she's progressing at all."

"I wouldn't know about that." Mr. Brierly brushed distastefully at an invisible speck of dirt on his stark white cuffs. "The point is that now he's hysterical too. Apparently the doctor at Adam House won't let him in, and he thinks they're doing something they shouldn't to his daughter."

"What nonsense," Anna said crossly. "Dr. Frank won't let him in because he upsets Thea. No other reason."

"Heaven knows what they get up to in these private clinics." His white hands picked up a fountain pen, turned it two or three times and put it down again.

"Anyway, the daughter's been asking for you, so you shouldn't have too much difficulty finding out."

"There's nothing to find out."

"Nevertheless, you have been asked for and I have agreed that you would go. This evening, if you'd be so kind."

Anna kept her mouth shut. Mr. Brierly in this mood was not to be argued with. After a pause to let her understand that his last statement was in fact an order, he continued, "I have decided that Mr. Schiller is to pass on the information you acquired today. Tomorrow, when they've become accustomed to the fact that their murder could just as well be suicide, I'll inform them as to Joseph Tulloch's identity. The news might be a little better received in reverse order. Anyway, that is Mr. Embury's suggestion. Mr. Hahn was in no condition to discuss policy."

Anna stirred uncomfortably in her hard chair. "What about the Tullochs?" she asked eventually. It was a subject that had been bothering her all day.

"It depends whether or not there was a suicide clause in his policy." Mr. Brierly opened his hands dismissively. "It's not our concern."

Anna had not been thinking of the insurance money. Now that Mr. Brierly reminded her she felt even worse. "It might eventually become our concern," she suggested. "If there is a suicide clause, anyone representing them will want to prove accident or murder, won't they? But what I was worried about is how they're going to feel when they're told their model husband and father's turned up dead a second time and in rather bizarre circumstances."

"Now that really isn't our concern. But I expect the Southampton police will send for one of them. Someone will have to identify Tulloch's body."

"Someone ought to warn them. It's a bit cruel, isn't it, leaving the police to spring it on them cold?"

Mr. Brierly's hands turned palm down on the blotter.

"I would advise you, Miss Lee, not to interfere. It's not our affair. And if, as you suggest, we eventually find ourselves giving opposing evidence in an insurance case, we don't want to compromise ourselves now. Besides, you are presently committed to Mr. Hahn. And I suggest you take yourself to Adam House forthwith. Mr. Hahn needs reassurance and we've wasted enough time. Was that all?"

"Was that all" meant "That is all" in Mr. Brierly's office cipher, and Anna went slowly downstairs thinking about what was supposed to be her concern and what wasn't. In the end she got in her car and drove straight to Maida Vale. Mr. Hahn's hysteria would have to wait a little longer.

Sam's mother was a tall thin woman. Her clothes hung on her as if she had recently lost some of what little weight she had to begin with. Even her round gold-framed spectacles looked a size too large. She had a green linen napkin in her hand when she opened the door. Anna had interrupted supper.

Mrs. Tulloch dabbed nervously at her lips and said, "Oh yes, Sam's told me about you. You're the detective looking for . . ." She wasn't thinking about what she was saying and obviously couldn't remember Thea's name. "Did you find her?" she asked distractedly. It wasn't as if she cared. It was just a matter of habit for her to express interest in other people's concerns. It would probably have been quite genuine at another time. But now it was only manners because she followed her question immediately by saying, "We're having supper. The children are still eating."

Someone called from the kitchen, and she replied, "A visitor. It's Miss . . . er, oh dear." She had forgotten Anna's name two minutes after being told it. Anna touched her arm and said, "It doesn't matter, Mrs. Tulloch. I'm sorry I disturbed your meal. Maybe I could come back another time."

"I'm so sorry," Mrs. Tulloch said, her face crumpling

as if forgetting Anna's name was the last in a series of unforgivable failures. Sam appeared from the lighted doorway at the end of the passage. He looked more worried and a lot older in his own home but his face brightened when he saw Anna.

"Oh, hello," he said, and then turned to Mrs. Tulloch, taking her arm gently. "It's all right, Mother, this is Anna. Remember? Why don't you go back to the kitchen. I've finished."

Mrs. Tulloch smiled at his gentleness, her drawn face transformed by gratitude. She went away like an obedient child. Sam said, "I'm glad you came. You've no idea how oppressive it is here with just the four of us. It's as if we've been locked in. Come into the study. No one'll interrupt us there." He opened a door and switched on the light. "You mustn't mind Mother," he went on, going into the room. "She can't seem to concentrate at the moment."

It was a small room with a big oak desk and a couple of easy chairs. One wall was entirely covered with chipboard and was used as a notice board.

"This was where Dad worked," Sam said. He turned on one bar of an electric fire and pulled the two chairs closer to it. The room had a clammy feel as if it had been kept shut up for weeks. "Sit down," he said. "I'll get you a cup of tea."

"Don't go," Anna said quickly. She thought that if he showed any more care or politeness she would be unable to tell him what she felt he had a right to know.

"What's up?" he asked, looking closely at her. "Is something wrong?"

"Yes," Anna said reluctantly. "And I don't know how to tell you about it." She sat down, and he took the chair opposite. "I don't think your mother can take it, and I don't know your sisters, so there's only you I can tell."

"Well, go on." Sam had a drawn look rather like his mother's. Anna took a deep breath and said, "Listen,

Sam, soon—tomorrow maybe—you're going to get a call from the police in Southampton, and I don't want you to be unprepared. Your father has turned up there and someone is going to have to identify the body."

"Southampton?" Sam broke in, completely mystified. "He drowned in North Devon. How on earth could he turn up in Southampton?"

Anna took another deep breath. "Not drowned," she said. "Shot. Your father didn't drown at Stony Point. I don't really know what he did, but he was found shot ten days later . . ."

"Ten days! Why didn't he come home?"

"Oh Sam," Anna said helplessly. "I don't understand why he did what he did. I only came across it accidentally because I was trying to trace Thea Hahn. But it seems clear that he spent at least the last of those ten days with her in Southampton. Maybe he was having a breakdown or something. I don't know. But they were both in the same hotel the night he died. And Sam, the gun was found beside him, and I'm pretty sure it's your grandad's Luger."

Sam stared at her with eyes that seemed unfocused. She hurried on. "Sam, who is your family solicitor? You've got to get him to help, perhaps break this to your mother. Sam?"

Sam wasn't looking at her any more. His head was bowed and he was shaking it rhythmically, rejecting everything she had said. She got up and stood by his chair with a hand on his shoulder. Behind him was the chipboard wall, busy with different coloured timetables, photographs, drawings, posters: posters for Amnesty International, Save the Children, Save the Whale, Save the Royal Court Theatre, South Coast Conservation Corps, Campaign for Nuclear Dis . . . "Oh Christ," Anna muttered, and looked again. There it was. Among all the evidence of Joseph Tulloch's good intentions, a poster for the South Coast Conservation Corps.

CHAPTER 30

"Sam!" Anna said urgently. "Don't just sit there. Please. We've got to try and make this something your family can cope with. Who is your family solicitor?"

"Uncle Robert." Sam cleared his throat and looked up. "Robert Vazey. What do we need him for? I don't understand anything at all."

"Because you can't handle this alone. You're going to need advice. Your uncle could deal with the police, even go to Southampton—spare your mother. Come on, Sam. Find me his number."

He got up and went to his father's desk and rummaged around for his phone book. When he had found the page he handed the book to Anna. There was a phone on the window-ledge beside the desk. She dialled the number, and when Robert Vazey answered she introduced herself and told him as concisely as she knew how what she had told Sam. He said he would come round right away. He sounded shocked but quite capable of grasping the implications of what she had said. His wife was Mrs. Tulloch's sister, he told her. He would bring her with him.

While she was speaking Sam stood close to her. Glancing at him every now and then, she saw that he was watching her lips intently as if, unable to trust his ears, he was lip-reading. When she had finished the call she took his hand and led him back to his chair.

After a while he said, "Was Dad having an affair with Thea Hahn? But he couldn't have. She's my age. And look—" he gestured around him, a sweeping motion of the hand that took in the wall with all the posters on it. "That's his life. He cared about everything except himself. I don't understand it. You must've made a mistake."

"I don't know anything about his relationship with Thea but, Sam, there is no mistake. She was there. That's all I can tell you certainly. But she's a strange girl, very unhappy. It's possible he saw through all her brilliance and felt sorry for her."

"That would figure." At once Sam sounded bitter. "He was a sucker for anyone he could feel sorry for. All she'd have to do was tell him a sob story."

"I don't think it would've been like that," she said softly. "Whatever happened had far more meaning than that. I know you're angry, and I know you don't understand. But don't make it mean and small. It won't help. It'll make all this even harder to accept."

"I don't want to accept it," Sam cried. "I want to be angry."

"Well, it happened so you've got to accept it some time. But you've every right to be angry. Just don't make it worse by thinking it was small." She searched her mind for something that might comfort him but she could think of nothing. After a few minutes Sam said, "I don't know why this is so awful. After all, I already knew he was dead."

"It's not the death, it's the leaving and deceit." She shut her mouth again, thinking that she had picked the least comforting thing she could possibly say. But surprisingly, he almost smiled. "That's it. That's it exactly. I knew you'd understand. It's not his death I've got to come to grips with, it's his life, isn't it?"

"You're right, Sam." Anna squeezed his hand gratefully. "He was a better man than most. But good men come a cropper too. And a good man has further to fall." They talked on quietly until the Vazeys arrived.

It was pitch dark when she got to Adam House. The night was chilly and her footsteps echoed in the empty hall. Quex was sitting on the refectory table reading a magazine stained by dozens of coffee cups. He jumped down from the table and said, "What happened? We were expecting you hours ago. Thea's father's threatening to take her away."

He stopped and stared at her. "Christ, Leo, you look shattered," he said more quietly. "Someone's put you through the wringer. What happened?"

"Where's Dr. Frank?" Anna didn't really want a long session with Quex. His sympathy unnerved her and there was still a lot to do.

"He's in his office," Quex said. "Come on, I'll take you up."

On the third floor they found Dr. Frank with his feet up on his couch. He was dictating from some scribbled notes into a tape-recorder. By his side was a plate bearing a tottering pile of cheese and tomato sandwiches. He took one, gave one to Anna and wordlessly passed the rest to Quex. He had obviously become very familiar with Quex's appetite and they were relaxed in each other's company. Anna was glad that at least one thing seemed to have worked well.

Dr. Frank said, "Thea's sleeping in the Treatment Wing tonight, under supervision. You've probably been told she tried to slash her wrists. What you won't have been told is that this happened just after a visit from her father. I've tried my damnedest to discourage his visits, but one can't keep the man away forever. He had to be told about the incident, of course, and unfortunately he came straight back."

"He sat by Thea's bed," Quex chipped in. "And he told her about how he'd take her away and they'd have a holiday in the south of France, just the two of them, and she went berserk. Tony had stitched the cuts in her arms, and she tried to pull all the stitches out with her teeth."

"I finally persuaded him to leave, and we've managed to get Thea calm and settled again, but I've had either him or that solicitor of his on the phone every half-hour since then, ranting about unethical behaviour and court orders. Can you talk to him, pacify him or something?"

"I'll try," Anna said. "Can I use your phone? I don't want to go to Wimbledon unless I'm absolutely forced to."

"Don't tell him you're ringing from here," Dr. Frank warned. "Or he'll think you're part of a conspiracy against him. We'll leave you alone if you want to call him now."

"No." Anna picked up the receiver and began to dial. "I'm going to tell him one or two things you ought to hear as well."

The conversation with Mr. Hahn began with a prolonged outburst against Dr. Frank. "He's taking my daughter away from me," Mr. Hahn said, among other things. "He's poisoning her mind. I must remove her from there at once."

Anna closed her eyes and let him talk, contributing a few sympathetic noises when the occasion demanded. After a while, when it sounded as if he was running out of things to complain about, she said, "I think I understand your feelings, Mr. Hahn. This must be dreadfully upsetting for you. But I have been to Adam House as you requested, and Thea is sleeping peacefully. She has been given no treatment that you would disapprove of." She looked at Dr. Frank who nodded confirmation. "No drugs," she went on. Dr. Frank nodded again. "Nothing like ECT or hypnosis or any of the things you're afraid of. In my opinion you chose this clinic very wisely. In the course of my investigations, I've heard nothing but good of it." She closed her eyes again, avoiding Dr. Frank's reaction, and went on carefully, "I think the misunderstanding has arisen because Thea reacts so strongly to you. And that may have given you a false impression about her state of mind at other times." She opened her eyes. Dr. Frank was nodding vigorously.

"Why does she react like that, if Dr. Frank is not poisoning her mind against me?" Mr. Hahn thundered at the other end of the line.

"I can't explain that, but I do know that Thea's behaviour has its roots in something that happened before Dr. Frank started treating her. For instance, you'll have heard by now that the man who was shot in Southampton was her tutor, Joseph Tulloch. Now I've seen pictures of him, and what is immediately striking is his resemblance to you."

Dr. Frank and Quex looked at each other. Mr. Hahn said, "You mean she may be mistaking me for the man who committed suicide?"

"I think that's quite likely," she said.

"She might even think I was a ghost or reincarnation. That would explain a lot."

"It would indeed." If he could be pacified, even temporarily, by such illusions she would leave it at that. He now turned the force of his invective against Joseph Tulloch, and as that could hurt nobody, Anna simply listened.

At last, when she was allowed to ring off, she turned to Dr. Frank and said, "He wants to think Thea's afraid of poor old Tulloch's ghost."

"Simple solutions for simple minds," Quex said happily. Dr. Frank smiled and said, "Someone will have to put him straight sometime. But if this means he's out of my hair for a while I'm very grateful. Thea needs all the time she can get. Now, if it wouldn't be breaking too many confidences, would you tell me what happened to her? And whether or not she's still in danger of being arrested?"

Anna told him everything she knew and ended by saying that she thought the danger to Thea was less than it had been the day before, but not entirely removed.

"It's a considerable improvement, though," Dr. Frank remarked when she had finished. "And thank you for the information. I'll try to put it to good use." He made no other comment on what she had told him, so after a pause she asked awkwardly, "Is Thea going to get better?"

He looked at her steadily for a few seconds and then said, "Look, I know you've had a long day, but would you like to come down and see her? She's been asking for you and it'd mean a lot to her if you just showed your face."

On the way to the second floor he spoke again. "It isn't realistic to talk about her getting better at the moment. I'm really only half way to understanding her problems. And even in the best of circumstances I wouldn't want you to think she can possibly come out of this unscathed. Given time, she may find a way of coping with life again. She is, at present, terribly damaged, and what happened with Tulloch is only the tip of a very big iceberg."

The Treatment Wing was the only part of Adam House that looked like a hospital. Cubicles with glass panels surrounded a central area where two nurses were playing cards. Only three of the cubicles were occupied.

"All quiet?" Dr. Frank asked cheerfully when one of the nurses got up to let them in.

"You're working late," the nurse said, leading the way to Thea's bed. "Yes, it's all quiet. I think your patient's sleeping now."

But Thea wasn't asleep. She opened her eyes drowsily when Dr. Frank and Anna crept in. She was lying on her back, her arms on top of the covers, neatly bandaged from elbow to wrist. When Anna approached she turned one of her hands palm up. Anna took it. "What've you been up to?" she said affectionately. "You're daft as a brush, aren't you? Worrying everyone like that." Thea smiled sleepily. She looked like a naughty little girl who knew she had already been forgiven.

"Go to sleep now," Anna went on. "And don't be such a wally next time." She felt as if she had spent all

evening saying stupid things. She held Thea's hand for
a while longer and wondered how Thea or Sam could
have any confidence in her at all.

Thea seemed to be asleep and Dr. Frank tapped her
on the shoulder. When they were walking back to the
hall Dr. Frank suddenly said, "You know, Quex is very
keen on you. He's a good man, but rather lonely."

"No, I didn't know," she answered gruffly. She couldn't
think why he had brought up the subject unless he was
warning her of something, but he said no more.

Quex was waiting patiently in the hall. "Shall we go
and get something to eat?" he suggested. "It's my treat."

She eyed him narrowly. She couldn't tell if he was
keen on her or not. He just looked hungry as usual. But
to be on the safe side, she said, "I'm too tired to eat. All
I want is a bath and bed."

He looked disappointed but not heartbroken. It was
strange, she thought, driving home, how suspiciously
you watched someone who was supposed to be keen on
you.

CHAPTER 31

"Would you mind following that cab over there? The
one that's just leaving now," Anna said. It was distinctly
annoying to find herself at Waterloo only an hour after
arriving in Woking, and forced to take a taxi because
her own car was miles away in a Surrey car park.

"What's your game?" the taxi-driver asked, humouring
her, but with a vast sigh. "I thought it was only American detectives and Secret Service got up to this lark.
Ladies ain't supposed to, unless that's your hubby's
fancy woman."

"Department policy," Anna said tensely. "Look, there's
a lot of traffic on the bridge. You'll lose her if you don't
stay close."

"You be me," the man said, offended. "You drive, I'll sit in the back. Think I'm wet behind the ears, don't you?"

"Sorry." She was instantly contrite. "You're doing terrific. I don't know how you manage."

"Takes practice," he told her as they rumbled over Waterloo Bridge. "How long I been on the cabs, you'll ask. Well, it's fourteen years come July. Ever since I left the Army."

"Amazing," Anna said, trying to distinguish Patricia Westerman's taxi from all the others. She hoped her driver was better at it than she was. The sun was high over the river, shining with a hard, clear light that was rare in England.

"You get much call for this sort of thing in your job?" the driver asked. "I'll give you my card. Your department could put me under contract. I always say there's too many foreigners up to no good in this country. I don't know why the government lets 'em all in. If I was you, I'd start with the Arabs. Ruined this country, they have."

There were black cabs everywhere: all down the Strand, the Mall, Constitution Hill and Knightsbridge. For one horrible minute Anna thought the driver was taking her all the way to Kensington High Street, which would have been exactly where she had started that morning. But he turned left on to Brompton Road and stopped outside Harrods.

"There you are, see," the driver said proudly. "Not such a schlepper, am I?"

To her astonishment she saw Mrs. Westerman disappearing into the brick and glass façade. She gave her driver the money she had ready in her hand and scurried in after her.

It was just her luck, Anna thought, weaving anxiously through the crowd trying to keep Mrs. Westerman in view. Just her luck that Mrs. Westerman should pick this of all days for a shopping trip to London. If Anna didn't lose her in Harrods she'd have many more chances in Selfridges, Marks and Spencers or Bond Street and her heart sank at the thought of all the taxi rides between. It would be just a matter of time before she disappeared completely.

At the moment though, Mrs. Westerman seemed content to wander through Harrods' ground floor. She finally settled on the stationery department and made a few small purchases. She bought only a couple of cards and an address book but persuaded the assistant to give her one of Harrods' distinctive plastic bags.

Anna cheered up a bit. It looked as if Mrs. Westerman was killing time before lunch. She was sleekly dressed, with the attention to detail suburban wives apply when setting out for the bright lights. The immaculate alligator shoes that matched her handbag so perfectly would be killing her after a couple of hours, Anna thought spitefully. Shoes like that kept taxi drivers in business.

After a brief tour around Garden Furniture Mrs. Westerman looked at her watch and made for the exit. She turned briskly down Beauchamp Place, past all the small elegant shops and went into the wine bar at the end. Anna peered through the glass door. She saw a man take his briefcase off the empty chair next to him so that Mrs. Westerman could sit down. It was the only empty chair in the place. Lunchtime drinkers were three deep at the bar. The man kissed Mrs Westerman on the mouth and patted her thigh. He was not Mr. Westerman.

Anna retired to the opposite side of the road and waited. It had not taken much effort that morning to find the South Coast Conservation Corps' telephone number. And it had taken even less time to establish that the Corps' respected chairman, Paul Knight, was not grieving for an injured wife. Paul Knight's wife had never felt better. The Corps meeting on Tuesday the 24th was cancelled because the chairman had been held up at a business meeting in Amsterdam. But a call to

Paul Knight's company told her that Paul Knight had not been to Amsterdam that month.

"If you want anything out of Mrs. Westerman," Mr. Brierly had remarked, "you'll have to get her at a disadvantage."

Mr. Embury, by now almost a permanent fixture in the office, had added, "What a pity Mr. Schiller isn't back from Southampton yet. He seems to be a man of great resourcefulness."

"I'm sure Miss Lee can keep the chair warm for him till he returns," Mr. Brierly said, frowning at Anna. "Perhaps, Miss Lee, you'd keep the lady in question under observation for the time being?"

Nothing was certain, Anna now thought gleefully. But there was a strong possibility that the thigh-patter in the wine bar was Paul Knight. And if being caught with him didn't put Mrs. Westerman at a disadvantage, nothing would.

The pair emerged at two o'clock and walked up to Brompton Road where they waved down a taxi. Taxis were easy to find on a dry day so close to Harrods and Anna got one too. She was determined not to lose them. There wouldn't be another opportunity as good as this if she followed Mrs. Westerman for a month.

They paid off the driver at a hotel in South Kensington close to Gloucester Road tube station. Anna watched them laughing in the hotel's revolving door, and that was the last she saw of them until ten to four.

When they came out they were no longer laughing. Each had the distracted air of someone late for an appointment. They went to the edge of the pavement, and the man began to look up and down for another taxi.

Anna stood a few feet behind them and called, "Mr. Knight!" The couple swung round. Paul Knight looked puzzled when he saw Anna. Mrs. Westerman looked horrified.

"What luck, bumping into you like this," Anna said

blithely. "I was hoping to ask you a few questions. You're the chairman of the Conservation Corps, aren't you?"

"I am," he said, bewildered.

"I do hope your wife's recovered from her accident."

"I beg your pardon?" he said. Mrs. Westerman tugged his sleeve excitedly and said, "Don't talk to her. She's a private detective."

"Oh Christ!" he said weakly. "What on earth do you want?"

"A few words with Mrs. Westerman, actually. But I don't want to interrupt anything."

"You're not interrupting anything," he said, recovering his composure. "I'm late for a board meeting. And don't be deceived by appearances. Mrs. Westerman and I were just discussing conservation policy. Weren't we, Mrs. Westerman?" A taxi cruised past with its yellow light shining. Knight hailed it.

"You're not going to leave me to deal with this alone," Mrs. Westerman wailed. Mr. Knight climbed hastily into the taxi saying, "So sorry, I must dash."

"What a gentleman!" Anna said. The taxi pulled away and vanished round the corner. "He doesn't look like the sort of chap who passes out in hotel rooms and leaves a lady to eat dinner by herself," Anna went on. "Oh well, mustn't be deceived by appearances, must I?"

"What do you want?" Mrs. Westerman clutched her alligator handbag to her chest like a talisman to ward off the evil eye. The Harrods bag dangled from her wrist.

"It's about poor Mr. Jones."

"What about him?" Mrs. Westerman looked flustered. "I told you, my meeting with him was accidental. I know nothing about him at all."

"But you do know about Joseph Tulloch, don't you? You should do. You've been a member of the same organization for three years."

"Oh God," Mrs. Westerman moaned. "How did you find out?"

"What on earth made you think I wouldn't? The question is—shall I ring the Southampton police and tell them you lied to them or shall we discuss this sensibly?"

"I suppose you think I've no alternative now you've seen me with Paul. Well, let me tell you, if you go telling tales to my husband I'll deny everything. He'll believe me, you know. He always believes me."

"Then you won't mind if I do go to him, will you? And the neighbours'll believe you too, won't they? And all the Woking and District Thespians. Look, I'm not interested in who you discuss conservation policy with unless you force me to be. I want to talk about Joseph Tulloch."

On the street people came and went, jostling the two women standing on the kerb. It was no place to talk. Anna stuck out her hand and stopped a passing cab. "Waterloo," she told the driver as they got in.

"But I haven't finished my shopping," Mrs. Westerman fumed, rearranging her skirt over smooth, dimpled knees. "This is outrageous."

Anna closed the glass panel between the driver and the two of them. "Don't make me give you a list of what really is outrageous in all this," she said sharply. "You're in no position to criticize. It's because of you, wriggling around lying to save your silly reputation, I've been running myself spare to get my client out of a hole. You don't have a reputation. All you've got's appearance." She looked out of the window and saw row after row of shop windows flash by: clothes displayed behind glass, china laid out on gaudy plinths, bright rugs hung out to catch the eye. There was no point in losing her temper with one woman whose sole motive was keeping up appearances when that was all half the western world thought about.

She sighed and said, "Look, just tell me what happened. Then, if you like, we can go through the whole thing again and I can show you how you can tell it to

the police without looking too bad. But I must have
your story and I'm not going to give up. You ask yourself how much damage I can do if I have to get it the
hard way." She leaned her head back against the leather
seat and gave Mrs. Westerman time to make up her
mind.

"You're a sneaking, dirty-minded, stringy little bitch,"
Mrs. Westerman said almost dreamily. A few mintues
later she exclaimed, "All right! Where do you want me
to begin?"

Anna sat up. "How well did you know Joseph Tulloch?"
she asked.

"Not well. He was a good-looking man, very clever,
but a bit of a prig. I saw him several times at Corps
meetings, and then, last year, he gave one or two
lectures at Open University summer school. He was
very helpful. But I've seen the type before. He gave all
his attention to the dreary ones: old ladies, people in
wheelchairs."

In other words he didn't fancy you, Anna thought
nastily. "Did you know he was going to be at the
Continental Gateway?" she asked.

"Of course not. And if Paul had been sober enough to
come down to dinner, obviously we'd have avoided
him. It would have been too embarrassing to have been
seen together."

"But as you were on your own you shared a table
with him."

"I told you—there was that bloody convention. I was
relieved to see someone I knew. He wasn't very good
company, though. He hardly said a word, seemed very
depressed. Later when I heard he'd been shot I thought
it must have been suicide. I was quite surprised that
the police were treating it so seriously.

"There was a tremendous fuss at the hotel that
morning—police, reporters, everyone gossiping. That's
why I lied and said I didn't know him. When I heard he
had registered under the name of Jones it gave me a
heaven-sent chance to stay uninvolved.

"I suppose I was shocked and I didn't think properly. I should have thought about what it might do to his family if he wasn't identified but by the time I did I had already spoken to the police and it was too late. You're quite right—I was only thinking about myself."

"Are you willing to tell the police that much?"

"I suppose I'll have to." Mrs. Westerman gazed despondently at a beautiful girl in a cerise silk boiler suit who was crossing Sloane Street in front of them. "I'm going to look awfully foolish, though. You just don't understand, do you, how bored and isolated a woman in my position gets? My husband's older than I am. He's away for days on end. Life seems to pass me by."

CHAPTER 32

The endless snake of traffic crawled steadily into Sloane Square. Anna said, "Life certainly does seem to pass you by. Don't you open your mail in the mornings or is it that you've got a really naff memory?"

"I beg your pardon?"

"Do me a favour," Anna said impatiently. "I talked to the Conservation Corps' secretary this morning. The news of Joseph Tulloch's death by drowning appeared in the monthly bulletin a week before you met him at the hotel. You were sent your copy. You could pretend you missed the item, but that wouldn't wash because according to the secretary you were on the committee that drafted a letter of condolence to his widow. So when you joined him that night you were sharing a table with a man you thought was dead. Weren't you just a tiny bit surprised?"

"You really *are* a frightful little cow, aren't you?" Mrs. Westerman leant forward and jerked the window down.

The wind ruffled her hair so she closed it quickly. "You're trying to trap me."

"You're trapping yourself. Why don't you just assume that I've done my homework? Start again. You knew Tulloch. You thought he'd drowned. You met him at the Continental Gateway. Weren't you surprised?"

"I was astonished, if you must know."

"What was his reaction?"

"He was absolutely shattered. I thought he was going to run from the table. He stood there stammering, as white as a sheet and I knew he had been up to something. Until then I thought there'd been some mistake, and we would laugh about it together." She opened her handbag and brought out an enamel and gold compact. She dabbed at her nose and studied her eyeshadow. The sight seemed to calm her, and when she spoke again it was more slowly. "He told me he had reached the end of his tether. He was overworked. There was never enough money no matter how much he added to his workload.

"He said he loved his children but he never had enough time to enjoy them. They were growing up without him. He said he had never been in love with his wife. She was a wonderful woman but he couldn't live up to her standards anymore.

"What he was describing was a sort of nervous collapse. I understood him completely. He wanted a fresh start but he couldn't leave his family in penury. He told me about the day he was sorting out his desk and he came upon his life insurance policy. It seemed like the answer to a prayer, he said. He was worth more dead than alive. He could start again, and his family, quite literally, would be better off without him. I was so sorry for him that when he asked me to promise I'd never tell a soul I'd seen him, of course I agreed. I would never have broken that promise if you hadn't forced me to."

"So that's the second reason you didn't tell the police who he was—loyalty."

"Sneer if you like." Mrs. Westerman put her compact away and shut the handbag with a decisive snap. "I don't suppose you've ever been in a situation where others depend on you for their happiness, while you are dying the death of the spirit—trapped by the needs of others and society's conventions. And I don't suppose you have the imagination to put yourself in his place. Well I have. I know what it's like."

"For Christ's sake, Mrs. Westerman!" Anna exploded. "What a load of bullshit." She sat forward and opened the sliding panel. "Victoria Street, please," she told the driver.

"Make your mind up," he grumbled. Anna slammed the panel closed.

"Where are we going now?" Mrs. Westerman asked.

"New Scotland Yard. I've given up on you. If you want to arse around—do it there. They've got more patience than I have."

Mrs. Westerman rapped on the panel with her wedding ring. "Waterloo!" she shouted through the glass. The taxi-driver braked and stopped in the middle of the road. Horns blared from behind. The driver turned in his seat and opened the panel himself. "Toss a coin," he advised. "Heads gets Waterloo. Tails we go to Victoria Street. I don't care which. Just don't muck me about."

"Waterloo," Mrs. Westerman urged, her mouth pale with anger and fear. "And hurry. I've a train to catch."

"That suit you, Miss?" the driver asked sarcastically, and when Anna nodded he shut the panel and started off with a jerk. Mrs. Westerman fell back in her seat.

"I'll never forgive you," she said, unclasping her handbag again and fishing out a handful of paper handkerchiefs.

"Last chance," Anna said implacably. "After that I swap to Plan B. If you don't like Plan A, you'll sodding loathe Plan B."

"You don't care what chaos you make of my life." Mrs. Westerman tickled her eyelids with a tissue. "I wasn't to know he was a mental case. I only went up to his room because I thought I could bring him a little comfort. I think he meant to kill me all along. Why couldn't he have trusted me?"

"Search me," Anna said, turning away to look at the Tate Gallery on her left. "So you went up to his room. Go on."

"He had a gun in his suitcase. I couldn't believe it—professors don't have guns. He pointed it at me. I swear he was going to shoot me. We struggled and the gun went off."

"Be careful," Anna warned. "That's all right as far as it goes. But where was the suitcase? Where were you, and where was he when he fell? Don't forget I've seen the room and the forensic report. So have the police. If you don't get the details right they're going to want to know why. You've got to tell a story that matches what was found later."

"You still don't believe me, do you?"

"You've got more sides than a honeycomb," Anna said tiredly. "I've almost stopped caring about the truth— just something that makes sense would do me for now."

"But I really do think he meant to kill me from the beginning," Mrs. Westerman insisted. "It was the only way he could be sure I wouldn't talk. He asked me up to his room for a drink. Well, I told you, Paul was sleeping in my room. It was early. I have a lot of energy you know. I didn't want to go back to my room just to listen to Paul snoring."

"Yes?"

"Well, we were sitting on the bed, drinking, Joseph had his arm round me. I thought we were getting on wonderfully. He told me I was just the sort of woman he'd left his wife for.

"Then all of a sudden, the door to the next bedroom opened and a girl walked in. She was wearing a cheap black dress with a gold chain round the waist. She looked like a little tart. It made me furious to think he'd led me on like that. And she just stood there staring at us with that blank expression young people have.

"I must have said something bitter—I can't remember exactly. But he started shouting, 'I'll kill you. I'll kill myself'—things like that. The gun wasn't in his case, it was in the drawer of the bedside table. He got it out. He was quite mad, you've got to believe that. Quite mad. We were fighting for the gun when it went off. I was only trying to defend myself. It was that bloody girl's fault. We were doing fine till she marched in."

"What did she do?"

"She just stood there like a dummy. But she'd seen everything. So I grabbed that silly chain she had round her waist and I made her look at him. I wanted to frighten her, you see. She would have run out and blabbed to the first person she met. I said, 'See what you've done,' and then I pushed her back to her room. I told her to pack up and get out, and if she ever told anyone I'd see she went to prison. It's the only thing girls like that understand."

"And did she pack up and go?"

"I didn't see what she did. I had to wash the blood off and get dressed. When I looked, though, her room was empty. At least she had brains enough to leave quietly."

"You washed?"

"I couldn't go through the corridors with blood all over me, could I? I panicked, I admit that. I was in a terrible state—frightened, weeping. I could only think about getting back to Paul and that no one should know I'd been there."

"How did you arrange that?"

"I used his shirt to wipe the things I might've touched. I know that sounds cold-blooded but it wasn't, I promise. I was like an automaton."

"What did you do with his passport?"

Mrs. Westerman swung round and stared at her.

"He was going to France," Anna said. "So he had a passport. What did you do with it?"

"I cut it up and put it down the garbage disposal when I got home. The stupid man had signed the register as Jones but he had his own passport. If the police found that they'd know who he was, and if they knew who he was they would know I was somehow connected. I had to take it with me. So long as they thought we were strangers they wouldn't be interested."

"You're right," Anna said, "it does sound cold-blooded. One minute you're in bed with the guy, and the next you're stuffing his passport down the drain."

"I wasn't in bed with him," Mrs. Westerman cried, real tears starting down her face.

"Then why did you say you had to get dressed?"

"Did I say that?" Mrs. Westerman wept. "Oh God, what am I going to do?"

The driver twisted round and rapped on the glass. "You can sit there as long as you like, ladies," he called. "But this here's Waterloo, and I thought you had a train to catch."

CHAPTER 33

"What the hell was Sam's dad doing in bed with Mrs. W.?" Quex's voice bounced off the tiles and boomed back at him. Two startled boys turned round to stare. Anna blushed and dived. The turquoise water buried her. She opened her eyes to the burn of chlorine, surfaced, and swam overarm to the shallow end.

Quex followed, thrashing along like a paddle-steamer. She watched him with a feeling of comic despair. Was there no venue, except perhaps the back row of a scrum, where he would not stand out like Gulliver in Lilliput? He arrived in a frenzy of white water to the

consternation of the tinies who clung like tadpoles to
the edge of the pool. He shook the water out of his ears
and stood up.

" 'Ere, lofty," a small boy protested. "You're standing
on my sister."

Quex fished a wailing tot from somewhere around his
knee and restored it to dry land. Anna pushed off and
breaststroked back to the deep end, feeling her muscles
stretch and relax. It was a lot better than exercising her
brain.

Quex caught up and barred her progress. "What was
Sam's dad doing . . ." he began, flicking soaked hair out
of his eyes and treading water furiously.

"Okay, okay," she said, resignedly swimming to the
side.

"Hardly what you'd call a rational act." He heaved
himself out, the muscles standing out on his back like
plaited loaves. He twitched Anna up beside him.

"You still expecting rational acts?" She watched the
water ripple around her dangling legs. "I don't think
Thea was the only one going off her noodle. If you take
Mrs. W.'s word for it, he was unable to resist her
massive charm. Or told another way, he lured her up
there to kill her. But if you ask me he probably thought
he was protecting Thea."

"Hardly a rational thought."

"Do give over," she sighed. "He'd've told Mrs. W. he
was alone. Then when she put the pressure on he was
left without excuses. And besides, maybe he thought if
she was involved in a guilty secret of her own, she
wouldn't shoot her mouth off about him. Poor sod."

"Well, with only her word to go by, we'll probably
never know." He stirred the water with his foot. "I say,
Leo—my leave's nearly over and I'll be going back to
Aberdeen shortly. Will you keep visiting Thea while
I'm gone?"

"I expect so." She shivered.

"Will you write to me? I want to stay in touch. My

life is far too episodic. It's hard to keep any continuity in it. While you're away your friends sort of disperse—marry, split up, stop writing. When you come back they've all reassembled elsewhere."

"The money must be brilliant, though."

"It is." He turned to face her. "Will you write, Leo?"

"I'm not much of a letter-writer." She looked at him directly too. He seemed rather more than hungry, but he was too sensitive to press further. "Okay," she said. "I'll try. Only don't expect any rational thoughts."

"Basho?" Dr. Frank said, turning the thin paperback over, his forehead pleating itself as he raised his eyebrows. *The Narrow Road to the Deep North?* Whatever made you think of that?"

"Quex sent it from Aberdeen," Anna said. "I didn't know what to bring. He says it's utter simplicity combined with deep meaning. I wouldn't know. I never heard of Basho before."

"Quex has some very sound instincts," Dr. Frank said thoughtfully. "But he also has a rather boyish enthusiasm for the insane which I find a little hard to swallow. Can you see Thea from here?"

Anna, perched on the windowsill, looked down into the garden. The resemblance of Adam House to a country hotel struck her again. It was early afternoon, just after lunch, and like hotel guests, the patients had gone out to sit in the sun to digest their meal. The only difference was that unlike hotel guests they didn't sit in pairs or groups to talk. Most of them were alone. Even from the distance of Dr Frank's office their isolation from each other was obvious.

Thea sat pressed against the trunk of a tree. It looked as if she were trying to take up as little space as possible. Her notebook was open and she was curled over it scribbling secretively. The sight of her was depressing.

"What she needs," she said almost without thinking, "is another childhood."

"You could help with that, if you wanted to." Dr. Frank smiled and reached for a sandwich. Today they were ham and cucumber. "Help yourself," he said, offering the plate. As Anna took one he went on, "She hasn't had much luck with older women. What with her mother and that dreadful Mrs. . . ."

"Patricia Westerman," Anna said. "She isn't all that dreadful, though. She's only doing what a lot of people do sometime or another: going to bed with the wrong men and lying to get out of trouble. It's only really dreadful when you think of the consequences." She looked out of the window again. Someone had wandered over to Thea and was standing over her, watching. Thea stopped writing and covered the notebook with her arm. The spectator wandered away.

"Sometimes there doesn't seem to be a lot of difference between good and bad," Anna went on. "Sometimes it seems any sort of action can cause harm."

"That doesn't sound like you." The Frank eyebrows waved like antennæ. "You've done all right. You've got the police off our backs. You've given Mr. Hahn something else to get obsessed about. You've bought us time. Maybe even enough for Thea's second childhood. Who knows?"

"But at the expense of the Tulloch family."

"You're not a historian," Dr. Frank said rather acidly. "You can't alter history. Tulloch was a mess in a tidy package long before he met Thea. If it hadn't been her, something else would've cracked him."

"Quex says Tulloch believed he already was a dead man," Anna remarked. "Guilt is the death of the spirit, Quex says, and Tulloch felt mortally guilty. Well, I suppose an antique Luger's hardly your standard honeymoon gear. Quex says he probably always had something like double suicide in mind."

"Quex isn't always wrong." Dr. Frank munched judiciously.

"Which means, in effect, that the dreadful Mrs. W. might've saved Thea's life."

"Speculation," he said briskly. "Quex is good at that. But you and I can't really afford the what ifs, can we? We just have to go full steam ahead and deal with the mess as we find it. Speaking of which, I've got a patient in five minutes." He got up and brushed the crumbs off his suit. He picked up the unfinished plate of sandwiches and stowed it out of sight in the bottom drawer of his desk. Anna giggled.

"I thought that was just what shrinks *didn't* do," she said. "Hiding the mess in a bottom drawer."

"Go away," Dr. Frank said, his toffee eyes crinkling up into a sheepish grin. "Go away and be a big sister to little girl lost down there." He bent over his desk and sorted through a pile of papers. Anna picked up her bag. He stopped her at the door and thrust a piece of paper into her hand saying, "This is from Thea's bottom drawer. Read it."

Anna read:

> His white life soaks the carpet.
> Spilled milk.
> He had not been born
> But life was the death of him.

"Chew on that," Dr. Frank said. "I can't explain so don't ask."

Anna didn't ask. She went downstairs.

Gauzy patches of light dappled the grass under the plane tree. Selwyn lay resplendent on the sunbed, lightly clad in a clean pair of winceyette pyjamas, a baby-blue shawl draped in languorous folds across his shoulders. He stared with disbelief into his glass of Rose's Lime Juice.

"This is bloody outrageous," he bellowed. "I thought at least she'd've put a finger of gin in it."

Anna stopped mowing and shook the sweaty hair away from the back of her neck. Bea skipped quickly out of earshot.

"There's vodka in there," Anna said, absolutely straight-faced. "You can't taste it because the lime juice is too strong."

"Oh well, that's all right then," he said, mollified. "Bloody doctors. First they mutilate a fellow's body, and then they have the gall to come between him and his grog."

An angry, intermittent buzzing drowned the sound of bird song. She picked up the bleeper and buried it deep beneath a heap of grass clippings.

"Aren't you going to answer that?" Selwyn asked, craning his neck to see what she was doing.

"Unreliable things, bleepers," Anna said absent-mindedly. "I called in six times yesterday, and the sodding thing had gone off of its own accord. Everyone else says the same. Beryl's getting quite fed up with them."

"What a liar you are," Selwyn said, pink with admiration. He looked suspiciously down at his glass. "Are you sure there's vodka in this?"

"Of course I'm sure." She met his eyes with unblinking candour. Upstairs the phone rang. She turned away and started to mow again.

ABOUT THE AUTHOR

LIZA CODY is a graphic artist and novelist who lives in Frome, a small English village. Her first novel, *Dupe*, was nominated for the 1981 Edgar Award for best mystery of the year and won the John Creasey Award for best first mystery published in England during 1980. Her other Anna Lee novels are *Bad Company* and *Stalker*.

• AN ANNA LEE MYSTERY •

If you enjoyed HEAD CASE, you will want to read these special advance preview chapters from UNDER CONTRACT, the new Anna Lee mystery by Liza Cody, which will be available as a Bantam paperback in July 1990, at your local bookseller.

UNDER CONTRACT

CHAPTER 4

Horowitz Management had its home on the top two
floors of a narrow building tightly wedged between
cutting-rooms and a porno cinema. The chaos and over-
crowding of Soho was reproduced upstairs in the reception area where girls, their make-up as thick as winter
woollies, dealt with scores of importuning punters, clam-
orous telephones and untidy piles of paper.

Anna was rescued from the mêlée by a man in his
fifties wearing a pink-striped shirt. "Anna Lee?" he
said, anxiously regarding her with watery blue eyes.
"Yes, good, did you bring the photos? Yes? Sadie, my
sweet, take these down to Whatsisname and get him to
run us off another thingy. Anna Lee. That's right. She's
joining the tour. And a couple of the sweatshirts. Medium? Yes, medium. I want everything ready when we
get back. Joanie darling, what day is it?"

"Chez Angelo," Joanie darling said without looking
up, "but, Mr. Horowitz . . ."

"Later, darling." He set off through the crush and
down the stairs like the White Rabbit. Anna trotted
after him. In the street he struggled into a squeaky new
leather coat, still moving at a brisk pace and remarking
breathlessly, "It never ends, it never ends, and what
for, I ask you? They've no idea, simply no idea." He
veered sharply across the road into a side street and then
dived into a basement restaurant. Down the steps he

went, now struggling out of the coat that had been hardly worth putting on. "Ah, Angelo," he said, out of breath, "nice to see you. My usual! Thank you, and a bottle of your . . . Over here, Anna, you can just squeeze through, can't you, darling? Sit, do sit, oh, your coat, yes, Angelo, the young lady's coat."

He collapsed into a chair at a cramped corner table and let out his breath. "*Oi veh*, what a life," he sighed, handing her a menu. "White meat, I recommend white meat and white wine here. Red inflames, you know. I wanted to get you on your own because what I've got to say is absolutely confidential and gossip runs round that office like a greyhound. You like music? What about Shona Una, have you heard of her?"

The sudden break in his conversation caught Anna unprepared. She cleared her throat and began, "She's pretty new, isn't she? I think *Bitterness* is great, but . . ."

"Well, that's something." He ran his hand over his sparse hair and looked at her closely for the first time. "Maybe you'll do. The last one they sent thought music began and ended with the Hallelujah Chorus and made no bones about it. Rubbed poor Roz up the wrong way. You've got to get along with Roz or we're wasting our time."

"Roz?" Anna asked, ducking as the waiter rushed and deposited a bottle of white wine on the table as he went. Mr. Horowitz poured a splash into two glasses. "Roz, Shona Una, what difference? Look, I'm worried about that girl. She's been on my books going on four years and she's been there or thereabouts club-wise ever since. Not a bad following. Nothing to write home about, but not bad. *Bitterness* was the big one, the lucky one, the one you pray at night for. Now we've got the LP and the tour and I don't want it all spoiled. You understand? We could be talking mega-mega. I'm not saying it *will* happen, but it might if nothing screws it up."

The waiter hovered over them, pencil poised. Anna, who had not had time to look at the menu, said, "The same," when Mr. Horowitz ordered. He smiled his approval. In spite of not having time to look at him properly either, Anna thought he was rather nice. The tired pouchy face managed to look quirky and kindly when it smiled. She said, "What might spoil it, Mr. Horowitz? What are you worried about?"

He sighed. "I can talk to you, can't I? You're young, but you know how to listen, don't you?" Anna nodded. She didn't have much choice. "You've got to be tolerant in this game," he went on with scarcely a pause. "They lead a strange life, these artists. Lots of pressure—image and so on. You may think it's superficial, but it's life and death in their business. And they're children, you know. Don't know fire burns. You read the music press? No? Well, who does? But there was a bit in *Sounds* about the gig in Birmingham. 'Shona Una—Will Bitterness Go Sour?' They could kill her, you know. She was late out. Kept the kids waiting. They don't like that, you know. There was the usual announcement about technical difficulties but it didn't wash."

"What happened?"

"She was locked in the dressing-room. All ready. But she just wouldn't come out. It was lucky I was there. I don't usually go—my ears, you know. But I drove up specially, this being the tour opening. Well, she let me in finally, but she was shaking and carrying on like Judy Garland. I don't know how we got her out there, but thank God, we did."

"And was she okay? What did she do out there?"

"What does a fish do in water? It swims. She was fine. She's a pro. But it did my heart no good at all. All that money, the record company, the promoter, sponsors. You wouldn't believe the money depending on that poor girl. Word gets round she's unreliable and she's dead, believe you me, she's one dead girl."

The waiter came with the food. Anna looked round while he served it. The restaurant was packed, mainly with men hunched over the tiny tables talking nineteen to the dozen. Forks flashed, glasses emptied, but everyone seemed to concentrate on talk rather than lunch.

While Mr. Horowitz had his fork in his mouth, she said, "This wasn't just nerves, was it? You wouldn't want my help with stage fright, would you? What happened before Birmingham?"

"Good girl." He chewed rapidly. "After *Bitterness* began to take off and before Birmingham things were beginning to roll. You know it's happening—the people you want to talk to are always in when you call, the money comes sniffing instead of the other way round. Success just round the corner. You can smell it. Wonderful. And Roz was loving it—interviews, photo calls. A girl like Roz, well, all those years begging for a mention somewhere, knocking on all those doors, and now they're knocking on hers. And then, suddenly, she shuts up. Doesn't answer the phone. When she does, it's 'Oh Danny, I'm not sure. Perhaps the timing's wrong. I'm not ready.' Not ready! What's she been doing all these years? Knitting mittens? And the deals! If she'd pulled out, it'd've been like Centre Point falling down. You've no idea what it takes to put a thing like this together."

The fork hung suspended in mid-air and sweat broke out on his upper lip. He suddenly looked quite unwell. Anna hurriedly poured him some more wine. He patted her hand. "Don't worry about me. I want you to look after Roz. I want to know what's wrong. That other one they sent suggested drugs. I'm not saying it isn't, but Roz's been a long time in this business. It wouldn't happen overnight. But anyway, if someone's giving her something she can't handle I want to be told. Or if it's a lover I don't know about, whatever. If I know what it is, I can sort it out. If I don't, I can't."

"You must've asked her yourself, Mr. Horowitz." Anna leaned forward. "What does she say?"

"She doesn't say anything. I won't say we're close, because we're not. Well, not particularly, but I always thought she trusted me. Now she treats me like the enemy. I say, 'What's up, Roz, tell Danny,' and she accuses me of interrogating her, sapping her confidence. You'd think I was trying to wreck her career. Me! So when the question of security for the tour came up I thought I'd put someone next to her, keep an eye on her, you know. Only they sent me this klutz in support stockings who doesn't know rock from reggae even.

"Roz isn't hard to get along with, or she wasn't till a few weeks ago, so what I'm asking is for you to get close to her, make yourself useful, find out what's on her mind."

Anna had only a hazy picture of Roz, and listening to Daniel Horowitz, she couldn't make up her mind whether he cared for her as a person or as a property. When she asked him about her, he gave the impression that either he did not know her individually or he was unwilling to describe her. He drifted too easily into trade descriptions. "Oh, she's creative, all right," he said, over pudding. "She writes some of her own material—I know what you're thinking, but she does. She's not really in the singer-songwriter category, though."

He had talked about her so often in those terms, attempted to sell her so many times, Anna thought, he was quite unable to think about her personally. At other times, though, she thought she saw an almost paternal anxiety. "She should see her family more often, make new friends away from the business. There are too many dogs around the bone here. Sincerity's a rare commodity, never mind what you read in interviews."

By the time coffee arrived Anna had decided she would just have to make up her own mind when she met her. Some warning notes were sounded here too. He fingered his saucer and looked a little evasive. "I'll call her later on and break the ice for you," he said. "She's staying at a friend's place for now. Don't go round there till I give the say-so, will you? And listen, as far as she's concerned you're part of general security, all right? I'll check with the tour manager too, so he'll be expecting you. And another thing: like I said, there's a lot of interests represented, Dog Records, Vanguard Promotions, etcetera. Now they're the people who want everything like clockwork. I wouldn't want anyone to know I'm concerned. Confidence—that's the name of the game. So watch who you talk to, all right? Anything wrong—you tell me, no-one else, not even the guys you work with. Anything iffy that gets out finds its way straight into the media, and then kaput!"

Back at the Horowitz office, Anna discovered that the "thingy" was a large white identification badge with her picture on it. "White's for security," Joanie darling said, handing it to Anna. "That's right, isn't it, Danny?"

"That'll get you in anywhere," Mr. Horowitz told her.

"I put in two T-shirts as well as the sweatshirts." Joanie darling produced a plastic carrier bag. She was more efficient than she looked. Anna took the bag.

"Okay." Mr. Horowitz drew her out of everyone's hearing. "You've got my private numbers, right? And I've got yours. Don't do anything till you hear from me. And . . ."

"Don't talk to anyone but you," Anna finished for him.

CHAPTER 5

The design on the sweatshirts was a silver-winged snake spitting out the words, "Shona Una UK Tour." It was the same on the T-shirts. The basic colour was black, and it looked as if one good wash would finish them for ever. Anna sighed and put them back in the bag.

The taxi stopped at her door. As she got out she saw Selwyn Price, a ludicrous figure in a green waterproof poncho and hat, pedalling his bike towards her. There was something wrong with his brakes. He took his feet off the pedals and tried to stop himself. His shoes slipped on the wet road so he tried to get off with the bike still moving.

Anna squatted on the kerb to untangle his left leg from the chain. His shoelace had come undone and was jammed in the links. She said, "You'll have to take your shoe off."

Selwyn stopped cursing and did as he was told. The taxi-driver said, "Do I get my money now or do we wait for the rest of the circus?" Anna paid him. Selwyn picked himself up and hopped over to the front door. Anna followed with the bicycle. Chain and shoe dragged noisily behind.

"What you want is a 'Just Married' sign," the taxi-driver called as he pulled away. "Or better yet—get the comic a pushchair."

Selwyn turned round to reply and put his unshod foot down in a puddle. As homecomings went, this was a little worse than usual. Anna bundled Selwyn, bike and shoe into the hall. He found the key and opened the door to his flat. "What're you doing home so early?" He wrung out his sock into Bea's carefully nurtured begonia. "And a taxi. Did someone die and leave you the cab fare? Where are you going?"

"Upstairs," Anna told him. "I'm going to get my tool kit. And then I'm going to fix your bike. You're a public nuisance, Selwyn Price. What's more, you're a bloody danger to yourself and anyone who comes within a half a mile of you. You've no sodding coordination."

"Well, nobody's perfect," Selwyn replied in a huff.

"Just average would be a big improvement." She ran up the stairs and let herself into her own flat. The air felt damp and chilly. She lit the gas fire and went to the kitchen to sort out some tools. If she had any sense of responsibility to mankind, she thought, she'd take the bike to bits and bury each one separately in the garden. They only thing that stopped her was the alarming thought that Selwyn might retaliate by taking driving lessons.

She had replaced Selwyn's chain so many times she could almost do it blindfolded. Grumbling and insulting him at the same time was part of the ritual. Selwyn expected it—he even enjoyed it. "I don't care what you say," he had admitted once, "so long as it's *me* you're talking about."

Today, however, he was oddly contrite. He even made her a cup of tea, which was completely out of character for him. Normally, his idea of hospitality was to point at the wine bottle and tell her to help herself—and while she was on her feet how about refilling *his* glass?

Now he hovered behind her, unusually subdued and offering to help. The offer aroused her suspicions. After a while he sat down on the stairs and said, "What do you do with your money, Leo?"

"What money?" Anna was surprised. Selwyn was simply not interested in money. That was Bea's responsibility. It came and it went. And so long as he had enough for the odd bottle, his paper and typewriter ribbons he didn't care where it came from or went to or in what quantities.

"Well, er, just money," he replied awkwardly. "I mean, haven't you got some put by . . . in a building society or something? Like candles. I mean, you've always got candles when there's a power cut, haven't you? You're a very practical person, Leo."

In fact she did have a small emergency fund. It was for the time when Martin Brierly either fired her or went broke himself. When thought about rationally, neither event was likely, but Anna was no more rational about her fears than anyone else. It wasn't much, just enough to last for a couple of weeks while she looked for another job.

"Is there an emergency?" she asked. Selwyn looked away, embarrassed. Anna turned back to the bike and rubbed at the rust which was causing the brakes to lock. Selwyn coughed and fidgeted. Finally he said, "Leo . . . you know Foolscap Press . . . ?"

"The one's who're publishing *Whole and Corners*?"

This was to be Selwyn's second collection of poems and he was very proud of it.

"Yes, and they've stolen my books," Selwyn said dramatically. "Well, held them hostage actually. And I can't raise the ransom."

"What on earth are you talking about?" She turned to look at him. He had his head in his hands. He groaned and said, "Foolscap's gone bust. They've got the liquidator in."

"What rotten luck," she said sympathetically. But there was worse to come, and by and by the story came out. In the first place, Selwyn had agreed to take his payment after publication and it was well past that date now. His books were printed and ready, but because Foolscap was in liquidation there was no money for him.

In the second place, the receiver had written to Selwyn asking if he had any claim on the company. But

Selwyn, with his mind on loftier things, had stuffed the unopened letter in his dressing-gown pocket. Bea had only found it this morning, when she was about to take the dressing-gown to the launderette. After Selwyn read it, he panicked.

"It was like finding a scorpion in the lucky dip," he told Anna glumly. "I was expecting a cheque, you see." In the letter the receiver told him that if he had a claim he must register it immediately. The deadline had expired last week.

Selwyn sweated and dithered over the phone all morning. Then, feeling he should tackle the receiver in person, he had pedalled in a frenzy over to Camden Lock to see him. There he was told that, since he had not registered as a creditor, he would lose not only the money Foolscap owed him but also his books. All fifteen hundred of them were now part of the company's assets. They would be sold and the proceeds would go to pay off other creditors.

"And that's robbery," Selwyn cried. "It's my work, isn't it? But all the profits will go to the printers and solicitors and I shan't see a penny."

Privately, Anna did not think there would be much by way of profits if his previous royalties were anything to go by. But she said, "So you thought you could buy the books back?"

"And sell them myself," Selwyn said. "But *Wholes and Corners* would've gone for £1.50 a copy. And if you multiply that by fifteen hundred it comes to . . . well, I worked it out on the way home and it's too much. Where will I get an amount like that? Unless you've got it, Leo . . . ?"

She did the sums in her head. She hadn't—nothing like it. She said, "I'm sorry, love. I haven't got that much." He hung his head. "But look," Anna went on, "usually, when a company goes broke, the assets are sold off at a cheaper price, aren't they? Maybe they won't want the face value."

"No?" Selwyn looked suddenly hopeful. "If you could lend me what you've got . . . and I could go round to all my friends, take up a collection . . ."

"Oh Lord." Anna's heart sank. She could imagine several people willing to lose their small savings on Selwyn's behalf. "Wait a minute. First you must talk to the receiver again. Find out what he's prepared to accept. It's no good borrowing till you know how much you've got to raise."

Selwyn's face fell. "I don't know if the receiver'll talk to me again." He shook his head dismally. "I was a bit upset when I saw him today. I called him 'an official receiver of stolen goods, thief, scoundrel, vulture pecking at the corpse of British Art, carrion eater.' I don't think he likes me." Anna had to laugh. It was so like Selwyn to leap before he looked. "Well, then you'll have to get Bea to represent you," she suggested. "She has a calm responsible approach. Officials like women like Bea."

Selwyn exploded. "You're not to tell Bea," he shouted. "She's not to know. She gave me a terrible earful when she found out about my not getting any money up front. Cruel, it was. She said a Foolscap was what I should wear and I was incompetent anyway. She said I'd do anything to get in print and it'd be vanity publishing next. Now she'll say I told you so and I'll do anything to avoid that!" He heaved himself off the stairs and disappeared into his living-room. From her position, stooped over the bicycle in the hall, Anna heard the muffled screech of a cork as it twisted out of a bottle. Selwyn, once more, had been driven to drink. Usually he didn't need much driving but today Anna had to admit there had been some provocation.

She tested the brakes, and when she was satisfied she

wiped her hands and joined Selwyn. His pint beer mug was filled to the brim with red wine and he stared dolefully at her from his armchair. Traitor, his look seemed to say. Anna ignored it.

"If you want your books, you'll have to find out how much they'll cost," she said reasonably. "And to find that out you'll have to get someone to deal with the receiver. Bea's involved in accounting and bookkeeping. She knows how to talk to people like that. So what if she says I told you so? She's only human, after all."

Selwyn poured wine down his throat and looked mutinous. Anna tried again. "If you could swallow your pride the way you swallow that plonk . . . Come on, Selwyn, be your age—you know it makes sense for Bea to handle this for you."

"No!" he shouted. "I'm not having her tell me what an idiot I am. She's always at it, and so are you. I'll handle this myself."

CHAPTER 6

"Dave McPhee," the wiry voice said. "What're you driving?"

"Pardon?" Anna said stupidly.

"Wheels, small fry, wheels. What you got?"

"Oh." She adjusted the receiver more comfortably to her ear and began to concentrate. What she had actually been thinking about before the phone rang was clothes. It had suddenly dawned on her while cleaning the grease from under her nails that she was about to enter a world where image was all important, where your credibility depended more on your clothes than on your competence. To get it wrong was to invite derision. Dave's question about her car made her realize that J. W. Protection had its own sense of style too.

Now he hooted with contempt. "A Renault Five? Wow! I'll have to stop calling you small fry, won't I . . . Tiddler?"

"From little tiddlers big fish grow," she said smartly.

He changed tack. "Have you met Superbitch yet?"

"Not yet. The client's arranging something."

"Well, don't hang about. We're shifting the whole circus up to Luton tomorrow p.m. and you'll be driving her. Done any security driving?"

"Some," Anna said cautiously. He sighed with exaggerated patience. "Well, not to worry, Tiddler. I'll explain procedure before we leave. And I suppose I'll have to draw a motor from the pool for you. Renault Five! Jeezus!"

"Gosh, thanks," she said sweetly. "But nothing vulgar, mind." She hung up, annoyed. She had never expected to use her own car. On a job like this a car to suit the client was always provided. She knew it, and she knew Dave was simply finding ways to make her look silly. She went back to thinking about clothes.

The only time she had seen Shona Una was in the *Bitterness* video on TV. All she could remember was a witch-like figure, dressed in what looked like black silk cobwebs, posed by a moonlit pool. A skeletal hand had emerged from the water making a slow oily ripple which spread until it touched Shona Una's bare feet. It was no help. Nobody could guess from that what she was really like.

Anna tried to think of the witch-like figure as Roz. But that didn't help either. She went into her bedroom and peered anxiously into her wardrobe. It was a fact of life, she thought, that there was nothing like the sight of your own clothes hanging deflated from a rail to make you feel inadequate. How could she possibly enter a world dominated by style wearing anything in there? People in that world dressed to attract attention. Anna dressed to avoid it.

She shut the cupboard door with a bang, thinking that even if she had a garment remotely suitable there would then be the problem of hair. Hers was uncoloured, unpermed, and altogether unremarkable when compared to what was fashionable. She wasn't going to do anything to alter it.

There was only one answer and that was to do nothing at all. A half-hearted attempt at trendiness was always a pitiful sight.

With nothing else to do she went back to the kitchen to make a pot of tea. Then she settled in the corner of the sofa with J.W.'s plastic file and tried to get familiar with the lists of names and tour dates.

At half past five she heard Bea come in from work, and about an hour later she came up for a chat, looking tired and cold. Anna made some more tea.

Bea said, "Selwyn's like a sick bear this evening. He's reading *Les Misérables*—in French, mark you. It's a fine thing to come home to, I must say!"

"He fell off his bike again," Anna told her. She didn't like keeping Selwyn's secrets from Bea. But sometimes she had to keep Bea's secrets from Selwyn too, so she supposed it worked out evenly. Bea launched into a story about a minor outrage at work. It was what she would have told Selwyn if he had been in a better mood: not very interesting, but the sort of story she had to get off her chest.

Anna listened patiently. It was dark outside and rainy wind spattered like gravel on the window. She felt suspended in time.

Release came when the telephone rang. Daniel Horowitz said, "Anna, sweetie? Good, listen . . . I've told Roz about you. She wasn't too pleased but she says she'll see you nowish. So look, darling, a low profile, please . . . nothing pushy, know what I mean? She's a tiny bit prickly. Tell her . . . no . . . tell her I've had some letters, crank letters. She'll think I'm an old woman, but she does anyway."

"And have you?" Anna managed to interrupt.

"What?"

"Had crank letters."

"Anna, darling, of course. Cranks write to famous people. That's how it goes."

Kinsey Millhone is...

"The best new private eye." —*The Detroit News*

"A tough-cookie with a soft center." —*Newsweek*

"A stand-out specimen of the new female operatives."
  —*Philadelphia Inquirer*

Sue Grafton is...

The Shamus and Anthony Award winning creator of Kinsey Millhone and quite simply one of the hottest new mystery writers around.

Bantam is...

The proud publisher of Sue Grafton's Kinsey Millhone mysteries:

THE MYSTERIOUS WORLD OF AGATHA CHRISTIE

Acknowledged as the world's most popular mystery writer of all time, Dame Agatha Christie's books have thrilled millions of readers for generations. With her care and attention to characters, the intriguing situations and the breathtaking final deduction, it's no wonder that Agatha Christie is the world's best-selling mystery writer.

NERO WOLFE STEPS OUT

Every Wolfe Watcher knows that the world's largest detective wouldn't dream of leaving the brownstone on 35th street, with Fritz's three star meals, his beloved orchids and the only chair that actually suits him. But when an ultra-conservative college professor winds up dead and Archie winds up in jail, Wolfe is forced to brave the wilds of upstate New York to find a murderer.

THE BLOODIED IVY
by Robert Goldsborough
☐ 27816 $3.95

and don't miss these other Nero Wolfe mysteries by Robert Goldsborough: